THE · BIG · BOOK · OF · FAIRY · TALES ·

THE · BIG · BOOK · OF · FAIRY · TALES ·

EDITED · BY · WALTER · JERROLD ·
· AND · ILLUSTRATED · BY ·
· CHARLES · ROBINSON ·
· AND ·
JANE HARVEY

LAMBOLL HOUSE
LONDON

This edition published 1987 by Lamboll House
a division of Bestseller Publications Ltd
Princess House, 50 Eastcastle Street
London W1

ISBN 1 85170 104 4

Printed and bound in Hungary

DEDICATION

TO
JOYCE

INTRODUCTION

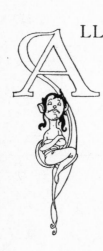

ALL the stories—told and re-told in many versions, familiar in their outline to everyone—which our great-grandparents told to their children are the stories in which our little ones delight. They have come to be known as nursery tales, because it is while children are still in the nursery that they, through them, are introduced to the wonderland of romance; and the annals of that wonderland have a truth transcending the truth of history; they take their place in the memory and directly or indirectly have their lessons, which may become blurred but are never forgotten.

INTRODUCTION

A collection of the best known of such fairy tales brings home to us the fact that the nursery knows no narrowing frontier lines of nationality or race. The world is its country, and anyone, from North or South, East or West, is sure of a hearty welcome so long as he can forget that he is anything but a story-teller. Thus it has come about that when we seek to bring together those fairy stories which in one form or another all of us heard or read in childhood, and all of us read or repeat to our children, we find that successive generations have granted and renewed the freedom of the nursery to story-tellers from far and wide.

An interesting and a motley company they would form, too, could they be brought together to lead their Giants and Fairies, their Princes and Princesses, their brave Heroes and beautiful Heroines in some grand Nursery Pageant! There we should see the splendid figure of an Oriental story-teller, he who first collected the thousand-and-one tales of the *Arabian Nights*; there would be the hunch-backed Greek slave Æsop, to whom it is believed we owe the many Fables associated with his name; there we should see the courtly Frenchman; Charles Perrault, the German Brothers Grimm, and that dearest of childhood's

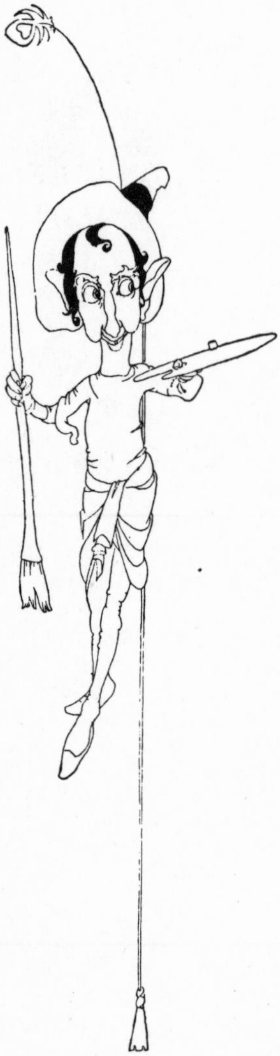

friends, the Danish Hans Andersen; as well as innumerable vague figures representing the unknown authors of well-known stories.

It is curious, by the way, that for the purposes of such a pageant we could not summon up the figure of an Englishman among our nursery story-tellers—except Robert Southey, the poet, who gave us *The Three Bears*. No one can tell who first wrote those of our stories that are English—*Jack the Giant-Killer*, *Jack and the Beanstalk*, or *Dick Whittington and his Cat*. There are many other people, known and anonymous, who would have to take part in any Pageant of Friends of the Nursery who have told fairy stories that are familiar to all our children.

A wise man once said that he would sooner write the ballads that his countrymen sang, than make their laws; to ballads he might well have added, or nursery tales. Many can learn to make laws; to few is it given to be able to tell stories that—told again and again—shall never grow stale.

Some of these stories have been told in many ways, by different people in different countries, until it is difficult to find where they started. Cinderella, for example, has had her romance set forth in various ways in various lands: with us she is Cinderella, in the French tales of Monsieur Perrault she is Cendrillon, in the German tales of Grimm she is Ashputtel. Then, too, the little man whose name had to be guessed, who is seen here as Rumpelstiltskin, is also known as Tom-Tit-Tot and by many other curious names; indeed this little story alone has provided a learned writer with enough material to make quite a big book.

Aladdin and Sindbad come from that wonderful treasure-house of tales, *The Arabian Nights.* From Hans Andersen we get the story of *The Ugly Duckling*; and from the same tender-hearted teller of tales we have the romance of *The Little Tin Soldier*, and the painful story of the little starved match-girl.

The terrible *Blue Beard* and the dainty *Beauty and the Beast* come from Monsieur Perrault, all of whose tales may be said to have become nursery favourites. But whoever may have been the first teller of any of these stories, his work lives immortal as childhood, even though his name may be forgotten.

WALTER JERROLD.

CONTENTS

CONTENTS

COLOURED PLATES

ILLUSTRATIONS

BLACK-AND-WHITE PLATES

ILLUSTRATIONS

TEXT ILLUSTRATIONS

ILLUSTRATIONS

ILLUSTRATIONS

ILLUSTRATIONS

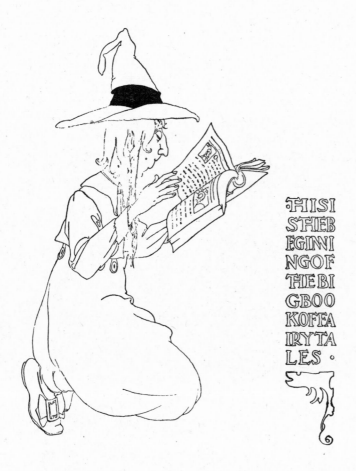

THIS IS THE BEGINNING OF THE BIG BOOK OF FAIRY TALES

Cinderella or The Little Glass Slipper

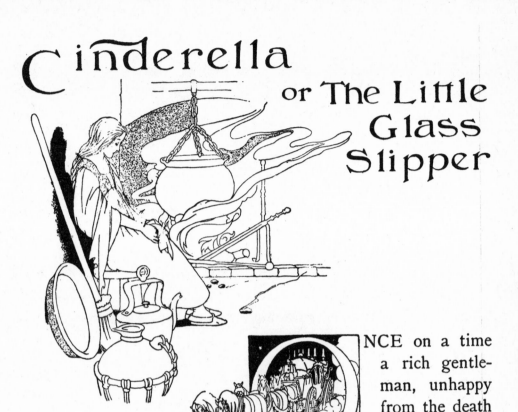

ONCE on a time a rich gentleman, unhappy from the death of his wife, resolved to marry again, that his little daughter, whom he dearly loved, might have some motherly care. Unfortunately his choice fell upon a proud, haughty, and selfish woman with two daughters much like herself. Not until the marriage was over did the stepmother show her true temper, and that she could not bear the pretty little girl whose goodness of heart contrasted with the selfishness and pride of her own daughters. She ordered the child to live in the kitchen, made her work with the servants, and forced her to sleep up in a garret without anything to make her comfortable. When the child had done her work she used to sit in the chimney corner among the cinders; so that she went by the name of Cinderella. And Cinderella, dirty and ragged as she was, was a thousand times prettier than her sisters, drest out in all their finery.

It happened that the king's son gave a ball, to which he invited all the persons of fashion in the country: Cinderella's stepsisters were of the number. He did not invite Cinderella, for he had never heard of her.

Nothing could exceed the joy of the two sisters; every moment was spent in fancying gowns, shoes, and head-dresses which would set them off to the greatest advantage. They talked of nothing but what they should wear.

On the morning of the ball, while Cinderella was busily engaged in dressing her sisters, they said to her:

"Should you not like to go to the ball?"

"Ah!" said she, "you are only laughing; it is not for such as I am to think of going to balls."

"You are right," said they; "folks might laugh, indeed, to see a Cinderella dancing in a ball-room."

At length the great moment arrived: the proud girls stepped into a beautiful carriage, and, followed by servants in rich liveries, drove to the palace. When they were out of sight, Cinderella sat down in a corner and began to cry.

Her fairy godmother suddenly appeared and asked what ailed her.

"I wish—I w-i-s-h—" sobbed poor Cinderella, without being able to say another word.

"You wish to go to the ball?"

"Alas, yes!" replied the poor child, sobbing still more.

"Well, well, be a good girl," said the godmother, "and you shall go. Run into the garden and bring me a pumpkin."

Cinderella brought the finest one she could. Her godmother scooped out the inside, leaving nothing but the rind; she then struck it with her wand, and the pumpkin instantly became a fine gilded coach. She next looked into the mouse-trap, where she found six lively mice. She told Cinderella to lift up the door of the trap very gently; and as the mice

passed out, she touched them one by one with her hand, and each immediately became a beautiful horse, of a fine dapple-grey mouse colour.

"Here, my child," said the godmother, "is a coach, and horses too; but what shall we do for a postilion?"

"I will run," replied Cinderella, "and see if there be not a rat in the rat-trap; if I find one, he will do very well for a postilion."

"Well thought of, my child!" said her godmother.

Cinderella brought the rat-trap, which contained three of the largest rats ever seen. The fairy chose the one which had the longest beard; and, touching him with her wand, instantly turned him into a smart, handsome postilion.

"Go again into the garden," she said, "and you will find six lizards behind the watering-pot; bring them hither."

This was no sooner done, than with a stroke they were changed into footmen, who all jumped up behind the coach in their laced liveries, and stood side by side as if they had been used to nothing else all their lives.

"Well, my dear," the fairy then said, "is not this such an equipage as you could wish for to take you to the ball? Are you not delighted with it?"

"Y-e-s," replied Cinderella with hesitation; "but must I go in these rags?"

Her godmother touched her with the wand, and her rags instantly became the most magnificent apparel, ornamented with the most costly jewels in the world. To these she added a beautiful pair of glass slippers, and bade her set out for the palace. The fairy, however, before taking leave of Cinderella, charged her on no account whatever to stay at the ball after the clock had struck twelve; as, should she stay but a single moment after that time, her coach would again become a pumpkin, her horses mice, her footmen lizards, and her fine clothes be changed to filthy rags. Cinderella did not fail to promise all her godmother wished, and, almost wild with joy, drove away to the palace.

As soon as she arrived, the king's son, who had been informed that a great unknown princess was come to the ball, presented himself at the door of her carriage, helped her out, and conducted her to the ball-room.

Cinderella no sooner appeared than everyone was silent. The dancing and music stopped, and everybody gazed at the beauty of the stranger. The King himself continually repeated to the Queen that it was a long time since he had seen so lovely a creature. The king's son conducted her to the most honourable seat, and soon after took her out to dance with him. She danced so gracefully that everyone admired her still more than before, and she was thought the most beautiful and accomplished lady ever beheld. After some time a delicious supper was served; but the young Prince was so busily employed in looking at her that he did not eat a morsel.

Cinderella seated herself near her sisters, paid them a thousand attentions, and offered them a part of the delicacies with which the Prince presented her; while they were quite astonished at these civilities from a strange lady.

As they were conversing, Cinderella heard the clock strike eleven and three-quarters: she rose from her seat, curtsied to the company, and hastened away as fast as she could.

As soon as she got home she flew to her godmother, and, thanking her, told her she would give the world to be able to go again to the ball the next day, for the king's son had entreated her to be there. While she was telling her godmother everything that had happened at the ball, her two sisters knocked a loud rat-tat-tat at the door, which Cinderella opened.

"How late you have stayed!" said she, yawning, rubbing her eyes, and stretching herself as if just awaked out of her sleep.

"If you had been at the ball," said one of the sisters, "let me tell you, you would not have been sleepy: there came thither the handsomest, yes, the very handsomest, princess ever beheld! She paid us many attentions, and made us partake of the sweetmeats the Prince gave her."

Cinderella asked her sisters the name of this princess. They replied, that nobody had been able to discover who she was; that the king's son was extremely grieved on that account, and had offered a large reward to any person who could find out whence she came.

"How very beautiful she must be!" said Cinderella. "How fortunate you are! Ah, could I but see her for a single moment! Dear sister, lend me only the yellow gown you wear every day, and let me go to see her."

"Oh, yes, I warrant you; lend my clothes to a Cinderella!

No, no; mind your business, and leave dress and balls to your betters."

The next day the two sisters again appeared at the ball, and so did Cinderella, but dressed more magnificently than before. The Prince was continually by her side, and said the most obliging things to her, so that the charming young creature was far from being tired; on the contrary, she was so delighted, that she forgot the charge her godmother had given her. Cinderella at last heard the striking of a clock, and counted one, two, three, on till she came to twelve, though she had thought that it could be but eleven at most. She got up and flew as nimbly as a deer out of the ball-room. The Prince tried to overtake her; but poor Cinderella's fright made her run the faster. However, in her hurry, she dropped one of her glass slippers, which the Prince stooped down and picked up.

Cinderella got home tired and out of breath, in her dirty old clothes, without either coach or footmen, and having nothing left of her magnificence but the fellow of the glass slipper which she had dropped.

Meantime the Prince enquired of all his guards at the palace gates, if they had seen a magnificent princess pass out, and which way she went? The guards replied, that no princess had passed the gates; that they had not seen a creature but a little ragged girl.

When the sisters returned, Cinderella asked if they had been as much amused as the night before, and if the beautiful princess had been there? They told her that she had; but as soon as the clock struck twelve she hurried away from the ball-room, and, in the haste she made, had dropped one of her glass slippers, which was the prettiest shape that could be; that the king's son had picked it up, and had done nothing but look at it all the rest of the evening; and that everybody believed he was violently in love with the handsome lady to whom it belonged.

A few days after, the Prince had it proclaimed, by sound of trumpet, that he would marry the lady whose foot should exactly fit the slipper he had found.

Accordingly messengers took the slipper, and carried it first to all the princesses; then to the duchesses—in short, to all the ladies of

the Court — but without success. They then brought it to the two sisters, who each tried all she could to squeeze her foot into the slipper; but this was quite impossible.

Cinderella, who was looking at them all the while, and knew her slipper, could not help smiling, and said:

"Pray, let me try it on."

Her sisters burst out laughing. "Very likely," said one of them, "that a clumsy foot like yours should fit the slipper of a beautiful princess."

The gentleman, however, who brought the slipper, turned round, looked at Cinderella, and, observing that she was very handsome, said, that as he was ordered by the Prince to try it on everyone till it fitted, it was but just that Cinderella should have her turn. Saying this, he made her sit down; and putting the slipper to her foot, it instantly slipped on, and he saw that it fitted her like wax.

The two sisters were amazed to see that the slipper fitted Cinderella; but how much greater was their astonishment when she drew out of her pocket the other slipper, and put it on!

Just at this moment the fairy entered the room, and, touching Cinderella's clothes with her wand, made her all at once even more magnificently dressed than when at the ball.

The sisters immediately perceived that she was the beautiful princess, and at once asked her forgiveness for the ill-treatment she had received from them. Cinderella tenderly embraced them, and said that she forgave them with all her heart.

Cinderella was then conducted to the young Prince, who, finding her more beautiful than ever, instantly desired her to accept his hand.

The marriage ceremony took place in a few days; and Cinderella, who was as amiable as she was handsome, gave her sisters magnificent apartments in the palace, and a short time after married them to two great lords of the Court.

Jack the Giant-killer

IN the days of King Arthur, St. Michael's Mount, which rises out of the sea some way from the mainland, was inhabited by an enormous giant, eighteen feet high and three yards in girth. He dwelt in a gloomy cavern on the top of the Mount, and was the terror of all Cornwall, for he used to wade over to the mainland in search of his prey. At his approach the people forsook their habitations; and when he had glutted his ferocious appetite upon their cattle, he would throw half a dozen oxen upon his back, and tie three times as many sheep and hogs round his waist, and so march back to his gloomy dwelling. The coast had been greatly impoverished by his ravages, when Jack, the son of a neighbouring farmer, bravely undertook to destroy the monster.

Jack furnished himself with a horn, a shovel, a pickaxe, and a dark lantern. In the beginning of a long winter's evening, he swam to the Mount, immediately fell to work, and before morning had dug a great pit. This he covered on the surface with sticks and straw, and, lightly strewing some of the earth over them, gave it the appearance of solid ground. Then, putting his horn to his mouth, he blew so loudly and so long that the giant awoke and came towards him, roaring in a voice like thunder:

"You impudent villain, you shall pay dearly for disturbing me. I will broil you for my breakfast."

Scarcely had he spoken these words than he tumbled headlong into the pit, and his fall shook the very foundations of the mountain.

"O ho! Mr. Giant, have you found your way so quickly to the bottom? How is your appetite now? Will nothing serve you for breakfast but broiling poor Jack?"

The giant making an effort to rise, Jack struck him such a terrible blow on the head with his pickaxe that he expired with a single groan. Jack threw the earth on him as he lay in the pit, and so buried him.

Now, when the people heard of this valiant deed, they declared that Jack should henceforth be called Jack the Giant-killer, and presented him with a sword and belt, upon which was embroidered, in letters of gold:

"This is the valiant Cornish man
Who slew the giant Cormoran".

The news soon spread, and another giant, called Blunderbore, vowed to be revenged, if it should ever be his fortune to get Jack into his power. This giant kept an enchanted

The Marriage Ceremony took place. (PAGE 10)

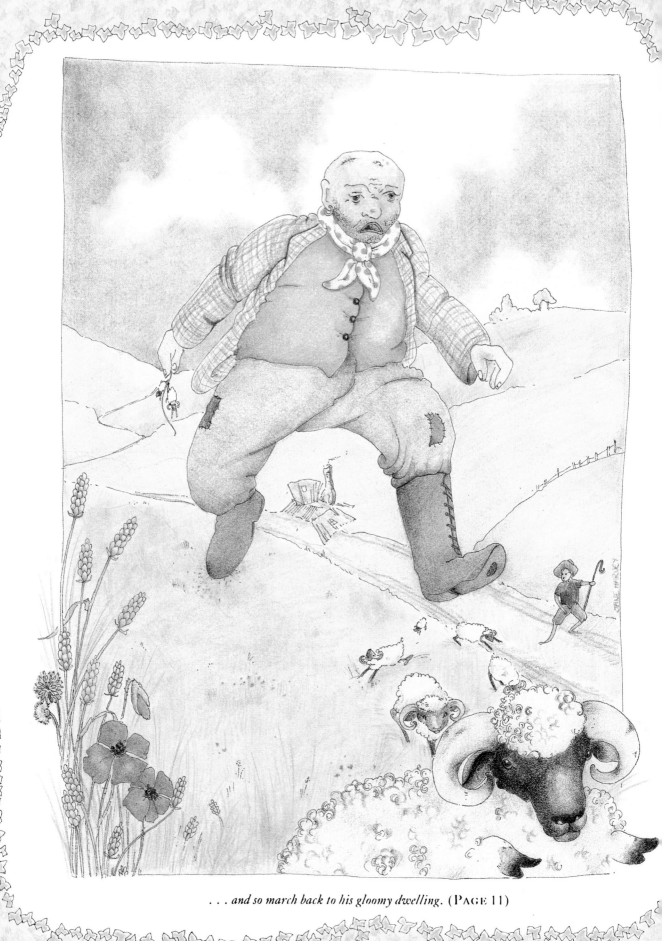

. . . and so march back to his gloomy dwelling. (PAGE 11)

castle in the midst of a lonely wood; and as Jack was travelling to Wales he passed through this wood, and, being weary, sat down to rest by the side of a stream, and fell asleep.

The giant found him there, and, knowing him to be Jack, lifted him up and laid him gently upon his shoulder to carry him to his enchanted castle. The rustling of leaves as they passed through the thicket awakened Jack, who, finding himself in the clutches of Blunderbore, was not a little frightened, though this was only the beginning of his terrors; for on entering the castle he beheld the floor covered with human skulls and bones.

The giant carried him into a large parlour, where he locked Jack up, and went to fetch a brother giant who lived in the same wood.

While he was absent, Jack heard dreadful shrieks and groans, and presently a mournful voice said:

"Haste, valiant stranger, haste away,
Lest you become the giant's prey.
On his return he'll bring another,
Still more furious than his brother—
A savage, cruel monster, who
Before he kills will torture you.
O valiant stranger! haste away,
Or you'll become these giants' prey."

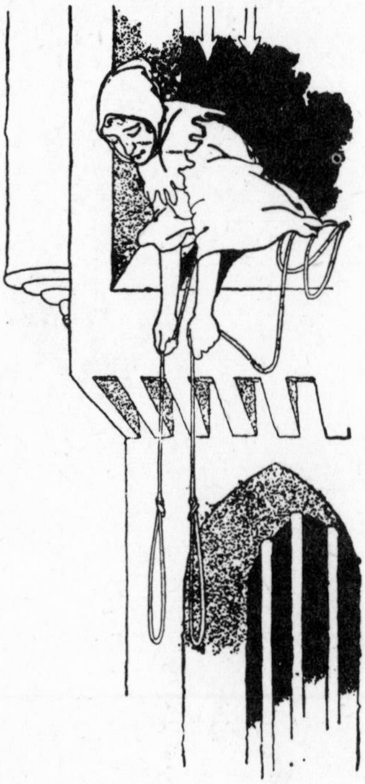

Poor Jack, affrighted, flew to the window immediately over the gates of the castle, and beheld the two giants coming arm in arm together.

"Now," thought Jack, "death or deliverance is at hand."

There were two strong cords in the room. At the end of each he made a large noose with a slip knot, and as the giants were unlocking the iron gates he threw the ropes over each of their heads, then, fastening the other ends to a beam in the ceiling, pulled with all his might till he had nearly strangled them. Seeing that they were both black in the face, and quite unable to make the least resistance, he drew his sword, and, sliding down the ropes, slew them both, and thus delivered himself from their intended cruelty.

Taking a great bunch of keys from the pocket of Blunderbore, Jack entered the castle, where he found three ladies tied up by the hair of their heads. They told him that their husbands had been murdered by the cruel giants, who had afterwards condemned them to be starved to death.

"Well," said Jack, "I have destroyed the monster and his wicked brother; and this castle, and all the wealth it contains, I give to you, in consideration of the dreadful sufferings you have undergone."

He then proceeded on his journey. At length, losing

his way, he was benighted in a lonely valley between lofty mountains, where, after wandering for some hours without seeing any habitation, he thought himself fortunate in finding a large house.

Jack knocked boldly at the gate, when, to his horror and amazement, there came forth a monstrous giant with two heads, who, however, accosted him very civilly. Jack told him that he was a traveller who had lost his way, and was kindly welcomed by the huge monster, and conducted into a chamber where there was a good bed.

Weary as he was, Jack could not go to sleep, and presently he heard the giant walking about the next apartment, and repeating to himself:

> "Though here you lodge with me this night,
> You shall not see the morning light;
> My club shall dash your brains out quite."

"Are these your tricks upon travellers!" thought Jack. "I hope to prove as cunning as you are." Then, getting out of bed, he groped about the room, and at length found in the chimney a large piece of wood, and, laying it in his place, hid himself in a corner of the room.

In the middle of the night the giant came with his enormous club, and struck several heavy blows on the bed, where Jack had cunningly laid the wood, and then returned to his own room, supposing he had broken all Jack's bones.

Early in the morning Jack put a bold face upon the matter, and walked into the giant's apartment to thank him for his lodging. The giant started at his approach, and with difficulty stammered out:

"Oh, dear me! is it you? How did you sleep last night? Did you hear anything, or see anything, in the dead of the night?"

"Nothing of any consequence," said Jack. "A troublesome rat, I believe, gave me three or four slaps with his tail, and disturbed me a little; but I soon went to sleep again."

The confused giant did not answer a word, but brought two great bowls of hasty pudding for their breakfast. Jack, unwilling to let the giant know that he was not able to eat as much as himself, contrived to button a leathern bag within his coat, into which he slipped the hasty pudding, while he pretended to put it into his mouth, and when breakfast was done, he said:

"Now I will show you a most extraordinary trick. I can heal all wounds with a touch. I could cut off my head and place it sound again on my shoulders. I will give you an example." Seizing the knife, he ripped up the leathern bag, and all the hasty pudding tumbled out upon the floor.

The Welsh giant, ashamed to be outdone by such a little fellow as Jack, cried: "Hur can do that hurself!" and, snatching up the knife, he plunged it into his stomach, and instantly dropped down dead.

Having thus outwitted the monster, Jack proceeded on his journey. A few days afterwards he met King Arthur's only son, who was travelling into Wales to deliver a beautiful lady from the power of a magician. Finding that the Prince was travelling without attendants, Jack begged leave to be his servant, to which request the youth consented.

The Prince was so generous that he gave money to every person he met; and at length, an old woman having begged of him the last penny he had, he turned to Jack, uneasy as to where they should lodge that night, saying: "How are we now to subsist on the journey?"

"Sir," said Jack, "be of good courage. Two miles farther there lives a huge giant, whom I know very well. He has three heads, and will fight five hundred men in

armour, and make them fly before him. Leave me to manage him, and do you wait here patiently till I return."

Jack rode on at full speed. On reaching the castle, he knocked with such force that he made the neighbouring hills resound. The giant, with a voice like thunder, roared out: "Who is there?"

"Only your poor cousin Jack."

"Well, what news with my poor cousin Jack?"

"Dear Uncle, heavy news."

"What heavy news can come to me? I am a giant with three heads, and can fight five hundred men in armour, and make them fly like chaff before the wind!"

"Alas!" said Jack, "here is the king's son coming with two thousand men in armour to kill you, and to destroy the castle."

"Oh, this is heavy news indeed! But I have a large vault underground, where I will hide myself, and thou shalt lock, bolt, and bar me in, and keep the keys till the king's son is gone."

Now Jack, having secured the giant in the vault, returned and fetched the Prince to the castle, and both made merry. That night they rested in very pleasant lodgings, whilst the poor giant lay trembling and shaking with fear in the vault underground.

Early in the morning Jack furnished the king's son with a fresh supply of gold and silver, and set him three miles forward on his journey. He then returned to let the giant out of the hole, who asked Jack what he should give him as a reward.

"Why," said Jack, "I desire nothing but the old coat and cap, together with the old rusty sword and the slippers, that are hanging at your bed's head."

"Then," said the giant, "thou shalt have them; and keep them for my sake, for they are things of excellent use. The coat will make you invisible; the cap will furnish you with knowledge; the sword cut asunder whatever you strike; and the shoes, of extraordinary swiftness, may be serviceable in times of danger; therefore take them with all my heart."

Jack thanked the giant, departed, and followed the Prince. Having overtaken him, they soon arrived at the dwelling of the beautiful lady who was under the dominion of a wicked magician. She received the Prince very courteously, and prepared a magnificent banquet for him; which being ended, she rose, and, taking an embroidered handkerchief, said:

"My lord, you must submit to the custom of my palace: to-morrow morning I command you to tell me on whom I bestow this handkerchief, or lose your head." She then put the handkerchief in her bosom, and retired.

The young Prince went to bed very sorrowful; but Jack put on his cap of knowledge, which instructed him that the lady was obliged, by the power of the enchantment, to meet the wicked magician every night in the middle of the forest. Jack instantly put on his coat of darkness and his shoes of swiftness, and was there before her. When the lady came she presented the handkerchief to the magician. Jack, with his sword of sharpness, instantly cut off his head; the enchantment was dissolved, and the lady restored to her former virtue and goodness.

She was married to the Prince with great pomp and solemnity on the following day, and soon after returned with her royal husband and a numerous company to the Court of King Arthur. The valiant hero, Jack, for the many and great exploits that he had done for the good of his country, was immediately made one of the Knights of the Round Table.

Having been hitherto successful in all his undertakings, Jack besought the King to furnish him with a horse and money, that he might travel in search of new and strange adventures.

"For," said he, "there are many giants yet living among the mountains, in the remote parts of Wales, to the unspeakable terror and distress of the people; therefore, should it please you to encourage me in my enterprise, I will speedily rid the kingdom of these giants and devouring monsters."

The King consented, and Jack departed, taking with him his cap of knowledge, his sword of sharpness, his shoes of swiftness, and his invisible coat, the better to perform the wonderful enterprise that lay before him.

He travelled over high hills and lofty mountains, and on the third day came to a large and spacious forest. Scarcely had he entered, when on a sudden he heard dreadful shrieks and cries. He pressed on through the trees, and beheld a monstrous giant dragging along by the hair of their heads a handsome knight and beautiful lady. Their tears and cries melted the heart of honest Jack to pity and compassion. He alighted from his horse, and, tying him to an oak tree, put on his invisible coat.

When he came up to the giant he made several strokes at him with the sword of sharpness, but could not reach

his body on account of the enormous height of the terrible creature. Still he wounded his thighs in several places, and at length, putting both hands to his sword, and aiming with all his might, he cut off both the giant's legs, just below the garter; and the trunk of his body, tumbling to the ground, made not only the trees shake, but the earth itself tremble.

Then Jack, setting his foot upon the monster's neck, exclaimed:

"Thou barbarous and savage wretch, behold I am come

to execute upon thee the just reward of all thy crimes!" and instantly plunged his sword into the giant's body. The huge monster gave a hideous groan, and died.

The courteous knight and his lady returned Jack hearty thanks for this deliverance, and invited him to their house, there to refresh himself after this dreadful encounter, and to receive a reward for his good services.

"No," said Jack, "I cannot be at ease till I find out the den that was the monster's habitation."

The knight, hearing this, grew sorrowful, and replied:

"Noble stranger, it is too much to make a second hazard. This monster lived in a den in yonder mountain, with a brother of his more fierce and cruel than himself; therefore, if you should go thither, and perish in the attempt, it would be a heartbreaking thing to both me and my lady. Let me persuade you to desist, and go with us."

"Nay," answered Jack, "if there be another, even if there were twenty, I would shed the last drop of blood in my body before one of them should escape my fury. When I have finished this task I will come to you."

So he mounted his horse, leaving the knight and his lady to return home, while he went in pursuit of the dead giant's brother. He had not ridden above a mile and a half before he came in sight of the mouth of the cavern, near to the entrance of which he beheld the other giant, sitting on a high stump, with a knotted iron club lying by his side, waiting for the return of his barbarous brother loaded with prey. His eyes appeared like terrible flames, his countenance was grim and ugly, and the bristles of his beard seemed to be wire, and his long locks of hair hung down upon his great shoulders like curling snakes or hissing adders.

Jack alighted from his horse, and, putting him into a thicket, with his coat of darkness approached somewhat nearer to behold this figure, and said softly:

"Oh, monster, are you there? It will not be long before I take you fast by the beard."

The giant could not see his foe, by reason of the invisible coat; so Jack, coming up close to him, struck a blow at his head with the sword of sharpness, but, missing his aim, only cut off the nose of the giant, who roared like loud thunder. Though he rolled his glaring eyes round on every side, he could not see whence the blow came; yet, taking up his iron club, he began to lay about him like one that was mad with pain and fury.

"Nay," said Jack, "I had better dispatch you presently." So, slipping behind him, and jumping nimbly upon the stump as the giant rose from it, he stabbed him in the back; when, after a few howls, he dropped down dead. Jack cut off his head, and sent it, with that of his brother, whom he had killed in the forest, to King Arthur, by a wagon which he had hired for that purpose.

Having thus dispatched these two monsters, Jack resolved to enter the cave in search of the giants' treasure. He passed through many turnings and windings, which led him at length to a great room, at the upper end of which was a boiling cauldron, and a large table whereat he supposed the giants used to dine.

He then came to an iron grate, where a window was secured with bars of iron, through which he beheld a number of miserable captives, who cried out:

"Alas, young man, art thou come to be one amongst us in this horrible den?"

"I hope," said Jack, "you will not tarry here long."

"Alas!" said an old man; "we are persons that have been taken by the giants that hold this cave, and we are kept till such time as they have a fancy for an extraordinary feast; and then the fattest of us all is slaughtered, and prepared for their devouring jaws. It is not long since they took three for the same purpose."

"Well," said Jack, "I have given them such a dinner that it will be long before they have occasion for any more. You may believe me, for I have slain them and have sent their monstrous heads in a wagon to the court of King Arthur."

In testimony of the truth of what he said, he unlocked the iron gate, and set the captives at liberty. Then, leading

them to the great room, he placed them round the table, and they feasted plentifully.

Supper being over, they searched the giant's coffers, the store of which Jack divided among the captives, who gratefully thanked him for their happy deliverance. The next morning they departed to their homes.

At the hour of sunrise Jack proceeded on his journey. He arrived at the knight's house about noon, and was received with joy by the grateful knight and his beautiful lady, who, in honour of Jack's victory, gave a splendid entertainment, to which all the nobility and gentry in that part of the country were invited. When the company were assembled, the knight related the noble exploits of Jack, and presented him with a most magnificent ring, on which was engraved the picture of the giant dragging the knight and the lady by the hair, with this motto:

"Behold, in dire distress were we,
Under a giant's fierce command;
But gain'd our lives and liberty
From valiant Jack's victorious hand".

Among the guests were five aged gentlemen, fathers to some of the miserable captives liberated by Jack from the dungeon of the giants. As soon as they understood that he was the person who had performed such wonders, the venerable men, with tears of gratitude, pressed round

to return him thanks for the happiness he had procured them and their families.

But suddenly a herald, pale and breathless with haste and terror, rushed into the midst of the company, and told them that Thundel, a ferocious giant with two heads, having heard of the death of his kinsmen, had come from the north to be revenged on Jack; and that he was now within a mile of the house, the country people all flying before him. At these tidings the boldest of the guests trembled with confusion and dismay, while the undaunted Jack brandished his sword and said:

"Let him come; I have a rod to chastise him also. You shall soon be spectators of this giant's death and destruction."

The good knight's house was situated on an island encompassed by a moat thirty feet deep and twenty wide, over which lay a drawbridge. Jack employed two men to cut the bridge on each side, almost to the middle, and then, dressing himself in his invisible coat, went against the giant with his sword of sharpness. As he came close up to him, though the giant could not see him by reason of his coat, yet he was sensible of some impending danger, which made him cry out:

> "Fa, fe, fi, fo, fum,
> I smell the blood of an Englishman;
> Be he alive, or be he dead,
> I'll grind his bones to make my bread."

"Say you so," said Jack. "You are a monstrous miller indeed."

"Art thou," cried the giant, "the villain who killed my kinsmen? I will tear thee with my teeth, and grind thy bones to powder."

"You must catch me first," said Jack; and, throwing off his coat of darkness and putting on his shoes of swiftness, he began to run, the giant following after and making the earth shake at every step.

Jack led him round and round the walls of the house, that the company might see the monster; and then, to finish the work, ran over the drawbridge, the giant pursuing him with his club. Coming to the middle, where the bridge had been cut on each side by Jack's order, with the very great weight of the giant's body, and the vast steps he took, it broke, and he tumbled into the water, and rolled about like a large whale.

Jack, standing by the moat, laughed at him, saying:

"I think you told me you would grind my bones to powder: when do you begin?"

The giant foamed with fury, and plunged from side to side of the moat, but could not get out to be revenged upon his adversary.

Jack at length ordered a cart-rope to be brought to him; he cast it over the giant's two heads, and by the help of a team of horses dragged him to the edge of the moat, where, in the presence of the knight and his guests, he cut off the monster's heads, and, before he ate or drank, sent them both to the Court of King Arthur.

After being hospitably entertained for some time longer, Jack set out again in search of new conquests. He travelled far without meeting any adventure, till, arriving at the foot of an exceedingly high mountain, he knocked at the door of a small and lonely house, when an old man, with a head as white as snow, arose and let him in.

"Good father," said Jack, "can you lodge a benighted traveller who has lost his way?"

"Yes," replied the hermit, "I can, if you will accept such accommodation as my poor house affords."

Jack therefore entered the hermitage, and the old man set before him bread and fruit for his supper. When Jack had satisfied his hunger, the hermit addressed him, saying:

There were once upon a time Three Bears, who lived in a wood.
(PAGE 32)

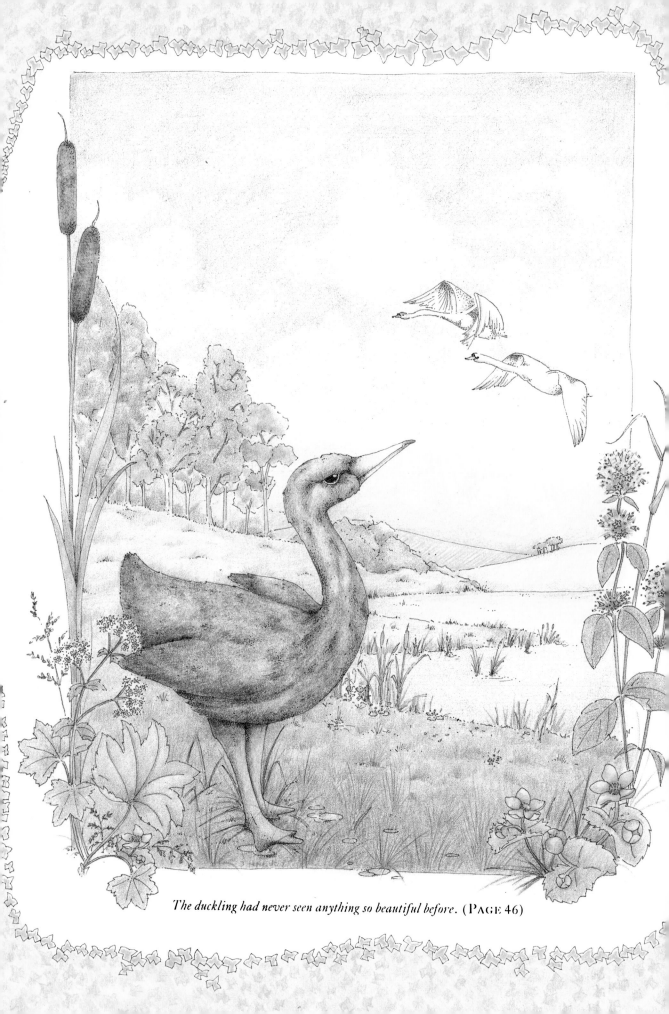

The duckling had never seen anything so beautiful before. (PAGE 46)

"My son, I well know you are the far-famed conqueror of giants, and on the top of this mountain is the enchanted castle of the giant Galligantus, who, by the help of a vile magician, gets many knights into his castle, where he transforms them into the shapes of various beasts. Above all, I lament the hard fate of a duke's daughter, whom they seized as she was walking in her father's garden, and brought hither

in a chariot drawn by two fiery dragons, and transformed her into the shape of a deer. Several knights have endeavoured to destroy the enchantment and deliver her; yet none has been able to accomplish it, by reason of two fiery griffins, who guard the gates of the castle, and destroy all who approach it. You, being furnished with an invisible coat, may pass undiscovered, and on the gates of the castle you will find engraved by what means the enchantment may be broken."

The old man having ended, Jack gave him his hand,

promising, at the hazard of his life, to break the enchantment, and free the lady. Having refreshed himself with a sound sleep, he arose early, put on his invisible coat, and prepared for the adventure.

When he had climbed to the top of the mountain, he discovered the two fiery griffins, between which he passed without danger, for they could not see him, because he had on his invisible coat. On the castle gate he found a golden trumpet, under which was written:

> "Whoever can this trumpet blow
> Shall cause the giant's overthrow".

Jack seized tne golden trumpet, and blew a shrill blast, which made the gates fly open, and the foundations of the castle tremble. The giant and the conjuror, knowing that their wicked practices were at an end, stood biting their thumbs and shaking with fear. Jack, with his sword of sharpness, slew the giant; and the magician mounted immediately into the air, and was carried away by a whirlwind. Thus was the whole enchantment dissolved, and all the knights and ladies who had been transformed into birds and beasts returned to their former shapes. The castle, though it seemed of vast strength, vanished away like smoke, and the head of the giant Galligantus was immediately conveyed to King Arthur.

The knights and ladies rested at the old man's hermitage, and the next day set out for the Court. Jack presented himself to the King, and related the history of all his fierce encounters. His fame ran through the whole country, and the King prevailed on the duke to give his daughter in marriage to Jack, protesting there was no one so deserving of her as he who had delivered her from so horrible a condition. The duke consented; and they were married, to the joy of all the kingdom. As a reward for the services which Jack had done the nation, the King gave him an estate, on which he and his lady lived the rest of their days in joy and contentment.

The Three Bears

THERE were once upon a time Three Bears, who lived in a wood. One of them was a Little, Small, Wee Bear; one was a Middle-sized Bear; and the other was a Great, Huge Bear. Each had a pot for its porridge: a little pot for the Little, Small, Wee Bear; a middle-sized pot for the Middle Bear; and a great pot for the Great, Huge Bear. Each had a chair to sit in: a little chair for the Little, Small, Wee Bear; a middle-sized chair for the Middle Bear; and a great chair for the Great, Huge Bear. Each had a bed to sleep in: a little bed for the Little, Small, Wee Bear; a middle-sized bed for the Middle Bear; and a great bed for the Great, Huge Bear.

One day, after they had made the porridge for their breakfast, they walked out into the wood while the porridge was cooling. While they were walking, a little old Woman came to the house. She could not have been a good, honest old Woman; for first she looked in at the window, and then she peeped in at the keyhole; and, seeing nobody in the house, she lifted the latch. So the little old Woman went in; and well pleased she was when she saw the porridge on the table. If she had been a good, little old Woman she would have waited till the Bears came home, and then, perhaps, they would have asked her to breakfast; for they were good Bears—a little rough or so, as the manner of Bears is, but for all that very good-natured and hospitable. But she was an impudent, bad old Woman and set about helping herself.

First she tasted the porridge of the Great, Huge Bear; but that was too hot, and she said a bad word about that. Then she tasted the porridge of the Middle Bear; but that was too cold, and she said a bad word about that. Then she went to the porridge of the Little, Small, Wee Bear, and tasted that; and that was neither too hot nor too cold, but just right; and she liked it so well that she ate it all up: but the naughty old Woman said a bad word about the little porridge-pot, because it did not hold enough for her.

Then the little old Woman sate down in the

chair of the Great, Huge Bear, and that was too hard. Then she sate down in the chair of the Middle Bear; that was too soft for her. Then she sate down in the chair of the Little, Small, Wee Bear, and that was neither too hard nor too soft, but just right. So she seated herself in it, and there she sate till the bottom of the chair came out, and down she came, plump upon the ground; and the naughty old woman said a wicked word about that too.

Then the little old Woman went upstairs into the bed-chamber in which the Three Bears slept. First she lay down upon the bed of the Great, Huge Bear; that was too high at the head for her. Next she lay down upon the bed of the Middle Bear; that was too high at the foot for her. Then she lay down upon the bed of the Little, Small, Wee Bear; and that was just right. So she covered herself up, and lay there till she fell fast asleep.

By this time the Three Bears came home to breakfast. Now the little old Woman had left the spoon of the Great, Huge Bear standing in his porridge.

"Somebody has been at my porridge!"

said the Great, Huge Bear in his great, rough, gruff voice. When the Middle Bear looked at his, he saw that the spoon was standing in it too.

"Somebody has been at my porridge!"

said the Middle Bear in his middle voice.

Then the Little, Small, Wee Bear, looked at his, and there was the spoon in the porridge-pot, but the porridge was all gone.

"So she covered herself up"

"Somebody has been at my porridge, and has eaten it all up!"

said the Little, Small, Wee Bear in his little, small, wee voice.

Upon this the Three Bears, seeing that someone had entered their house, and eaten up the Little, Small, Wee Bear's breakfast, began to look about them. Now the little old Woman had not put the hard cushion straight when she rose from the chair of the Great, Huge Bear.

"Somebody has been sitting in my chair!"

said the Great, Huge Bear in his great, rough, gruff voice.

And the little old Woman had squatted down on the soft cushion of the Middle Bear.

"Somebody has been sitting in my chair!"

said the Middle Bear in his middle voice.

And you know what the little old Woman had done to the third chair.

"Somebody has been sitting in my chair, and has sate the bottom of it out!"

said the Little, Small, Wee Bear in his little, small, wee voice.

Then the Three Bears went upstairs. Now the little old Woman had pulled the pillow of the Great, Huge Bear out of its place.

"Somebody has been lying in my bed!"

said the Great, Huge Bear in his great, rough, gruff voice.

And the little old Woman had pulled the bolster of the Middle Bear out of its place.

"Somebody has been lying in my bed!"

said the Middle Bear in his middle voice.

And when the Little, Small, Wee Bear came to look at his bed, there was the bolster in its place, and the pillow in its place upon the bolster, and upon the pillow was the little old Woman's ugly, dirty head—which was not in its place, for she had no business there.

"Somebody has been lying in my bed, and here she is!"

said the Little, Small, Wee Bear in his little, small, wee voice.

The little old Woman had heard in her sleep the great, rough, gruff voice of the Great, Huge Bear; but she was so fast asleep that it was no more to her than the roaring of wind, or the rumbling of thunder. And she had heard the middle voice of the Middle Bear, but it was only as if she had heard someone speaking in a dream. But when she heard the little, small, wee voice of the Little, Small, Wee Bear, it was so sharp, and so shrill, that it awakened her at once. Up she started; and when she saw the Three Bears on one side of the bed, she tumbled herself out at the other, and ran to the window. Now the window was open, because the Bears, like good, tidy Bears, as they were, always opened their bed-chamber window when they got up in the morning. Out the little old Woman jumped; and whether she broke her neck in the fall, or ran into the wood and was lost there, or found her way out of the wood, I cannot tell. But the Three Bears never saw anything more of her.

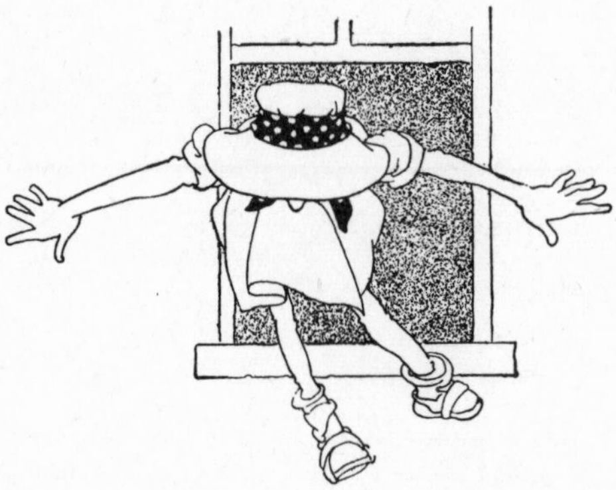

The Ugly Duckling

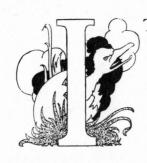

IT was summertime, and it was beautiful in the country! The sunshine fell warmly on an old house, surrounded by deep canals, and from the walls down to the water's edge there grew large burdock leaves, so high that children could stand upright among them without being seen. This place was as wild and lonely as the thickest part of the wood, and on that account a duck had chosen to make her nest there. She was sitting on her eggs; but the pleasure she had felt at first was now almost gone, because she had been there so long.

At last the eggs began to crack, and one little head after another appeared. "Quack, quack!" said the duck, and all got up as well as they could, and peeped about from under the green leaves.

"How large the world is!" said the little ones.

"Do you think this is the whole of the world?" said the mother. "It stretches far away beyond the other side of the garden, down to the pastor's field; but I have never been there. Are you all here?" And then she got up. "No, I have not got you all; the largest egg is still here. How long, I wonder, will this last? I am so weary of it!" And then she sat down again.

The great egg burst at last. "Peep, peep!" said the little one, and out it tumbled. But oh! how large and ugly it was! The duck looked at it. "That is a great, strong creature," said she; "none of the others are at all like it."

The next day there was delightful weather, and the sun was shining warmly when mother-duck with her family went down to the canal. Splash! she went into the water. "Quack, quack!" cried she, and one duckling after another jumped in. The water closed over their heads, but all came up again, and swam quite easily. All were there, even the ugly grey one was swimming about with the rest.

"Quack, quack!" said the mother-duck. "Now come with me, I will take you into the world; but keep close to me, or someone may tread on you; and beware of the cat."

When they came into the duckyard, two families were quarrelling about the head of an eel, which in the end was carried off by the cat.

"See, my children, such is the way of the world," said the mother-duck, whetting her beak, for she too was fond of roasted eels. "Now use your legs," said she, "keep together, and bow to the old duck you see yonder. She is the noblest born of them all, and is of Spanish blood, which accounts for her dignified appearance and manners. And look, she has a red rag on her leg; that is considered a

special mark of distinction, and is the greatest honour a duck can have."

The other ducks who were in the yard looked at them and said aloud: "Only see! now we have another brood, as if there were not enough of us already. And, fie! how ugly that one is; we will not endure it." And immediately one of the ducks flew at him, and bit him on the neck.

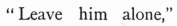

"Leave him alone," said the mother; "he is doing no one any harm."

"Yes; but he is so large and ungainly."

"Those are fine children that our good mother has," said the old duck with the red rag on her leg. "All are pretty except that one, who certainly is not at all well favoured. I wish his mother could improve him a little."

"Certainly he is not handsome," said the mother, "but he is a very good child, and swims as well as the others, indeed rather better. I think in time he will grow like the others, and perhaps will look smaller." And she stroked the duckling's neck, and smoothed his ruffled feathers. "Besides," added she, "he is a drake; I think he will be very strong; so he will fight his way through."

"The other ducks are very pretty," said the old duck.

"Pray make yourselves at home, and if you find an eel's head you can bring it to me."

And accordingly they made themselves at home.

But the poor duckling who had come last out of his egg-shell, and who was so ugly, was bitten, pecked, and teased by both ducks and hens. And the turkey-cock, who had come into the world with spurs on, and therefore fancied he was an emperor, puffed himself up like a ship in full sail, and marched up to the duckling quite red with passion. The poor thing scarcely knew what to do; he was quite distressed because he was so ugly.

So passed the first day, and afterwards matters grew worse and worse. Even his brothers and sisters behaved unkindly, saying: "May the cat take you, you ugly thing!" The ducks bit him, the hens pecked him, and the girl who fed the poultry kicked him. He ran through the hedge, and the little birds in the bushes were frightened and flew away. "That is because I am so ugly," thought the duckling, and ran on. At last he came to a wide moor, where lived some wild ducks. There he lay the whole night, feeling very tired and sorrowful. In the morning the wild ducks flew up, and then they saw their new companion. "Pray who are you?" asked they; and the duckling greeted them as politely as possible.

"You are really very ugly," said the wild ducks; "but that does not matter to us if you do not wish to marry into our family."

Poor thing! he had never thought of marrying. He only wished to lie among the reeds, and drink the water of the moor. There he stayed for two whole days. On the third day there came two wild geese, or rather goslings, for they had not been long out of their egg-shells, which accounts for their impertinence.

"Hark-ye," said they, "you are so ugly that we like you very well. Will you go with us and become a bird of passage? On another moor, not far from this, are some dear, sweet, wild geese, as lovely creatures as have ever said 'hiss, hiss'. It is a chance for you to get a wife; you may be lucky, ugly as you are."

Bang! a gun went off, and both goslings lay dead among the reeds. Bang! another gun went off, and whole flocks of wild geese flew up from the rushes. Again and again the same alarming noise was heard.

There was a great shooting party. The sportsmen lay in ambush all around. The dogs splashed about in the mud, bending the reeds and rushes in all directions. How frightened the poor little duck was! He turned away his head, thinking to hide it under his wing, and at the same moment a fierce-looking dog passed close to him, his tongue hanging out of his mouth, his eyes sparkling fearfully. His jaws were wide open. He thrust his nose close to the duckling, showing his sharp white teeth, and then, splash, splash! he was gone—gone without hurting him.

"Well! let me be thankful," sighed the duckling. "I am so ugly that even a dog will not bite me."

And he lay still, though the shooting continued among the reeds. The noise did not cease till late in the day, and even then the poor little thing dared not stir. He waited several hours before he looked around him, and then hastened away from the moor as fast as he could.

Towards evening he reached a little hut, so wretched that it knew not on which side to fall, and therefore remained standing. He noticed that the door had lost one of its hinges, and hung so much awry that there was a space between it and the wall wide enough to let him through. As the storm was becoming worse and worse, he crept into the room.

In this room lived an old woman, with her tom-cat and her hen. The cat, whom she called her little son, knew how to set up his back and purr. He could even throw out sparks when his fur was stroked the wrong way. The hen had very short legs, and was therefore called "Chickie Shortlegs"; she laid very good eggs, and the old woman loved her as her own child.

The next morning the cat began to mew and the hen to cackle when they saw the new guest.

"What is the matter?" asked the old woman, looking round. Her eyes were not good, so she took the duckling to be a fat duck who had lost her way. "This is a capital catch," said she. "I shall now have duck's eggs, if it be not a drake. We must wait and see." So the duckling was kept on trial for three weeks; but no eggs made their appearance.

The duckling sat in a corner feeling very much dispirited, till the fresh air and bright sunshine came into the room through the open door, and these gave him such a strong desire to swim that he could not help telling the hen.

"What ails you?" said the hen. "You have nothing to do, and therefore brood over these fancies; either lay eggs, or purr, then you will forget them."

"But it is so delicious to swim," said the duckling, "so delicious when the waters close over your head, and you plunge to the bottom."

"Well, that is a queer sort of pleasure," said the hen; "I think you must be crazy. Not to speak of myself, ask the cat—he is the wisest creature I know—whether he would like to swim, or to plunge to the bottom of the water. Ask your mistress: no one is cleverer than she. Do you think she would take pleasure in swimming, and in the waters closing over her head?"

"You do not understand me," said the duckling.

"What! we do not understand you! So you think yourself wiser than the cat and the old woman, not to speak of myself! Do not fancy any such thing, child, but be thankful for all the kindness that has been shown you. Are you not lodged in a warm room, and have you not the advantage of society from which you can learn something? Believe me, I wish you well. I tell you unpleasant truths, but it is thus that real friendship is shown. Come, for once give yourself the trouble either to learn to purr, or to lay eggs."

"I think I will take my chance, and go out into the wide world again," said the duckling.

"Well, go then," said the hen.

So the duckling went away. He soon found water, and swam on the surface and plunged beneath it; but all other animals passed him by, on account of his ugliness. The autumn came: the leaves turned yellow and brown; the wind caught them and danced them about; the air was cold; the clouds were heavy with hail or snow, and the raven sat on the hedge and croaked. The poor duckling was certainly not very comfortable!

One evening, just as the sun was setting, a flock of large birds rose from the brushwood. The duckling had never seen anything so beautiful before; their plumage was of a dazzling white, and they had long, slender necks. They were swans. They uttered a singular cry, spread out their long, splendid wings, and flew away from these cold regions to warmer countries, across the sea. They flew so high, so very high! and the ugly duckling's feelings were very strange. He turned round and round in the water like a wheel, strained his neck to look after them, and sent forth such a loud and strange cry that it almost frightened himself. Ah! he could not forget them, those noble birds! those happy birds! The duckling knew not what the birds were called, knew not whither they were flying, yet he loved them as he had never before loved anything. He envied them not. It would never have occurred to him to wish such beauty for himself. He would have been quite contented if the ducks in the duckyard had but endured his company.

And the winter was so cold! The duckling had to swim round and round in the water to keep it from freezing. But every night the opening in which he swam became smaller, the duckling had to make good use of his legs to prevent the water from freezing entirely. At last, wearied out, he lay stiff and cold in the ice.

Early in the morning there passed by a peasant, who saw him, broke the ice in pieces with his wooden shoe, and carried the duckling home to his wife.

The duckling soon revived.

The children would have played with him, but he thought they wished to tease him, and in his terror jumped into the milk-pail, so that the milk was splashed about the room. The good woman screamed and clapped her hands. He flew first into the tub where the butter was kept, and thence into the meal-barrel, and out again.

The woman screamed, and struck at him with the tongs; the children ran races with each other trying to catch him, and laughed and screamed likewise. It was well for him that the door stood open; he jumped out among the bushes, into the new-fallen snow, and lay there as in a dream.

But it would be too sad to relate all the trouble and misery he had to suffer during the winter. He was lying on a moor among the reeds when the sun began to shine warmly again. The larks were singing, and beautiful spring had returned.

Once more he shook his wings. They were stronger than formerly, and bore him forward quickly; and, before he was well aware of it, he was in a large garden where the apple trees stood in full bloom, where the syringas sent forth their fragrance, and hung their long green branches down into the winding canal. Oh! everything was so lovely, so full of the freshness of spring!

Out of the thicket came three beautiful white swans. They displayed their feathers so proudly, and swam so lightly! The duckling knew the glorious creatures, and was seized with a strange sadness.

"I will fly to them, those kingly birds!" said he. "They will kill me, because I, ugly as I am, have presumed to approach them; but it matters not. Better be killed by them than be bitten by the ducks, pecked by the hens, kicked by the girl who feeds the poultry, and have so much to suffer during the winter!" He flew into the water and swam towards the beautiful creatures. They saw him and shot forward to meet him. "Only kill me," said the poor duckling, and he bowed his head low, expecting death. But what did he see in the water? He saw beneath him his own form, no longer that of a plump, ugly, grey bird—it was that of a swan!

It matters not to have been born in a duckyard if one has been hatched from a swan's egg.

The larger swans swam round him and stroked him with their beaks, and he was very happy.

Some little children were running about in the garden. They threw grain and bread into the water, and the youngest exclaimed: "There is a new one!" The others also cried out: "Yes, a new swan has come!" and they clapped their hands, and ran and told their father and mother. Bread and cake were thrown into the water, and everyone said: "The new one is the best, so young and so beautiful!" and the old swans bowed before him. The young swan felt quite ashamed, and hid his head under his wing. He was all too happy, but still not proud, for a good heart is never proud.

He remembered how he had been laughed at and cruelly treated, and he now heard everyone say he was the most beautiful of all beautiful birds. The syringas bent down their branches towards him, and the sun shone warmly and brightly. He shook his feathers, stretched his slender neck, and in the joy of his heart said: "How little did I dream of so much happiness when I was the ugly, despised duckling!"

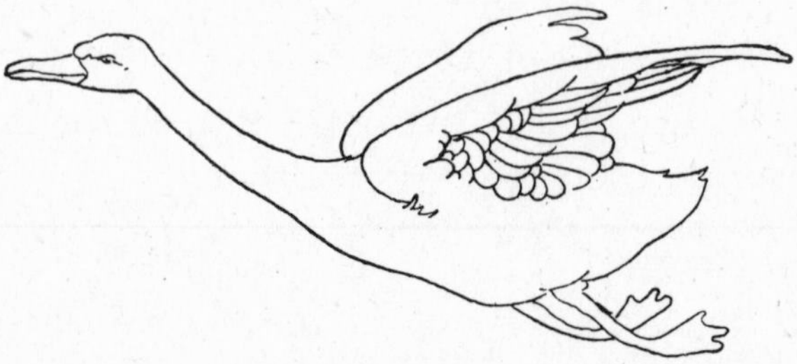

Briar Rose or The Sleeping Beauty

ONCE upon a time there lived a King and Queen who grieved because they had no child. One day, when the Queen was walking along the river bank, she saw a poor little fish that had thrown itself out of the water, and lay nearly dead on the bank. The Queen took pity on the fish, and put it back into the river. Before it swam away it lifted its head out of the water, and said:

"I know what your wish is, and it shall be fulfilled in return for your kindness to me—you will soon have a daughter."

What the little fish had foretold soon came to pass, and the Queen had a little girl, so beautiful that the King could not cease looking on her for joy, and said he would hold a feast, and show the Princess to all the land. So he asked his kinsmen, and nobles, and friends, and neighbours. But the Queen said:

"I will have the fairies also, that they may be kind and good to our daughter."

Now there were thirteen fairies in the kingdom; but, as the King and Queen had only twelve golden dishes for them to eat from, they were forced to leave one of the fairies without an invitation. So twelve came, each with a high red cap, and red shoes with high heels, and a long white wand. After the feast was over, they gathered round and gave all their best gifts to the little Princess. One gave goodness, another beauty, another riches, and so on, till she had all that was good in the world.

Just as eleven of them had done blessing her, a great noise was heard in the courtyard, and the thirteenth fairy came, with a black cap, and black shoes, and a broomstick in her hand; and presently she came into the dining-hall. As she had not been invited, she was very angry, and scolded the King and Queen, and set to work to take her revenge. She cried out:

"The King's daughter shall, in her fifteenth year, be wounded by a spindle, and fall down dead!"

Then the twelfth of the friendly fairies, who had not yet given her gift, came forward and said that the evil wish must be fulfilled, but that she could soften its mischief; so her gift was, that when the spindle wounded the King's daughter, she should not really die, but only fall asleep for a hundred years.

However, the King hoped to save his dear child from the threatened evil; so he ordered that all the spindles in the country should be bought up and burnt. But all the gifts of the first eleven fairies were in the meantime fulfilled; for the Princess was so beautiful, and well-behaved, and good, and wise that everyone loved her.

THE SLEEPING BEAUTY

On the day she was fifteen years old, the King and Queen were not at home, and she was alone in the palace. So she roved about by herself, till at last she came to an old tower, to which there was a narrow staircase ending at a little door. In the door was a golden key, and when she turned it the door sprang open, and there sat an old lady busily spinning.

"How now, good mother?" said the Princess. "What are you doing?"

"Spinning," said the old lady, and nodded her head; humming a tune, while buzz! went the wheel.

"How prettily that little thing turns round!" said the Princess, and took the spindle and began to try and spin. But scarcely had she touched it, before the fairy's prophecy was fulfilled; the spindle wounded her, and she fell down on the ground.

She was not dead, but had only fallen into a deep sleep; and the King and the Queen, who just then came home, and all their Court, fell asleep too; and the horses slept in the stables, and the dogs in the court fell asleep too; the pigeons

on the housetop; and the very flies slept upon the walls. The fire on the hearth left off blazing, and went to sleep; the jack stopped; the spit that was turning about with a goose upon it for the King's dinner stood still; and the cook, who was pulling the kitchen boy by the hair, to give him a box on the ear, let him go, and both fell asleep; the butler, who was slyly tasting the ale, fell asleep with the jug at his lips; and thus everything stood still and slept soundly.

A large hedge of thorns soon grew round the palace, and every year it became higher and thicker, till at last the old palace was surrounded and hidden, so that not even the roof or the chimneys could be seen. But there went a report through all the land of the beautiful sleeping Briar Rose (for so the King's daughter was called); so that, from time to time, several kings' sons came and tried to break through into the palace. This, however, none of them could ever do, for the thorns and bushes laid hold of them, as it were with hands, and there they stuck fast, and died wretchedly.

After many years there came a king's son, and an old

man told him the story of the thicket of thorns, and how a wonderful palace stood behind it, and how a beautiful princess, called Briar Rose, lay there asleep with all her Court. He told, too, how many princes had come, and had tried to break through the thicket, but that they had all stuck fast in it, and died. The young Prince said:

"All this shall not frighten me. I will go and see this Princess Briar Rose."

Now that very day the hundred years ended; and as the Prince came to the thicket, he saw nothing but beautiful flowering shrubs, through which he went with ease, and they shut in after him as thick as ever. He came at last to the palace, and there in the court lay the dogs asleep; and the horses were standing in the stables; and on the roof sat the pigeons fast asleep with their heads under their wings. When he came into the palace, the flies were sleeping on the walls; the spit was standing still; the butler had the jug of ale at his lips, going to drink; the maid sat with a fowl in her lap ready to be plucked; and the cook in the kitchen was still holding up her hand, as if she were going to beat the boy.

He went on farther, and all was so still that he could hear every breath he drew; till at last he came to the old tower, and opened the door of the little room in which Briar Rose was; and there she lay, fast asleep, on a couch by the window. She looked so beautiful that he could not take his eyes off her, so he stooped down and gave her a kiss. But the moment he kissed her she opened her eyes and awoke, and smiled upon him; and they went out together; and soon the King and Queen also awoke, and all the Court, and gazed on each other with great wonder. And the horses shook themselves, and the dogs jumped up and barked; the pigeons took their heads from under their wings, and looked about, and flew into the fields; the flies on the walls buzzed again; the fire in the kitchen blazed up; round went the jack, and round went the spit with the goose for the King's dinner upon it; the butler finished his draught of ale; the maid went on plucking the fowl; and the cook gave the boy the box on his ear.

And then the Prince and Briar Rose were married, and the wedding feast was given; and they lived happily together ever after.

Aladdin or the Wonderful Lamp

ALADDIN, the only son of a poor widow in China, was an idle lad who played about in the streets instead of helping his mother to earn their livelihood. One day he was observed by a stranger who thought he would be just the boy to serve as a tool. Now this stranger was a magician, and going up to Aladdin he pretended that he was his uncle, gave him some gold, and said that he would come to his home that evening. Aladdin's mother had never heard that her husband had a brother, but believed all that the stranger said, while as for Aladdin he was delighted on learning that his newly-found uncle was going to buy him new clothes and set him up in a shop.

The next morning the stranger came again, took Aladdin and fitted him out finely, gave him many nice things to eat, and then took him for a long walk, telling him all manner of diverting stories the while. At length they reached the

entrance of a narrow valley bounded on each side by bare lofty mountains. Aladdin then began to be frightened, and suggested that they should go back from so dreadful a place.

"No," said the Magician, seizing hold of the boy's arm, "no going back at present."

Aladdin followed his uncle still farther into the valley, till they seemed to be surrounded with high black mountains. Suddenly the Magician stood still, and in a rough voice commanded Aladdin to gather some sticks for a fire. Aladdin obeyed, trembling, and when he had collected a large heap, the Magician set them on fire. Presently the blaze rose high, and the Magician threw some powder into the midst of it, and pronounced mystical words, which Aladdin did not understand. Instantly they were surrounded by a thick smoke; the earth shook beneath their feet, the mountain burst asunder and discovered a broad flat stone with a large brass ring in the middle of it. Aladdin was so terrified that he was going to run away, but the Magician gave him a box on the ear that knocked him down. Poor Aladdin got up again, and, with tears running down his cheeks, said:

"What have I done, Uncle, that you should use me so cruelly?"

"I did not mean to strike thee so severely," said the Magician. "But thou shouldst not think of running away from me, when I only brought thee hither to do thee a service. Know that under this stone lies hid a treasure that will make you richer than the greatest monarch on the earth, and of which I alone know how to make you master."

Aladdin forgot his box on the ear when he heard of the treasure, and eagerly promised to do whatever he was desired to perform.

"Come then," said the Magician, "take hold of the brass ring, and lift up that stone."

When the stone was pulled up, there appeared a deep hollow cave, and a narrow flight of steps.

"Go," said the Magician, "down into that cavern. At the bottom you will find a door, which will lead you into a large, vaulted place, divided into three great halls, full of silver and gold coin. Pass through quickly, for if you touch anything they contain, you will meet with instant death. At the end of the third hall you will see a fine garden; cross the garden by a path that will bring you upon a terrace, where you will see a lighted lamp, standing in a niche. Take the lamp down, and put out the light, and when you have thrown away the wick, and poured out the oil, put the lamp into your bosom, and bring it to me. If you wish for any of the fruit of the garden, you may gather as much as you please." Having said this, the

Magician put a ring on Aladdin's finger, and told him it was a preservative against all evil, if he faithfully obeyed his directions.

"Go down boldly," he added, "and we shall both be rich and happy all the rest of our lives."

Aladdin jumped into the cave, went down the steps, and found the three halls, as the Magician had described them. He went through them without touching anything, crossed the garden without stopping, took down the lamp from the niche, threw out the wick and the oil, and, as the Magician had desired him, put the lamp into his bosom. As he came down from the terrace he was greatly surprised to observe that the branches of the trees were loaded, as he thought, with beautiful pieces of glass of all colours, that dazzled his eyes with their lustre; and though he would rather have found peaches, figs, and grapes, yet these pieces of coloured glass were so very pretty that he could not help filling his pockets, and two purses his uncle had given him, with them.

"Pray, Uncle," said Aladdin, when he came to the steps, "give me your hand to assist me in getting out."

"Yes, yes, but give me the lamp first," said the Magician.

"I cannot, dear Uncle, till I am out of this place," replied Aladdin.

"Wretch," roared the Magician in a fury, "deliver it this instant!"

"No, I will not," said Aladdin, "till you have helped me out of the cave."

The Magician's eyes flashed fire.

"Villain, thou shalt repent thy obstinacy!" he exclaimed, stretching out his arm to strike Aladdin, when some powder

. . . and there she lay, fast asleep, on a couch by the window.
(PAGE 56)

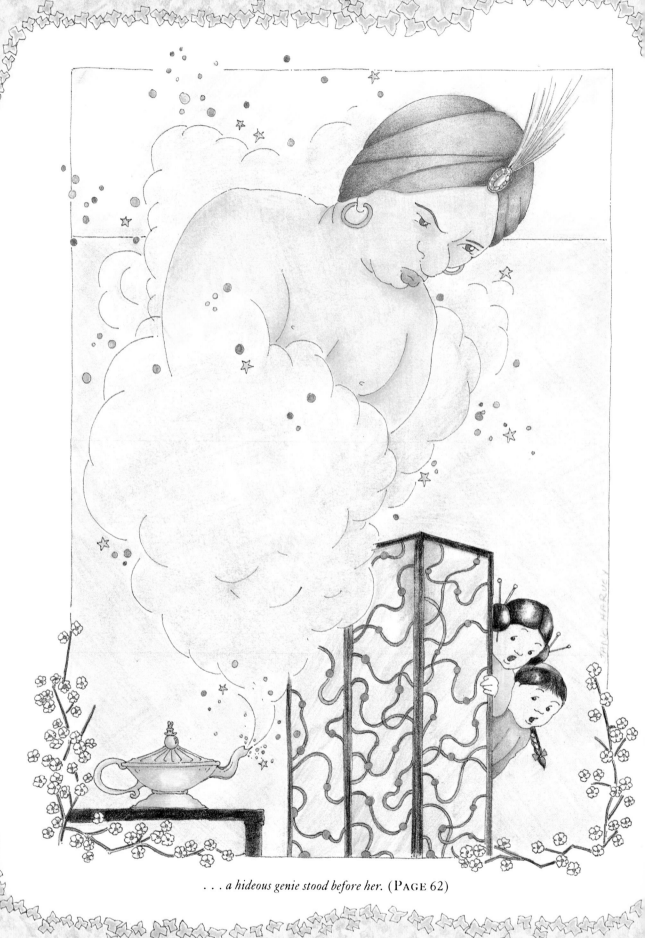

. . . a hideous genie stood before her. (PAGE 62)

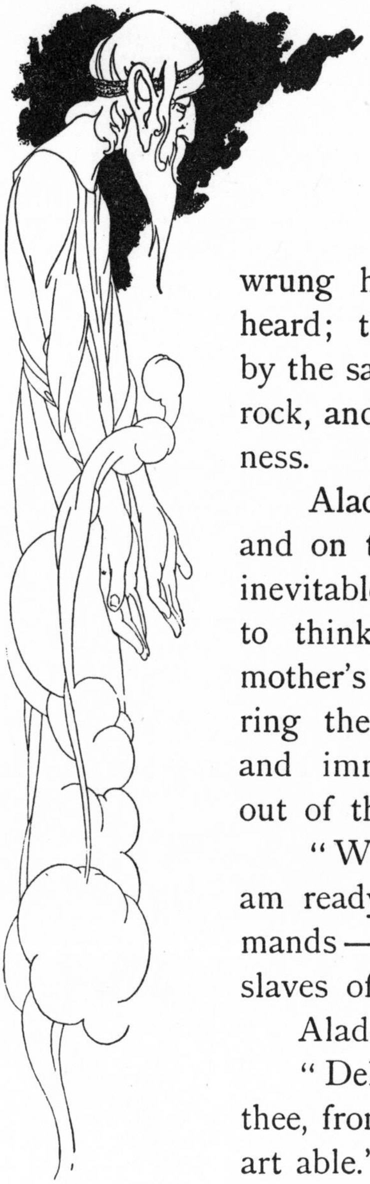

he still held in his hand dropped into the fire; the rock shook with thunder, the great stone moved again into its place, and Aladdin remained buried alive in this cavern of treasure. In vain he cried and wrung his hands: his cries could not be heard; the doors of the halls were closed by the same enchantment that had closed the rock, and he was left to perish in total darkness.

Aladdin remained in this state two days, and on the third day looked upon death as inevitable. Clasping his hands with agony, to think of his own destruction and his mother's sorrow, he chanced to press the ring the Magician had put on his finger, and immediately an enormous genie rose out of the earth, and said:

"What wouldst thou have with me? I am ready to obey thy commands — I and the other slaves of the ring."

Aladdin, trembling, said:

"Deliver me, I beseech thee, from this place, if thou art able."

He no sooner spoke than the earth opened, and he found himself on the very spot where he had been brought by the Magician. When at home again he hastened to relate to his mother all that had befallen him.

"Ah, my son," she cried, "that man was no brother of thy father's! He was a wicked enchanter, that meant to make thee useful to him in some bad purpose or other. Let it be a warning to thee, Aladdin, to work for thy own subsistence, and then thou wilt not want the assistance of deceitful strangers."

Aladdin, having promised his mother to attend to her advice, entreated her to bring him some food, as he was almost starved. Alas! the poor woman had neither food nor money in the house, for while her son had been absent she had neglected her spinning to search for him.

"Well, Mother," said Aladdin, "do not mind. Dry your tears, and reach me the lamp I put on the shelf just now, and I will go and sell it."

The woman took down the lamp, and, thinking it would sell better if it were cleaner, began to rub it with sand. Instantly a hideous genie stood before her, and said, in a voice like thunder:

"What wouldst thou? I am ready to obey thy commands—I and all the other slaves of the lamp."

Aladdin, having seen the former genie, was less frightened than his mother, who fainted away, while he said boldly:

"I am hungry; bring me something to eat."

The genie disappeared, and presently returned with twelve large plates of silver, full of the most savoury meats, six white loaves, two bottles of wine, and two silver drinking cups. Having placed them all in order on a table, he vanished.

Aladdin, sprinkling some water on his mother, entreated her to arise and eat of the goodly banquet.

"What!" cried the old woman, looking around in amazement; "has the Sultan been informed of our poverty, and sent us all these fine things from his table?"

"Come, Mother," replied Aladdin, "let us eat now, and talk after."

Accordingly they wasted no time, and, having dined plentifully, set aside enough to serve them for two days more.

On hearing that the genie had provided their repast, Aladdin's mother besought him to sell the lamp, and have nothing to do with genies; but Aladdin was resolved not to part with the lamp, which he perceived to be of infinite value, both from the service he had just received, and from the eagerness of the Magician to get possession of it. He assured his mother, however, that he would never use it except in great necessity, but would endeavour to get some employment. At night they were greatly surprised to see the bright light that issued from the heap of pieces of coloured glass that Aladdin had laid in a corner;

they were not aware that they were really jewels of immense value, and the mother and son went as quietly to sleep as if no such treasure had been in their possession. On the following morning Aladdin sold one of his silver plates to a Jew, to purchase a few necessaries that were wanting in their dwelling.

One day Aladdin heard a proclamation commanding all the people to retire into their houses, as the beautiful Princess Balroudour, whom no one must look upon, was coming to the public baths. Aladdin was a long way from home; people were running this way and that, and he was at a loss where to go; and hearing the drums and trumpets that preceded the Princess, he ran into a large hall and hid himself behind a folding door. This was the entrance to the baths; and as soon as the Princess passed the gate she pulled off her veil, thinking she was only surrounded by her own slaves. There was a crevice in the door, which permitted Aladdin to see the Princess, and her beauty made so deep an impression on him that he could think of nothing else for days afterwards, and neglected his employment and his meals. At length he could conceal his love no longer.

"Mother," said he, "I love the Princess Balroudour, and you must demand her for me in marriage of the Sultan."

The old woman concluded he must be mad; but on his repeating that he was resolved to be the husband of the lovely Princess, she could not forbear laughing, and bid him remember he was the son of Mustapha, the tailor, and no prince or governor who could pretend to be the son-in-law of the Sultan.

"Mother," said Aladdin, "I am not so poor as you imagine. Since I have frequented the jewellers' shops I

have learnt to know the value of those things I used to call pieces of glass; it is with those things that I intend to purchase the goodwill of the Sultan."

Aladdin's mother laughed again, and refused to hear anything more of such foolish projects. Poor Aladdin meanwhile pined almost to death, and when his mother saw him nearly at the last gasp she promised she would go to the Sultan, if that would restore him. Aladdin, overjoyed, sent her to borrow a large china dish, which he filled with the finest jewels from his heap; and having tied it up carefully in two napkins, the poor old woman set out for the Sultan's palace with a heavy heart, fearing to be punished for her presumption. Being come to the divan, where the Sultan was administering justice, she placed herself opposite the throne, and waited till her turn should come to be called forward. When the Vizier bade her approach she fell on her knees and besought the Sultan's pardon, who commanded her to speak on and fear nothing. She then related the story of her son's falling in love with the Princess, and

the advice she had given him, stopping at every three words to entreat the Sultan's forgiveness, who only smiled, and asked what was tied up in the napkin. When the dish was uncovered the Sultan started with surprise; he had never before seen jewels of such size or lustre.

"Your son," he said, "can be no ordinary person if he can afford to make such presents as these."

The Vizier approached, and whispered something to the Sultan, who nodded, and, turning to Aladdin's mother, said:

"Tell your son that he shall have the Princess Balroudour in marriage as soon as he sends me forty basins of massy gold filled with such jewels as these, carried by forty black slaves, who shall be led by forty white slaves, all magnificently clothed. Hasten and declare my will to your son."

Aladdin's mother retired in grief and consternation. She was surprised to see that her son only smiled at the Sultan's demand; she concluded, therefore, he had already got the better of his foolish passion, and went joyfully to market. As soon as she was gone, Aladdin rubbed the lamp, and the genie stood before him, whom he commanded to bring the basins of gold, the jewels, and the black slaves and white, as the Sultan had required; and presently the house was filled with the splendid train of slaves, magnificently dressed, bearing basins of massy gold, filled with the rarest jewels.

When Aladdin's mother returned from market she trembled to see these wonderful things; but as her son entreated her to make haste back to the divan, she stayed to ask no questions, and put herself at the head of the procession, which drew after it all the idle and curious people of the city. When she entered the divan she prostrated herself at the foot of the throne, and said:

"Sire, my son Aladdin is sensible that this present he sends Your Majesty is much below the worth of the Princess Balroudour; but he hopes Your Majesty will accept it as token of his submission to your royal commands."

The Sultan was not able to reply, he was so taken up with the beauty of the slaves, who looked like so many kings, and whose habits were even richer than his own; at length he said:

"Bring your son hither, that I may bestow on him the hand of my daughter."

Aladdin again summoned the genie of the lamp, who transported him invisibly to a fine bath of rosewater, and dressed him in the most sumptuous apparel. A horse, with saddle and housings of pure gold, surpassing the best in the Sultan's stables, was provided for him. He had a train of slaves ready, finely mounted, and bearing magnificent presents for the Princess.

Aladdin mounted his horse, and so great a change had the care of the genie made in his appearance that no one knew him to be poor Aladdin, the tailor's son, but took him for some mighty prince, accustomed to grandeur and magnificence all his life. When the Sultan beheld him he was no less surprised at his good mien, fine shape, and dignity of demeanour than at the elegance and costliness of his apparel. Aladdin would have thrown himself at the feet of the Sultan, but was prevented by the Sultan's embracing him and seating him on his right hand.

They conversed together during some hours, and the Sultan was so charmed with his good sense and modesty that he proposed to marry the young lovers that very evening. To this, however, Aladdin objected, saying it was necessary that he should build a palace to receive his Princess; and he entreated the Sultan would grant him a piece of ground opposite the gates of the royal palace for this purpose. The Sultan agreed to this, and they separated.

When the Sultan arose the next morning, great was his amazement to behold, opposite to his own, a palace of the purest architecture, and half the inhabitants of the city already gathered in crowds to gaze on the wonder. He was presently informed that Aladdin waited to conduct His Majesty to his new palace. The Sultan was more and more amazed at every step; for the walls were built of wedges of gold and silver, and the ornaments were of jasper, agate, and porphyry, intermixed with diamonds, rubies, emeralds, amethysts, and everything that was most rare and beautiful. The treasury was full of gold coin, the offices filled with domestics, the stables with the finest horses and carriages, with grooms and equerries in splendid liveries. The Sultan acknowledged that the wealth of all his dominions was not equal to the purchase of such costly rarities as the hall, with twenty-four windows, of Aladdin's palace could produce.

Aladdin and the Princess were speedily married, and lived very happily; but the fame of his magnificence spread to all corners of the world, and at length reached Africa and the ears of the Magician, who was at no loss to know the source of Aladdin's riches. He disguised himself, and travelled to China. Having come to the city where Aladdin lived, he bought a number of beautiful lamps, and, when he knew that Aladdin was out hunting, he went under the windows of the Princess's apartments, crying:

"Lamps! lamps! New lamps for old!"

"Oh," said one of the slaves, "let us try if the fool means what he says! There is an ugly old lamp on the cornice of the hall of twenty-four windows; we will put a new one in its place if the old fellow will really give us one."

The Princess agreed, and away ran one of the slaves with the lamp to the Magician, who willingly gave her the best he had among his new ones, and retired to enjoy the triumph of his revenge.

As soon as night arrived, he summoned the genie of the lamp, and commanded him to transport him, the palace, and the Princess to the remotest corner of Africa. The order was instantly obeyed.

It is impossible to describe the confusion, grief, and dismay of the Sultan when he arose to find the beautiful palace vanished and his daughter lost. All the people of the city ran in terror through the streets, and a number of soldiers were sent in search of Aladdin, who was not returned from hunting.

On hearing that his palace and his wife were gone, Aladdin fainted away, and was soon after dragged before the Sultan like a criminal, and would have been beheaded had not the Sultan been afraid to enrage the people.

"Go, wretch," cried the Sultan; "I grant thee thy life; but if ever thou appearest before me again, thy death shall be the consequence, unless in forty days thou bringest me tidings of my daughter."

Aladdin left the palace, not knowing whither to turn. At length he stopped at a brook to wash his eyes; as he stooped to the water his foot slipped, and, catching hold of a piece of rock, he pressed the Magician's ring, and the genie of the ring appeared before him, saying:

"What wouldst thou?"

"Oh, genie," cried Aladdin, "bring my palace back where yesterday it stood!"

"What you command," answered the genie, "is not in my power. I am only the

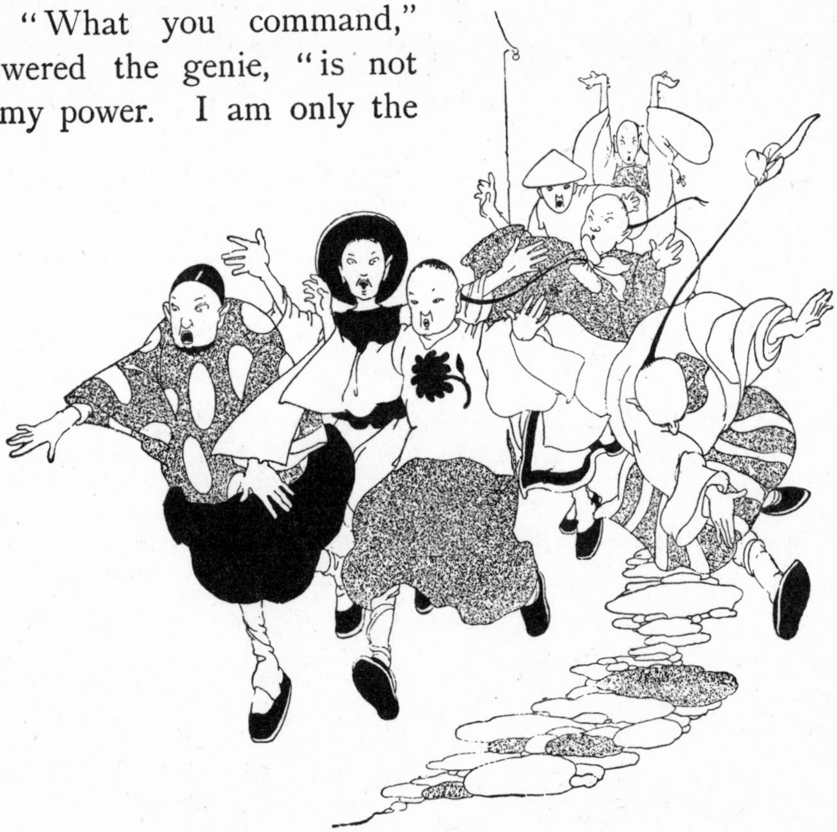

genie of the ring; you need the genie of the lamp for that service."

"Then I command thee," said Aladdin, "to transport me to the place where it stands now."

Instantly Aladdin found himself beside his own palace, in a meadow not far from a great city.

The Princess Balroudour was walking backward and forward in her own chamber, weeping for the loss of Aladdin. Happening to approach the window, she beheld him under it, and, making a sign to him not to betray his joy, she sent a slave to bring him in by a private door. The Princess and her husband having mingled their tears and embraces, Aladdin said:

"Tell me, my Princess, what is become of an old lamp I left on the cornice of the hall of four-and-twenty windows?"

The Princess related the manner in which her slaves had exchanged it for a new one, and added that she feared all her misfortunes were owing to that lamp, since she observed that the tyrant, in whose power she was, always carried it in his bosom. Aladdin, convinced that it was his old enemy the Magician who had got possession of the lamp, contrived with the Princess means of getting it from him.

Aladdin went into the city, disguised as a slave, and procured a powder that, on being swallowed, would cause a death-like sleep, and the Princess invited the Magician to sup with her. He was quite delighted with her kindness; and while they were at table, she ordered a slave to bring two cups of wine, which she had herself prepared; and after pretending to taste the one she held in her hand, she asked the Magician to change cups, as was the custom, she said, between lovers in China. He joyfully seized her goblet, and, drinking it all at a draught, fell senseless on the floor.

Aladdin was at hand to snatch the lamp from his bosom; and having thrown the traitor out, the genie was summoned, and in an instant the Princess, the palace, and all that it contained, were transported to their original place. The very morning of the return of Aladdin's palace, the Sultan had risen by break of day to indulge his sorrow; when, to his unspeakable joy, he beheld the vacancy filled up! During a whole week nothing was to be seen but illuminations, fireworks, balls, and entertainments throughout the city, in honour of Aladdin's safe return.

Aladdin did not forget now to carry the lamp always about him, and things went on very well for some time. But the Magician, having slept off his potion, and found the lamp and the palace gone, once more

set out for China. Having come to the end of his journey, he went to the cell of a holy woman named Fatima, renowned through the city for her sanctity, and her cure of headache. The cruel Magician, having killed the old woman and buried her, dressed himself in her garments, and, having stained his face and eyebrows, walked out into the city, and counterfeited so well that everybody believed him to be the holy woman. At length he approached the palace, and the Princess, hearing Fatima was in the street, sent her slaves to invite the holy woman into the palace.

The pretended Fatima was kindly entertained by the Princess, who led her through the apartments of the palace, and showed her the magnificent hall of twenty-four windows.

"Princess," said the false Fatima, "forgive my offering my opinion, but I think if a roc's egg were hung up in the middle of the dome, this hall would have no parallel in the four quarters of the world, and your palace would be the wonder of the universe."

"My good Fatima," said the Princess, "what sort of a bird is a roc, and where may one get an egg?"

"Princess," replied Fatima, "it is a bird of prodigious size, which inhabits the top of Mount Caucasus: the architect that built your palace can get you one."

The pretended Fatima would now have withdrawn, but the Princess insisted on her continuing in the palace some days. That very evening, Aladdin, who had been absent on a journey, returned home sooner than was expected, and found the Princess somewhat melancholy. He begged to know the cause, and she confessed she was wishing she could have the dome of the grand hall ornamented with a roc's egg.

"Beautiful Princess," said Aladdin, "your wish shall be gratified."

He instantly withdrew to the hall of four-and-twenty windows, and, calling for the genie of the lamp, said:

"Good genie, I command thee, in the name of the lamp, to hang up a roc's egg in the centre of this dome."

The genie, on hearing these words, uttered so loud and

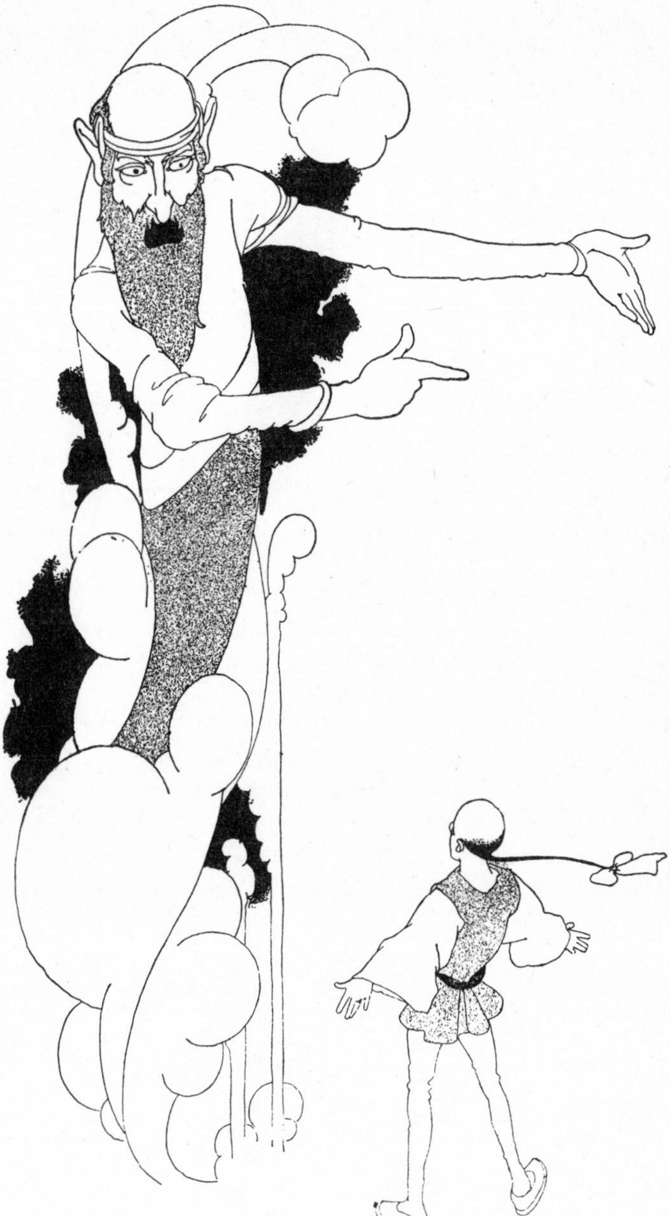

terrible a cry, that the palace shook with the noise, and Aladdin had nearly fallen to the ground.

"What!" said he; "after everything I and my fellow slaves have done to serve thee, dost thou command me to bring my master and hang him up in the midst of this dome? This attempt deserves my utmost vengeance, and I would reduce your palace to a heap of ashes, but that I know you are not the contriver of this wish. The African Magician is now under your roof, disguised as the holy woman Fatima, whom he has murdered.

Go, punish his crimes, or your own destruction is certain."

The genie vanished, and left Aladdin in the utmost agitation. He was not long in deliberating on the means of destroying his enemy. He went to his wife's apartment, and, throwing himself upon a sofa, complained of a violent headache. The Princess, delighted with the idea of being able to relieve her husband's pain, exclaimed that the good Fatima was in the palace, and then ran to bring her.

The pretended Fatima came with one hand lifted up as if to bless Aladdin, while the other grasped a dagger concealed in her garment. Aladdin kept an eye on her, and, as soon as she came near him, seized the hand that held the dagger, and stabbed the traitor to the heart.

The Princess began to scream and tear her hair with grief, to think her husband had killed the holy Fatima; till Aladdin, snatching off the hood of the cloak, showed her the wicked Magician concealed beneath. Her grief was then changed to joy that they had escaped his wicked snares; and shortly after, the Sultan dying without a son, Aladdin and the Princess Balroudour ascended the throne, reigned together many years, and left behind them a numerous, virtuous, and illustrious progeny.

'I see two men on horseback.' (PAGE 83)

. . . a strange hut made of bread, with roof of cake, and windows of barley-sugar. (PAGE 91)

The Story of Blue Beard

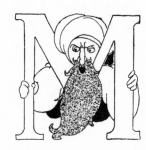

MANY years ago there was a very rich man who had a singular blue beard, which made him very ugly. Being left a widower, he wished to marry one of the two beautiful daughters of a neighbouring lady, and at length the younger of these girls consented to be his wife.

About a month after the marriage, Blue Beard told his bride that he must leave her for a time, as he had some business to attend to at a distance. He gave her his keys, and told her to make free of everything and entertain her friends while he was absent, but ended by drawing one key from the bunch and saying:

"This small key belongs to the room at the end of the long gallery—and that, my dear, is the one room you must not enter, nor even put the key into the lock, without disaster. Should you disobey, your punishment would be dreadful."

Blue Beard set out on his journey, and for a time his wife found pleasure in showing her friends all her magnifi-

cence; but again and again she wondered as to what could be the reason why she was not to visit the room at the end of the long gallery. At length her curiosity became such that she could not resist the temptation to take just one peep within the forbidden door. When she reached the door she stopped for a few moments to think of her husband's warning, and that he would not fail to keep his word should she disobey him. But she was so very curious to know what was inside, that she determined to venture in spite of everything.

Accordingly, with a trembling hand, she put the key into the lock, and the door immediately opened. The window shutters being closed, she at first saw nothing; but in a short time she perceived that the floor was covered with clotted blood, on which the bodies of several dead women were lying. (These were all the wives whom Blue Beard had married, and murdered one after another!) She was ready to sink with fear, and the key of the door, which she held in her hand, fell on the floor. When she had somewhat recovered from her fright, she took it up, locked the door, and hastened to her own room, terrified by what she had seen.

As she observed that the key had got stained with blood in falling on the floor, she wiped it two or three times to clean it; still, however, the blood remained: she next washed it; but the blood did not stir: she then scoured it with brick-dust, and afterwards with sand. But notwithstanding all she could do, the blood was still there; for the key was a fairy, who was Blue Beard's friend, so that as fast as she got the stain off one side it appeared again on the other.

Early in the evening Blue Beard returned, saying he had not proceeded far before he was met by a messenger, coming to tell him that the business was concluded without his presence being necessary, upon which his wife said

everything she could think of to make him believe that she was transported with joy at his unexpected return.

The next morning, he asked for the keys. She gave them, but, as she could not help showing her fright, Blue Beard easily guessed what had happened.

"How is it," said he, "that the key of the closet upon the ground floor is not here?"

"Is it not?" said the wife. "I must have left it on my dressing table."

"Be sure you give it me by and by," replied Blue Beard.

After going several times backwards and forwards, pretending to look for the key, she was at last obliged to give it to Blue Beard. He looked at it attentively, and then said:

"How came this blood upon the key?"

"I am sure I do not know," replied the lady, turning as pale as death.

"You do not know?" said Blue Beard sternly. "But I know well enough. You have been in the closet on the ground floor. Very well, madam; since you are so mightily fond of this closet, you shall certainly take your place among the ladies you saw there."

His wife, almost dead with fear, fell upon her knees, asked his pardon a thousand times for her disobedience, and entreated him to forgive her, looking all the time so sorrowful and lovely that she would have melted any heart that was not harder than a rock.

But Blue Beard answered:

"No, no, madam; you shall die this very minute."

"Alas," said the poor creature, "if I must die, allow me, at least, a little time to say my prayers!"

"Come down instantly, or I will fetch you"

"I give you," replied the cruel Blue Beard, "half a quarter of an hour—not one moment longer."

When Blue Beard had left her to herself, she called her sister; and, after telling her that she had but half of quarter of an hour to live:

"Prithee," said she, "Sister Ann" (this was her sister's name), "run up to the tower, and see if my brothers are not in sight; they promised to come and visit me to-day; and if you see them, make a sign for them to gallop on as fast as possible."

Her sister instantly did as she was desired, and the terrified lady every minute called out:

"Sister Ann, do you see anyone coming?"

And her sister answered:

"I see nothing but the sun, which makes a dust, and the grass, which looks green."

In the meanwhile, Blue Beard, with a great scimitar in his hand, bawled as loud as he could to his wife:

"Come down instantly, or I will fetch you."

"One moment longer, I beseech you," replied she, and again called softly to her sister:

"Sister Ann, do you see anyone coming?"

To which she answered:

"I see nothing but the sun, which makes a dust, and the grass, which looks green."

Blue Beard again bawled out:

"Come down, I say, this very moment, or I shall come and fetch you."

"I am coming; indeed I will come in one minute," sobbed his unhappy wife. Then she once more cried out:

"Sister Ann, do you see anyone coming?"

"I see," said her sister, "a cloud of dust a little to the left."

"Do you think it is my brothers?" continued the wife.

"Alas, no, dear sister," replied she, "it is only a flock of sheep!"

"Will you come down or not, madam?" said Blue Beard, in the greatest rage imaginable.

"Only one moment more," answered she. And then she called out for the last time:

"Sister Ann! do you see no one coming?"

"I see," replied her sister, "two men on horseback coming to the house; but they are still at a great distance."

"God be praised!" cried she; "it is my brothers. Give them a sign to make what haste they can."

At the same moment Blue Beard cried out so loud for her to come down, that his voice shook the whole house.

The poor lady,

with her hair loose and her eyes swimming in tears, came down, and fell on her knees to Blue Beard, and was going to beg him to spare her life, but he interrupted her, saying: "All this is of no use, for you shall die;" then, seizing her with one hand by the hair, and raising the scimitar he held in the other, he was going with one blow to strike off her head.

The unfortunate creature, turning towards him, desired to have a single moment allowed her to recollect herself.

"No, no," said Blue Beard; "I will give you no more time, I am determined. You have had too much already."

Again he raised his arm. Just at this instant a loud knocking was heard at the gates, which made Blue Beard wait for a moment to see who it was. The gates were opened, and two officers entered, and, with their swords in their hands, ran instantly to Blue Beard, who, seeing they were his wife's brothers, endeavoured to escape from their presence; but they pursued and seized him before he had got twenty steps, and, plunging their swords into his body, he immediately fell dead at their feet.

The poor wife, who was almost as dead as her husband, was unable at first to rise and embrace her brothers. She soon, however, recovered; and, as Blue Beard had no heirs, she found herself the possessor of his great riches.

She employed a portion of her vast fortune in giving a marriage dowry to her sister Ann, who soon after became the wife of one by whom she had long been beloved. Another part she employed in buying captains' commissions for her two brothers; and the rest she presented to a most worthy gentleman whom she married soon after, and whose kind treatment soon made her forget Blue Beard's cruelty.

Hansel and Grethel

ONCE as a poor woodman went to cut wood in the forest he heard a little cry; so he followed the sound, till at last he looked up a tree, and on one of the branches sat a tiny child. Its mother had fallen asleep, and a vulture had taken it out of her lap and flown away with it, and left it on the tree. The woodcutter climbed up, took the child down, and found it was a pretty little girl; and he said to himself: "I will take this child home, and bring her up with my son Hansel." So he brought her to his cottage, and called her Grethel, and the two children were so fond of each other that they were never happy except when together.

But the woodcutter became very poor, and had nothing in the world he could call his own; indeed he had scarcely

bread enough for his wife and the two children to eat. At last the time came when even that was all gone, and he knew not where to seek help in his need. At night, his wife said to him: "Husband, listen to me, and take the two children out early to-morrow morning; give each of them a piece of bread, and then lead them into the midst of the wood, where it is thickest, make a fire for them, and go away and leave them to shift for themselves, for we can no longer keep them here." And she would not let him have any peace until he came into her hard-hearted plan.

Meantime the poor children, lying awake restless, and weak from hunger, heard all that Hansel's mother said to her husband. "Now," thought Grethel to herself, "it is all up with us", and she began to weep. But Hansel crept to her bedside, and said: "Do not be afraid, Grethel, I will find some help for us." Then he got up, put on his jacket, and opened the door and went out.

The moon shone upon the little court before the cottage, and the white pebbles glittered like daisies on the meadows. So he stooped down, and put as many as he could into his pocket, and then went back to the house. "Now, Grethel," said he, "rest in peace!" and he went to bed and fell fast asleep.

HANSEL AND GRETHEL

Early in the morning the woodman's wife came and awoke them. "Get up, children," said she, "we are going into the wood; there is a piece of bread for each of you, but take care of it, and keep some for the afternoon."

Grethel took the bread, and carried it in her apron, because Hansel had his pocket full of stones; and they made their way into the wood.

After a time, Hansel stood still and looked towards home; and after a while he turned again, and so on several times. Then his father said: "Hansel, why do you keep turning and lagging about so?"

"Ah, Father," answered Hansel, "I am stopping to look

at my white cat, that sits on the roof, and wants to say goodbye to me."

"You little fool!" said his mother; "that is not your cat; it is the morning sun shining on the chimney-top."

Now Hansel had not been looking at the cat, but had all the while been lingering behind to drop from his pocket one white pebble after another along the road.

When they came into the midst of the wood, the woodman said: "Run about, children, and pick up some wood, and I will make a fire to keep us warm."

So they piled up a heap of brushwood, and set it on fire; and the mother said: "Now set yourselves by the fire, and go to sleep, while we go and cut wood in the forest. Be sure you wait till we come and fetch you." Hansel and Grethel sat by the fireside till the afternoon, and then ate their pieces of bread. They fancied the woodman was still in the wood, because they thought they heard the blows of his axe; but it was a bough which he had cunningly hung in such a way that the wind blew it against the other boughs; and so it sounded as the axe does in cutting. They waited till evening; but the woodman and his wife kept away, and no one came to fetch them.

When it was dark, Grethel began to cry; but Hansel said: "Wait till the moon rises." And when the moon rose he took her by the hand, and there lay the pebbles along the ground, glittering like new pieces of money, and marking out the way. Towards morning they came again to the woodman's house, and he was glad in his heart when he saw the children, for he had grieved at leaving them alone.

Not long afterwards there was again no bread in the house, and Hansel and Grethel heard the wife say to her husband: "The children found their way back once, and I took it in good part; but now there is only half a loaf of bread left for them in the house; to-morrow you must take them deeper into the wood, that they may not find their way out, or we shall be starved."

It grieved the husband in his heart to do as his selfish wife wished, and he thought it would be better to share their last morsel with the children; but, as he had done as she said once, he did not dare now to say no. When the children heard their plan, Hansel got up, and wanted to pick up pebbles as before. But when he came to the door, he found his mother had locked it. Still he comforted Grethel, and said: "Sleep in peace, dear Grethel! God is very kind, and will help us."

Early in the morning, a piece of bread was given to each of them, but smaller than the one they had before.

Upon the road Hansel crumbled his in his pocket, and often stood still and threw a crumb upon the ground. "Why do you lag so behind, Hansel?" said the woodman; "go your ways on before."

"I am looking at my little dove that is sitting upon the roof, and wants to say goodbye to me."

"You silly boy!" said the wife; "that is not your little dove; it is the morning sun, that shines on the chimney-top."

But Hansel went on crumbling his bread, and throwing it on the ground. And thus they went on farther into the wood.

There they were again told to sit down by a large fire, and go to sleep; and the woodman and his wife said they would come in the evening and fetch them away. In the afternoon, Hansel shared Grethel's bread, because he had strewed all his upon the road; but the day passed away, and evening passed away, and no one came to the poor children. Still Hansel comforted Grethel and said: "Wait till the moon rises; and then I shall be able to see the crumbs of bread which I have strewed, and they will show us the way home."

The moon rose; but when Hansel looked for the crumbs they were gone, for hundreds of little birds in the wood had found them and picked them up. Hansel, however, set out to try and find his way home; but they soon lost themselves, and went on through the night and all the next day, till at last they lay down and fell asleep. Another day they went on as before, but still did not come to the end of the wood; and they were as hungry as could be, for they had had nothing to eat.

In the afternoon of the third day they came to a strange

little hut, made of bread, with roof of cake, and windows of barley-sugar. "Now we will sit down and eat till we have had enough," said Hansel; "I will eat off the roof for my share; do you eat the windows, Grethel; they will be nice and sweet for you." Whilst Grethel, however, was picking at the barley-sugar, a pretty voice called softly from within:

"Tip, tap! who goes there?"

But the children answered:

"The wind, the wind,
That blows through the air!"

and went on eating. Now Grethel had broken out a round pane of the window for herself, and Hansel had torn off a large piece of cake from the roof, when the door opened, and a little old fairy came out. At this Hansel and Grethel were so frightened that they let fall what they had in their hands. But the old lady nodded to

them, and said: "Dear children, come in with me; you shall have something good."

So she led them into her little hut, and brought plenty to eat—milk and pancakes, with sugar, apples, and nuts; and then two beautiful little beds were got ready, and Grethel and Hansel laid themselves down, and thought they were in heaven. But the fairy was a spiteful one, and made her pretty sweetmeat house to entrap little children. Early in the morning she went to their little beds; and though she saw the two sleeping, and looking so sweetly, she had no pity on them, but was glad they were in her power. Then she took up Hansel, and fastened him in a coop by himself, and when he awoke he found himself behind a grating, shut up safely, as chickens are; but she shook Grethel, and called out: "Get up, you lazy little thing, and fetch some water; and go into the kitchen, and cook something good to eat. Your brother is shut up yonder. I shall fatten him, and when he is fat, I think I shall eat him."

When the fairy was gone, poor Grethel watched her time,

and got up, and ran to Hansel, and told him what she had heard, and said: "We must run away quickly, for the old woman is a bad fairy, and will kill us."

But Hansel said: "You must first steal away her fairy wand, that we may save ourselves if she should follow; and bring the pipe, too, that hangs up in her room."

Then the little maiden ran back, and fetched the magic wand and the pipe, and away they went together. So when the old fairy came back, and could see no one at home, she sprang in a great rage to the window, and looked out into the wide world (which she could do, far and near), and a long way off she spied Grethel, running away with her dear Hansel. "You are already a great way off," said she; "but you will still fall into my hands."

Then she put on her boots, which walked several miles at a step, and scarcely made two steps with them before she overtook the children; but Grethel saw that the fairy was coming after them, and, by the help of the wand, turned her friend Hansel into a lake of water, and herself into a swan, which swam about in the middle of it. So the fairy sat herself down on the shore, and took a great deal of trouble to decoy the swan, and threw crumbs of bread to it; but it would not come, and she was forced to go home in the evening without taking her revenge. Then Grethel changed herself and Hansel back into their own forms, and they journeyed on until the dawn; and then the maiden turned herself into a beautiful rose, that grew in the midst of a quickset hedge; and Hansel sat by the side.

The fairy soon came striding along. "Good piper," said she, "may I pluck yon beautiful rose for myself?"

"Oh yes!" answered he. "And then," thought he to

himself, "I will play you a tune meantime." So when she had crept into the hedge in a great hurry, to gather the flower—for she well knew what it was—he pulled out the pipe slily, and began to play. Now the pipe was a fairy pipe, and, whether they liked it or not, whoever heard it was obliged to dance. So the old fairy was forced to dance a merry jig, on and on, without any rest, and without being able to reach the rose. And as he did not cease playing a moment, the thorns at length tore the clothes from off her body, and pricked her sorely, and there she stuck quite fast.

Then Grethel set herself free, and on they went; but she grew tired, and Hansel said: "Now I will hasten home for help."

And Grethel said: "I will stay here in the meantime, and wait for you." Then Hansel went away.

But when Grethel had stayed in the field a long time, and found he did not come back, she became quite sorrowful, and turned herself into a little daisy, and thought to herself: "Someone will come and tread me under foot, and so my sorrows will end." But it so happened that, as a shepherd was keeping watch in a field, he saw the daisy; and, thinking it very pretty, he took it home, placed it in a box, and said: "I have never found so pretty a daisy before." From that time everything throve wonderfully at the shepherd's house. When he got up in the morning, all the household work was ready done: the room was swept and cleaned, the fire made, and the water fetched; and in the afternoon, when he came home, the cloth was laid, and a good dinner ready for him. Although it pleased him, he was at length troubled to think how it could be, and went to a cunning woman who lived hard by, and asked what he should do. She said: "There must be witchcraft in it. Look out to-morrow early, and see if anything stirs about in the room: if it does, throw a white cloth at once over it, and then the witchcraft will be stopped." The shepherd did as she said, and the next morning saw the box open, and the daisy come out; then he sprang up quickly, and threw a white cloth over it. In an instant the spell was broken, and Grethel stood before him, for it was she who had taken care of his house for him; and she was so beautiful that he asked her if she would marry him. She said "No", because she wished to be faithful to her dear Hansel; but she agreed to stay and keep house for him till Hansel came back.

Time passed on, and Hansel came back at last; for the spiteful fairy had led him astray, and he had not been able for a long time to find his way to Grethel. Then he and Grethel set out to go home; but, after travelling a long way, Grethel became tired, and she and Hansel laid themselves down to sleep in an old hollow tree. But as they slept, the fairy—who had got out of the bush at last—came by; and, finding her wand, was glad to lay hold of it, and at once turned poor Hansel into a fawn.

Soon Grethel awoke, and found what had happened. She wept bitterly over the poor creature; and the tears rolled down his eyes too, as he laid himself beside her. Then she said: "Rest in peace, dear fawn; I will never, never leave thee." So she took off her golden necklace, and put it round his neck, and plucked some rushes, and plaited them into a soft string to fasten to it, and led the poor little thing by her side when she went to walk in the wood; and when they were tired they came back, and lay down to sleep by the hollow tree; but nobody came near them except the little dwarfs that lived in the wood, and these watched over them.

At last one day they came to a cottage; and Grethel having looked in, and seen that it was empty, thought to herself: "We can stay and live here." Then she went and gathered leaves and moss to make a soft bed for the fawn; and every morning she went out and plucked nuts and berries for herself, and sweet shrubs and tender grass for her friend. In the evening, when Grethel was tired, she laid her head upon the fawn for her pillow, and slept; and if poor Hansel could but have his right form again, she thought they should lead a very happy life.

They lived a long while in the wood by themselves, till it chanced that the king of that country came hunting there. And when the fawn heard all around the echoing of the horns, and the baying of the dogs, and the merry shouts of the huntsmen, he wished very much to go and see what was going on. "Ah, sister," said he, "let me go out into the wood; I can stay no longer!" And he begged so long that she at last agreed to let him go. "But," said she, "be sure to come to me in the evening. I shall shut the door, to keep out those wild huntsmen, and if you tap at it and say: 'Sister, let me in!' I shall know you; but if you don't speak, I shall keep the door fast." Then away sprang the fawn. The king and his huntsmen saw the

beautiful creature, and followed but could not overtake him; for when they thought they were sure of their prize, he sprang over the bushes, and was out of sight.

As it grew dark he ran home to the hut and tapped, and said: "Sister, let me in!" Then she opened the door.

Next morning, when he heard the horn of the hunters, he said:

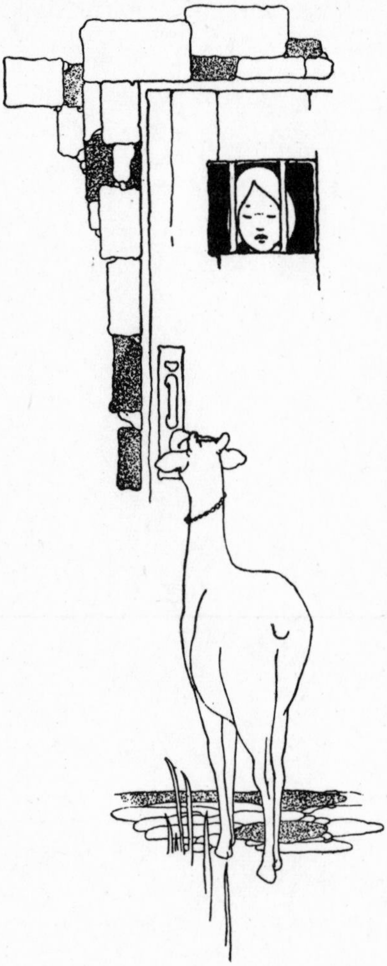

"Sister, open the door; I must go again." Then she said: "Come back in the evening, and remember what you are to say." When the king and the huntsmen saw the fawn with the golden collar again, they gave him chase; but he was too quick for them. The chase lasted the whole day; but at length the huntsmen nearly surrounded him, and one of them wounded him in the foot, so that he became sadly lame, and could hardly crawl home. The man who had wounded him followed close behind, and hid himself, and heard the little fawn say: "Sister, let me in!" upon which the door opened, and soon shut again. The huntsman went to the king and told him what he had seen and heard; then the king said: "To-morrow we will have another chase."

Grethel was frightened when she saw that her dear fawn was wounded; but she washed the blood away, and put some healing herbs on it, and said: "Now go to bed, dear fawn, and you will soon be well again." The wound was so slight that in the morning there was nothing to be seen of it; and when the horn blew, the little thing said: "I can't stay here; I must go and look on. I will take care that none of them shall catch me."

But Grethel said: "I am sure they will kill you this time: I will not let you go."

"I shall die of grief," said he, "if you keep me here. When I hear the horns, I feel as if I could fly."

Then Grethel was forced to let him go. So she opened the door with a heavy heart, and he bounded out.

When the king saw him, he said to his huntsmen: "Now chase him all day long, till you catch him; but let none of you do him any harm." The sun set, however, without their being able to overtake him, and the king called away the huntsmen, and said to the one who had watched: "Now come and show me the little hut." So they went to the door and tapped, and said: "Sister, let me in!" Then the door opened, and the king went in, and there stood a maiden more lovely than he had ever seen. Grethel was frightened to see that it was not her fawn, but a king with a golden crown, that was come into her hut; however, he spoke kindly to her, and took her hand, and said: "Will you come with me to my castle and be my wife?"

"Yes," said the maiden, "I will go to your castle, but I cannot be your wife; and my fawn must go with me. I cannot part with that."

"Well," said the king, "he shall come and live with you all your life, and want for nothing." Just then in sprang the fawn; and they left the hut in the wood together.

Then the king took Grethel to his palace, and on the way she told him all her story. And then he sent for the fairy, and made her change the fawn into Hansel again; and he and Grethel loved one another, and were married, and lived happily together all their days in the good king's palace.

Jack and the Beanstalk

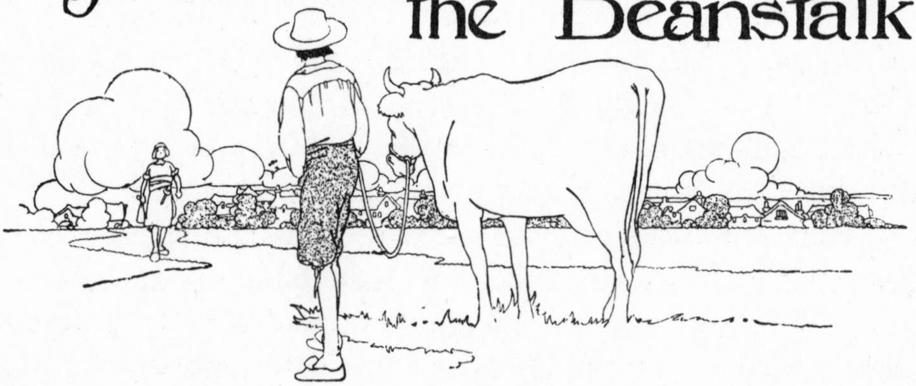

JACK was the only son of a poor widow woman; he was a lazy and extravagant lad, and did not realize that he should have been working to support his mother instead of leaving her to work for him. At length they had nothing left but a cow, and the poor woman sent Jack to sell it at the neighbouring market.

As he was going along, Jack met a butcher who, finding he wished to sell the cow, offered in exchange for it a hatful of curious coloured beans. Jack thought this a fine bargain, and hurried home to his mother. The poor, disappointed woman upbraided him angrily, kicked the beans in a passion out of the cottage door, and they both went supperless to bed.

Early next morning Jack woke to find leaves shadowing his window. He ran downstairs, and saw that some of the beans had taken root and sprung up to a great height. The immense stalks had so entwined that they formed a ladder, the top of which seemed to be lost in the clouds.

JACK AND THE BEANSTALK

Jack set out climbing, and reached the top of the beanstalk quite exhausted. Looking around, he found himself in a strange, barren country, not a tree, shrub, house, or living thing to be seen. However, he walked on, hoping to see a house where he might beg something to eat and drink. Presently an infirm-looking woman approached: he saw that she was old and poor. She accosted Jack, enquiring how he came there; and he related the circumstances of the beanstalk. She then asked if he recollected his father. He replied he did not, and added there must be some mystery relating to him, for he had frequently asked his mother who his father was, but that she always burst into tears, and appeared violently agitated; nor did she recover herself for some days after. One thing he could not avoid observing upon those occasions, which was that she always carefully avoided answering him, and seemed afraid of speaking, as if there were some secret connected with his father's history. The old woman replied:

"I will reveal the whole story; your mother must not. But before I begin I require a solemn promise on your part to do what I command. I am a fairy, and if you do not perform exactly what I require, your mother and yourself shall both be destroyed."

Jack promised to fulfil her injunctions exactly, and the fairy continued:

"Your father, though only a private gentleman, was as rich as a prince, and deserved all he possessed, for he only lived to do good. There lived, a great many miles off, a giant who was altogether as wicked as your father was good; who was in his heart envious, covetous, and cruel; but who had the art of concealing those vices.

"Hearing of your father, he was determined to ingratiate himself into his favour. Your father credited the lying story he told, gave him handsome apartments in his own house, and caused him and his wife to be treated like visitors of consequence. Things went on in this way some time, the giant becoming daily more impatient to put his plan into execution. At last a favourable opportunity presented itself. Your father's house was at some distance from the seashore, but with a good glass the coast could be seen distinctly. The giant was one day using the telescope; the wind was very high; he saw a fleet of ships in distress off the rocks; he hastened to your father, mentioned this, and eagerly requested he would send all the servants he could spare to relieve the sufferers. Everyone was instantly dispatched, except the porter and your nurse. The giant then joined your father in the study, and appeared to be delighted—he really was so. Your father recommended a favourite book, and was handing it down; the giant took the opportunity, and stabbed him; he instantly fell dead. The giant left the body, found the porter and nurse, and presently dispatched

them. You were then only three months old. Your mother had you in her arms in a remote part of the house, and, ignorant of what was going on, went into the study. How was she shocked on discovering your father a corpse! She was stupefied with horror. The giant found her in that state, and hastened to serve her and you as he had done her husband; but she fell at his feet, and in a pathetic manner besought him to spare your life.

"The cruel giant for a short time was struck with remorse, and spared your lives; but first he made her swear solemnly that she never would inform you who your father was, or answer any questions concerning him, assuring her that if she did he would put both of you to death in the most cruel manner. Your mother took you in her arms and fled as quickly as possible. She was scarcely gone, when the giant repented that he had suffered her to escape: he would have pursued her instantly, but he had his own safety to provide for, as it was necessary he should be gone before the servants returned. He knew where to find all your father's treasure, soon loaded himself and his wife, set the house on fire in several places, and, when the servants returned, the house was burnt to the ground.

"Your poor mother, forlorn, abandoned, and forsaken, wandered with you many miles from this scene of desolation, and settled in the cottage where you were brought up; and it was owing to her fear of the giant that she has never mentioned your father to you.

"I became your father's guardian at his birth; but fairies have laws to which they are subject as well as mortals. A short time before the giant went to your father's, I transgressed; my punishment was a total suspension of power for a limited time—an unfortunate circumstance, as it prevented my succouring your father. The day on which you met the butcher, as you went to sell your mother's cow, my power was restored. It was I who secretly prompted you to take the beans in exchange for the cow. By my power the beanstalk grew to so great a height and formed a ladder. I need not add that I inspired you with a strong desire to ascend the ladder.

"The giant lives in this country. You are the person appointed to punish him for all his wickedness. You will have dangers and difficulties to encounter, but must persevere in avenging the death of your father, or you will always be miserable. As to the giant's possessions, you may seize all with impunity, for everything he has is yours, though now you are unjustly deprived of it. Go along the road; you will soon see the house where your cruel enemy lives. Remember the severe punishment that awaits you if you disobey my commands."

So saying, the fairy disappeared, leaving Jack to pursue his journey.

He walked until after sunset, and soon, to his great joy, spied a large mansion. A plain-looking woman was standing at the door. He accosted her, begging she would give him a morsel of bread and a night's lodging. She expressed great surprise on seeing him, said it was quite uncommon to see a human being near their house, for it was well known that her husband was a large and powerful giant, and that he would never eat anything but human flesh if he could possibly get it; that he did not think anything of walking fifty miles to procure it, usually being out all day for that purpose.

Jack hoped to elude the giant, and again entreated the woman to take him in for one night only, and hide him in the oven. The woman at last suffered herself to be persuaded, for she was of a compassionate disposition. She gave him plenty to eat and drink, and took him into the house.

A long gallery through which they passed was very dark, just light enough to show that, instead of a wall on one side, there was a grating of iron which parted off a dismal dungeon, whence issued the groans of poor victims whom the giant reserved in confinement for his own voracious appetite. Poor Jack was half-dead with fear, and gave himself up for lost. At the farther end of the gallery there

was a winding staircase, which led them into a spacious kitchen. A good fire was burning in the grate, and Jack, not seeing anything to make him uncomfortable, here forgot his fears, and was beginning to enjoy himself, when he was aroused by a loud knocking at the house door. The giant's wife ran to secure him in the oven, and then made what haste she could to let her husband in, and Jack heard him accost her in a voice like thunder, saying:

"Wife, I smell fresh meat."

"Oh, my dear," she replied, "it is nothing but the people in the dungeon!"

The giant appeared to believe her, and walked downstairs into the very kitchen where poor Jack was, who shook, trembled, and was more terrified than he had yet been. At last the monster seated himself by the fireside, whilst his wife prepared supper. By degrees Jack recovered himself sufficiently to look at the giant through a crevice. When supper was ended, the giant desired his wife to bring him his hen. A beautiful hen was brought, and placed upon the table. Jack observed that every time the giant said "Lay", the hen laid an egg of solid gold. The giant amused himself a long time with the hen; meanwhile his wife went to bed. At length the giant fell fast asleep by the fireside, and snored heavily.

At daybreak, Jack, finding the giant not likely to be soon roused, crept softly out of his hiding place, seized the hen, and ran off with her. He met with some difficulty in finding his way out of the house, but at last reached the road in safety, without fear of pursuit. He easily found the way to the beanstalk, and descended it better and quicker than he expected. His mother was overjoyed to see him.

"And now, Mother," said he, "I have brought home that which will quickly make you rich without any trouble. I hope I have made you some amends for the affliction I have caused you through my idleness, extravagance, and folly."

The hen produced them as many eggs as they desired; they sold them, and in a little time became very rich.

For some months Jack and his mother lived happily together; but he longed to climb the beanstalk, and pay the giant another visit, in order to carry off some more of his treasures. A few mornings later he rose very early, put on a disguise, and, unperceived by anyone, climbed the beanstalk. He was greatly fatigued when he reached the top, and very hungry. He reached the giant's castle late in the evening; the woman was standing at the door as usual. Jack accosted her, at the same time telling her a pitiful tale, and requested that she would give him victuals and drink, and a night's lodging. She told him what he knew before, concerning her husband, and also that she one night admitted a poor, hungry, distressed boy, who was half-dead with travelling; that he stole one of the giant's treasures;

and ever since that her husband was worse than before, and used her very cruelly, upbraiding her continually with being the cause of his loss. Jack did his best to persuade the woman to admit him, and found it a very hard task; but at last she consented, and, as she led the way, Jack observed that everything was just as before. She took him into the kitchen, and hid him in an old lumber closet. The giant returned at the usual time, and walked in so heavily that the house was shaken to the foundation. He seated himself by the fire, saying:

"I smell fresh meat!"

The wife replied that it was the crows, who had brought a piece of carrion, and laid it at the top of the house upon the leads.

While supper was preparing, the giant was very ill-tempered and impatient, frequently lifting up his hand to strike his wife for not being quick enough. She, however, was always so fortunate as to elude the blow. He was also continually upbraiding her with the loss of his hen. Then, having eaten till he was quite satisfied, he said to his wife:

"I must have something to amuse me, either my bags of money or my harp."

After a great deal of ill humour, and having teased his wife some time, he commanded her to bring his bags of gold and silver. Jack, as before, peeped out, and presently the woman brought two bags into the room; they were of an immense size—one filled with new guineas, the other with new shillings. They were placed before the giant: he reprimanded his wife most severely for staying so long. The poor woman replied, trembling with fear, that they were so heavy she could scarcely lift them, and that she had nearly fainted owing to their weight. This so exasperated the giant that he raised his hand to strike her. She, however, escaped, and went to bed, leaving him to count over his treasures by way of amusement.

First the bag containing the silver was emptied, and the contents placed upon the table. Jack viewed the glittering heaps with delight, and heartily wished the contents in his own possession. The giant reckoned the silver over and over again, then put it all carefully into the bag, which he made secure. The other bag was opened next, and the guineas placed upon the table. If Jack was pleased at the sight of the silver, he felt much more delighted when he saw such a heap of gold. The gold was put up as the silver had been before, and, if possible, more securely. The giant snored aloud; Jack could compare his noise to nothing but the roaring of the sea in a high wind when the tide is coming in. At last, concluding him to be asleep, and therefore secure, Jack stole out of his hiding place, and approached in order to carry off the two bags of money. Just as he laid his hand upon one of them, a little dog started out from under the giant's chair, and barked most furiously, so that Jack gave himself up for lost. Fear riveted him to the spot; instead of running,

he stood still, expecting his enemy to awake every moment; but the giant continued in sleep, and the dog grew weary of barking. Jack looked round, saw a large piece of meat, which he threw to the dog, who took it into the lumber closet which Jack had just left.

He found himself thus delivered from a noisy and troublesome enemy; and, as the giant did not awake, Jack seized both the bags, and carried them away. He reached the house door in safety, and found it quite daylight. The only difficulty he had arose from the weight of the bags, and they were so heavy he could hardly carry them. Jack was overjoyed when he found himself near the beanstalk; he soon reached the bottom, and immediately ran to seek his mother. An old woman said she was at a neighbour's, ill of a fever, and directed him to the house where she was. He was shocked on finding her apparently dying, and could scarcely bear his own reflections on knowing himself to be the cause. On being told of his return, she began to recover gradually. Jack presented her with his two bags, and they lived happily and comfortably for some time. Notwithstanding the comfort, Jack's mind dwelt upon the beanstalk; he could not think of anything else. His mother found that something preyed upon his mind, and endeavoured to discover what it was; but Jack knew too well what the consequence would be of disclosing the cause of his melancholy. He did his utmost to conquer the great desire he felt for another journey. However, finding the inclination grow too powerful for him, he began to make secret preparations; and, on the longest day, arose as soon as it was light, ascended the beanstalk, and reached the top with some trouble. He found the road and journey much as before. He arrived at the giant's mansion late in the evening, and found the wife standing at the door. Jack had disguised himself so completely that she did not appear to have the least recollection of him. However, when he pleaded hunger and poverty in order to gain admittance, he found it very difficult indeed to persuade her. At last he prevailed, and was concealed in the copper. When the giant returned in the evening, he said:

"I smell fresh meat!"

Jack felt quite composed, as he had said so before, and was soon satisfied; however, the giant started up suddenly, and, notwithstanding all his wife could say, searched all around the room. Whilst this was going on, Jack was

ready to die with fear; and when the giant approached the copper, and even put his hand upon the lid, Jack thought his death warrant was signed. But fortunately the giant ended his search there, without moving the lid of the copper, and seated himself quietly by the table. This fright nearly overcame poor Jack; he was afraid of moving or even breathing, lest he should be heard and captured.

The giant at last ate a great supper. When he had finished his meal he commanded his wife to fetch his harp. Jack peeped under the copper lid, and saw the most wonderful and beautiful harp that could be imagined. The giant said "Play", and it instantly played without being touched. The music was very fine; Jack was delighted, for he had never heard anything like it before, and felt more anxious to get the magic harp into his possession than either of the former treasures. The sweet music lulled the giant into a sound sleep, and the woman went into the back-kitchen. Jack quickly made up his mind, got out of the copper, and took the harp. But the harp, however, was a fairy, and called out loudly: "Master! master! master!"

The giant awoke, stood up, and tried to pursue Jack, but he had drunk so much wine that he could not stand. Poor Jack ran as fast as he could.

In a little time the giant was sufficiently recovered to walk slowly, or rather to reel, after him; had he been sober he must have overtaken Jack instantly; but, as he then was, Jack contrived to be the first at the top of the beanstalk. The giant, roaring with anger, and calling to him all the way, was sometimes very near him.

The moment Jack set his foot on the beanstalk he

called at the top of his voice for a hatchet. One was brought directly. He soon reached the ground. Just at that instant the giant was beginning to come down; but Jack, with his hatchet, cut the beanstalk close off to the root,

which made the giant fall headlong into the garden, and the heavy fall killed him.

Jack's mother was delighted when she saw the beanstalk destroyed and the wicked giant overcome. At that instant the good fairy appeared; she first addressed Jack's mother, and explained every circumstance relating to the journeys up the great beanstalk. The fairy then charged Jack to be a dutiful and affectionate son to his mother, and to follow his father's good example in everything, which was the only way to be respectable and happy in this life. After giving this advice she took her leave of them and disappeared from their sight. Jack humbly and with his whole heart begged his mother's pardon for all the sorrow and affliction he had caused her, promising faithfully to be very dutiful and obedient to her for the future. He proved as good as his word, and was a pattern of affectionate behaviour and attention to parents. His mother and he lived together a great many years, and continued to be always very happy.

BQ dinner with
n potatoes
TO GRATIN
175 mL
1
h plum tomato,
nly sliced
redded Swiss cheese 125 mL
hopped fresh parsley
Freshly cracked pepper
tir over medium-high heat
ok and
all.
Shirriff
Classic
Scallope
(Sears reg. $10)
these sizes:
8x10
Vallets.
fee. Session
ll applicable
free item.
rohibited.
offers.
1997.
0 00000 27708 2
FSINMY0437-1
COUPON AT TIME OF SESSION

n bun

MUSHROOM POTA

ICK
ASY
CIPE

1 tbsp	vegetable oil	15 mL	
2 1/2 cups	sliced fresh mushrooms	625 mL	
1	clove garlic, minced	1	
1	pkg (175 g) Shirriff* Scalloped Potatoes	1	
2 1/4 cups	water	550 mL	

3/4 cup	milk
1	fres
	thi
1/2 cup	sh

1. Heat oil in medium saucepan. Add mushrooms and garlic; cook and s until tender and any liquid has evaporated.
2. Add package of sauce mix, potato slices, water and milk to pan. Co stir until mixture boils. Reduce heat, cover and simmer 20 min; stir occasionally.
3. Spoon potato mixture into 6-cup (1.5 L) shallow baking dish. Arrange tomato slices on top of the potatoes; sprinkle cheese ove
4. Broil until cheese melts and bubbles. Sprinkle with parsley and pepper. Let stand 10 min before serving. Makes 6 servings.

PREPARATION TIME: 10 MIN. **COOKING TIME:** 25 MIN

*Registered trade-mark / **oetker** ltd - Licensee

Little Chicken Kluk

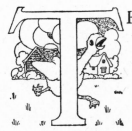

THERE was once a little chicken called Kluk. A nut fell on his back, and gave him such a blow that he rolled on the ground. So he ran to the hen, and said: "Henny Penny, run, I think all the world is falling!"

"Who has told thee that, little chicken Kluk?"

"Oh, a nut fell on my back, and struck me so that I rolled on the ground."

"Then let us run," said the hen.

So they ran to the cock, and said: "Cocky Locky, run, I think all the world is falling."

"Who has told thee that, Henny Penny?"

"Little chicken Kluk."

"Who told thee that, little chicken Kluk?"

"Oh, a nut fell on my back, and struck me so that I rolled on the ground."

"Then let us run," said the cock.

So they ran to the duck, and said: "Ducky Lucky, run, I think all the world is falling."

"Who told thee that, Cocky Locky?"

"Henny Penny."

"Who has told thee that, Henny Penny?"

"Little chicken Kluk."

"Who has told thee that, little chicken Kluk?"

"Oh, a nut fell on my back, and struck me so that I rolled on the ground."

"Then let us run," said the duck.

So they ran to the goose, and said: "Goosy Poosy, run, I think all the world is falling."

"Who has told thee that, Ducky Lucky?"

"Cocky Locky."

"Who has told thee that, Cocky Locky?"

"Henny Penny."

"Who has told thee that, Henny Penny?"

"Little chicken Kluk."

"Who has told thee that, little chicken Kluk?"

"Oh, a nut fell on my back, and struck me so that I rolled on the ground."

"Then let us run," said the goose.

Then they ran to the fox, and said: "Foxy Coxy, run, I think all the world is falling."

"Who has told thee that, Goosy Poosy?"

"Ducky Lucky."

"Who has told thee that, Ducky Lucky?"

"Cocky Locky."

"Who has told thee that, Cocky Locky?"

"Henny Penny."

"Who has told thee that, Henny Penny?"

"Little chicken Kluk."

"Who has told thee that, little chicken Kluk?"

"Oh, a nut fell on my back, and struck me so that I rolled on the ground."

"Then let us run," said the fox.

So they all ran into the wood. Then the fox said: "I must now count and see if I have got you all here. I, Foxy Coxy, one; Goosy Poosy, two; Ducky Lucky, three; Cocky Locky, four; Henny Penny, five; and little chicken Kluk, six; Hei! that one I'll snap up." He then said: "Let us run."

So they ran farther into the wood. Then said he: "Now I must count and see if I have got you all here. I, Foxy Coxy, one; Goosy Poosy, two; Ducky Lucky, three; Cocky Locky, four; Henny Penny, five; Hei! that one I'll snap up."

And so he went on till he had eaten them all up.

The Little Match Girl

IT was the last evening of the year. In the cold and darkness a poor little girl, with bare head and feet, was wandering about the streets, her feet quite red and blue with the cold. In her tattered apron she carried a bundle of matches, and there were a good many more in her hand. No one had bought any of them the livelong day—no one had given her a single penny. Trembling with cold and hunger, she crept on, the picture of sorrow.

The snowflakes settled on her long, fair hair, which fell in ringlets over her shoulders; but she thought neither of her own beauty, nor of the cold. Lights shone from every window, and the smell of roast goose reached her, for it was New Year's eve, and it was of that she thought.

In a corner formed by two houses, one of which came a little farther forward than the other, she sat down, drawing her feet close under her, but in vain—she could not warm them. She dared not go home—she had sold no matches, earned not a single penny, and her father would certainly beat her; besides, her home was almost as cold as the street—it was an attic; and, although the larger of the many holes in the roof were stopped up with straw and rags, the cold wind came whistling through. Her hands were nearly frozen. A match would warm them, perhaps, if she dared light it. She drew one out, and struck it against the wall. It was a bright, warm light, like a little candle, and she held her hands over it. It was quite a wonderful light. It seemed to that poor little girl as though she were sitting before a large iron stove with polished brass feet and brass ornaments. So beautifully did the fire within burn that the child stretched out her feet to warm them also. Alas! in an instant the flame had died away, the stove vanished, and the little girl sat cold and comfortless, with the remains of the burnt match in her hand.

A second match was struck; it kindled and blazed, and wherever its light fell the wall became transparent as a veil, and the little girl could see into the room. She saw the table spread with a snowy-white tablecloth and set with shining china dinner dishes. A roast goose, stuffed with apples and dried plums, stood at one end, smoking hot, and—pleasantest of all to see—the goose, with knife and fork still in her breast, jumped down from the dish, and waddled along the floor right up to the poor child. The match was burnt out, and only the thick, hard wall was beside her.

She lighted a third match. Again the flame shot up, and now she was sitting under a most beautiful Christmas-tree, far larger, and far more prettily decked out than the one she had seen last Christmas-eve through the glass doors of the rich merchant's house. Thousands of wax tapers lighted up the branches, and tiny painted figures, such as she had seen in the shop windows, looked down from the tree upon her. The child stretched out her hands towards them and the match went out. Still, however, the Christmas candles burned higher and higher, till they looked to her like the stars in the sky. One of them fell, the light streaming behind it like a long, fiery tail.

"Now someone is dying," said the little girl softly, for she had been told by her old grandmother, the only person who had ever been kind to her—but she was now dead,—that

whenever a star falls a soul flies up to God. She struck another match against the wall and the light shone round her, and in its brightness she saw her dear dead grandmother, gentle and loving as always, but bright and happy as she had never looked during her lifetime.

"Grandmother!" said the child, "oh, take me with you! I know you will leave me as soon as the match goes out—you will vanish like the warm stove, like the New Year's feast, and like the beautiful Christmas-tree." And she hastily lighted all the remaining matches in the bundle, lest her grandmother should disappear. And the matches burned with such a splendour, that noonday could scarcely have been brighter. Never had the good old grandmother looked so tall and stately, so beautiful and kind. She took the little girl in her arms, and they both flew away together radiant with happiness. They flew far above the earth higher and higher, till they were in that place where neither cold, nor hunger, nor pain is ever known,—in the presence of God.

But in the cold morning hour, crouching in the corner of

the wall, the poor little girl was found—her cheeks glowing, her lips smiling—frozen to death on the last night of the Old Year. The New Year's sun shone on the lifeless child; motionless she sat there with the matches in her lap, one bundle of them quite burnt out.

"She has been trying to warm herself, poor thing!" some people said; but no one knew of the sweet visions she had beheld, or how gloriously she and her grandmother were celebrating their New Year's festival.

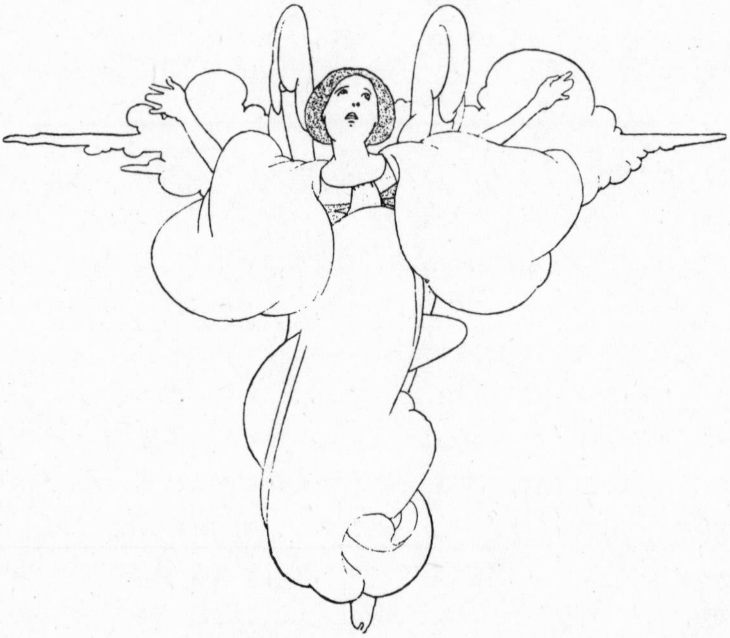

Beauty and the Beast

THERE was once a merchant who had six children, three boys and three girls. The three daughters were all handsome, but particularly the youngest; so very beautiful indeed was she, that everyone, during her childhood, called her the Little Beauty, and being still the same when she was grown up, nobody called her by any other name; which made her sisters extremely jealous. This youngest daughter was not only handsomer than her sisters, but was better tempered also.

Owing to some accident the merchant suddenly lost his fortune, having nothing left but a small cottage in the country. He said to his daughters, the tears all the time running down his cheeks:

"My children, we must go and live in the cottage, and try

to get a subsistence by labour, for we have no other means of support left!"

When they had removed to their cottage, the merchant and his three sons employed themselves in the fields and garden, that they might have corn and vegetables for their support. Beauty rose by four o'clock, lighted the fires, cleaned the house, and got the breakfast for the whole family. When she had done her work she amused herself with reading, playing on the harpsichord, or singing as she spun. Her sisters were at a loss what to do to pass the time away! they breakfasted in bed, and did not rise till ten, when they walked out, but finding themselves very soon tired, would frequently sit down under a shady tree, and lament the loss of their carriage and fine clothes.

The family had lived in this manner about a year, when the merchant received a letter, which informed him that one of his richest vessels, which he thought lost, had arrived in port. This made the two sisters almost mad with joy. When they found it necessary for their father to take a journey to the ship they begged he would bring them on his return some new gowns, caps, rings, and all sorts of

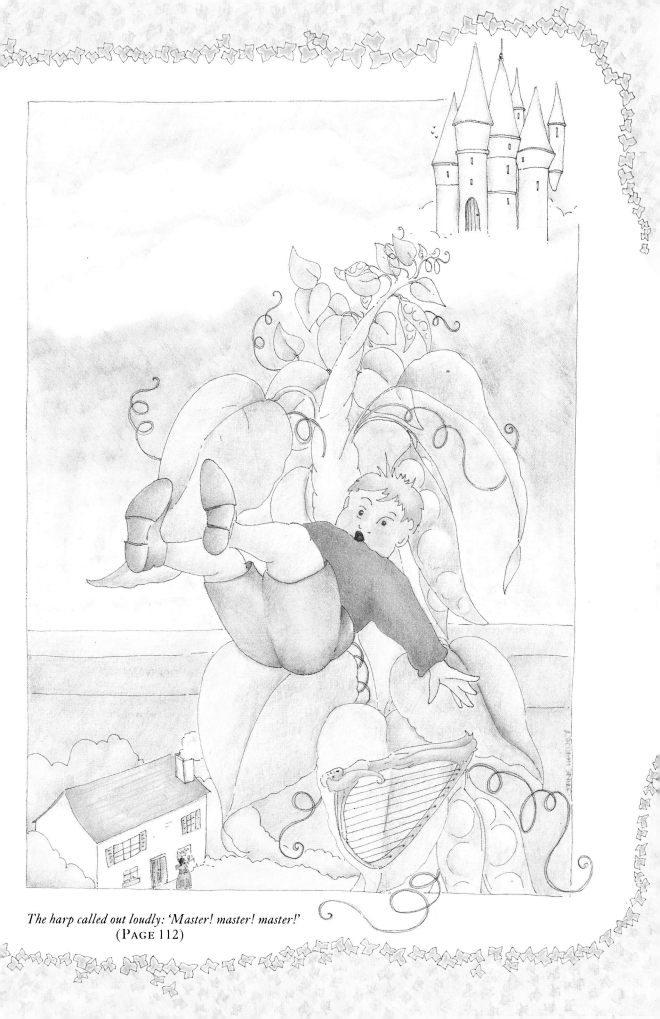

The harp called out loudly: 'Master! master! master!'
(PAGE 112)

A nut fell on his back. (PAGE 115)

trinkets. Beauty asked for nothing; for she thought that the ship's cargo would scarcely purchase all that her sisters wished for.

"You, Beauty," said the merchant, "ask for nothing; what can I bring you?"

"Since you are so kind as to think of me, dear father," answered she, "I should be obliged to you to bring me a rose, for we have none in our garden."

It was not that Beauty wished for a rose, but she was unwilling to condemn, by her example, the conduct of her sisters, who would have said she refused only to be praised. The merchant took his leave, and set out on his journey; but, on arriving at the port, some dishonest persons went to law with him about the merchandise; so after a great deal of trouble he returned to his cottage as poor as he had left it. When he was within thirty miles of his home, and thinking of the happiness he should enjoy in again embracing his children, his road lay through a thick forest, and he lost himself. All at once, happening to look down a long avenue, he discovered a light, but it seemed at a great distance. He pursued his way towards it, and found it proceeded from a splendid palace brilliantly illuminated. He quicked his pace, and was surprised to find not a single creature in any of the outer yards. His horse, which followed him, finding a stable with the door open, entered, and, being nearly starved, helped himself to a plentiful meal of oats and hay. His master then tied him up, and walked towards the house, which he entered, without, to his great astonishment, seeing a living creature: pursued his way to a large hall, in which was a good fire, and a table provided with the most delicate dishes, on which was laid a single cover.

As snow and rain had wetted him to the skin, he approached the fire.

"I hope," says he, "the master of the house or his servants will excuse the liberty I take, for it surely will not be long before they make their appearance."

He waited a considerable time, and still nobody came: at length the clock struck eleven; and the merchant, overcome with hunger and thirst, helped himself to a chicken, of which he made but two mouthfuls, and then to a few glasses of wine, all the time trembling with fear. He sat till the clock struck twelve, and not a creature had he seen. He now took courage, and began to think of looking a little farther about him: accordingly, he opened a door at the end of the hall, and entered an apartment magnificently furnished, which opened into another, in which there was an excellent bed; and finding himself quite overcome with fatigue, he resolved to shut the door, undress, and get into it. It was ten o'clock the next morning before he thought of rising; when, what was his astonishment at seeing a handsome suit of clothes entirely new, in the place of his own, which were quite spoiled!

"No doubt," said he to himself, "this palace belongs to some good fairy, who has taken pity on my unfortunate situation."

He looked out of the window; and instead of snow, he saw the most delightful flowers. He returned to the hall where he had supped, and found a breakfast table, with chocolate ready prepared.

"Truly, my good fairy," said the merchant aloud, "I am extremely indebted to you for your kind care of me."

Having made a hearty breakfast, he took his hat, and was going toward the stable to pay his horse a visit. As he passed under one of the arbours, which was loaded with roses, he recollected Beauty's request, and gathered a bunch of them to carry home. At the same instant he heard a most horrible noise, and saw such a hideous Beast approaching him, that he was ready to sink with fear!

"Ungrateful man!" said the Beast in a terrible voice; "I have saved your life by receiving you in my palace, and in return you steal my roses, which I value more than all my other possessions. With your life you shall atone your fault: you shall die in a quarter of an hour!"

The merchant fell on his knees, and, clasping his hands, said:

"My lord, I humbly entreat your pardon: I did not think it could offend you to gather a rose for one of my daughters."

"I am not a lord, but a beast," replied the monster; "I do not like compliments, but that people should say what they think; so do not imagine you can move me with your flattery. You say, however, that you have daughters; I will pardon you, on condition that one of them shall come hither and die in your

place: do not attempt to argue with me, but go; and if your daughters should refuse, swear to me that you will return in three months."

The merchant had no intention to let one of his daughters die in his stead; but thought that, by seeming to accept the Beast's condition, he should have the satisfaction of once again embracing them. He accordingly swore, and the Beast told him he might set off as soon as he pleased: "but," added he, "it is my will that you should not go empty-handed. Go back," continued he, "to the chamber in which you slept, where you will find an empty chest: fill it with whatever you like best, and I will get it conveyed to your own house."

The Beast then went away, and the good merchant said to himself:

"If I must die, yet I shall have the consolation of leaving my children some provision."

He returned to the chamber in which he had slept; and having found a great quantity of pieces of gold, filled the chest with them to the very brim, locked it, and, mounting his horse, left the palace. The horse of itself took a path across the forest, and in a few hours they reached the merchant's house. His children gathered round him as he dismounted, but the merchant, instead of embracing them with joy, could not, as he looked at them, refrain from weeping. He held in his hand the bunch of roses, which he gave to Beauty, saying:

"Take these roses, Beauty; little do you think how dear they have cost your unhappy father;" and then gave an account of all that had happened in the palace of the Beast. The two eldest sisters immediately began to shed tears, and to reproach Beauty, who they said would be the cause of her father's death.

"See," said they, "the consequence of the pride of the little wretch; why did she not ask for fine things as we did? But, forsooth, she must distinguish herself; and though she will be the cause of her father's death she does not shed a tear."

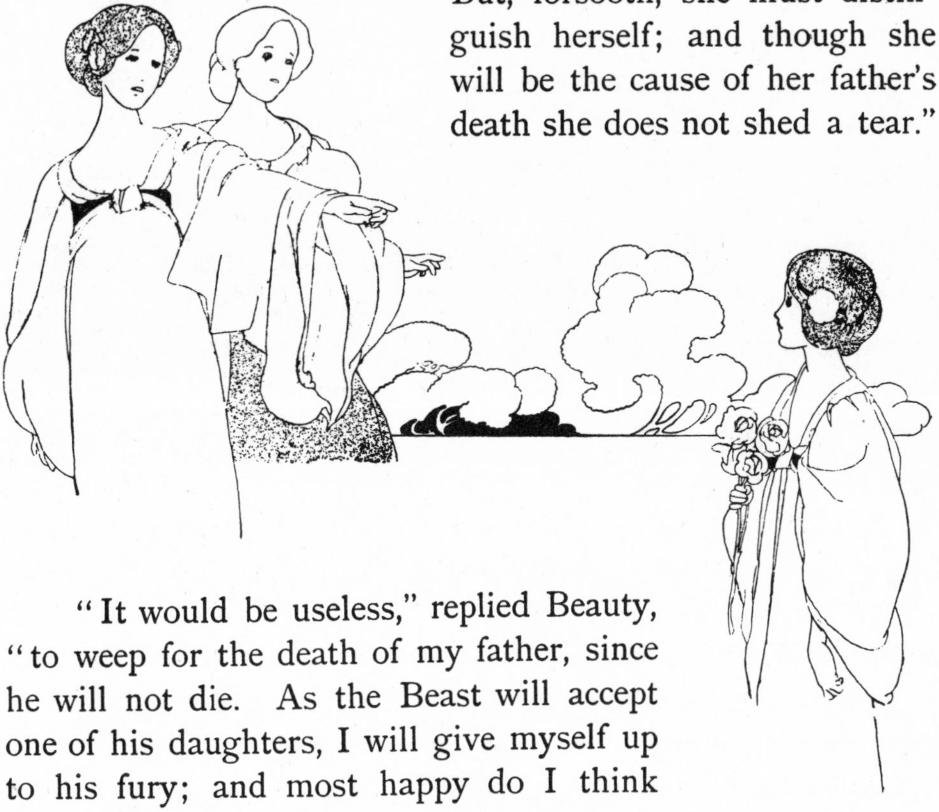

"It would be useless," replied Beauty, "to weep for the death of my father, since he will not die. As the Beast will accept one of his daughters, I will give myself up to his fury; and most happy do I think myself in being able at once to save his life, and prove my tenderness to the best of fathers."

"No, sister," said the three brothers, "you shall not die: we will go in search of this monster, and he or we will perish."

"Do not hope to kill him," said the merchant; "for his power is by far too great for this to be possible. I am charmed with the kindness of Beauty, but I will not suffer her life to be exposed. I am old, and cannot expect to live much longer: I shall therefore have lost but a few years of my life, which I regret only for my children's sake."

"Never, my father," cried Beauty, "shall you go to the palace without me; for you cannot prevent my following you: though young, I am not overfond of life, and I had much rather be devoured by the monster than die of the grief your loss would occasion me."

The merchant tried in vain to reason with Beauty, for she was determined to go. He was, indeed, so afflicted with the idea of losing his child, that he never thought of the chest filled with gold; but, retiring to his chamber at night, to his great surprise, perceived it standing by his bedside. He now determined to say nothing to his eldest daughters of the riches he possessed; for he knew very well they would immediately wish to return to town: but he told Beauty his secret, who informed him that two gentlemen had been visiting at their cottage during his absence, who had a great affection for her two sisters. She entreated her father to marry them without delay; for she was so sweet-tempered, that she loved them notwithstanding their unkind behaviour, which she forgave with all her heart.

When the three months had passed, the merchant and

Beauty prepared to set out for the palace of the Beast; the two sisters rubbed their eyes with an onion, to make-believe they shed a great many tears: but both the merchant and his sons shed them in reality. Beauty did not weep, for she thought this would only increase their affliction. They reached the palace in a few hours: when the horse, without bidding, entered the stable, and the merchant with his daughter proceeded to the large hall, where they found a table provided with every delicacy, and with two covers laid on it. The merchant had little appetite; but Beauty, the better to conceal her sorrow, placed herself at table, and, having helped her father, began to eat, thinking all the time, that the Beast had surely a mind to fatten her before he ate her up, since he had provided such good cheer. When they had finished their supper they heard a great noise; and the good old man began to bid his poor child farewell, for he knew it was the Beast coming to them. Beauty, on seeing his form, could not help being terrified, but tried as much as possible to conceal her fear. The monster asked her if she had come willingly; she replied, trembling still more:

"Y-e-s."

"You are a good girl," replied he, "and I think myself much obliged to you. Good man," continued he, "you may leave the palace to-morrow morning, and take care to return to it no more. Good-night, Beauty!"

"Good-night, Beast!" answered she; and the monster withdrew.

"Ah! dear child," said the merchant, embracing her, "I am half dead at the thoughts of your being sacrificed to this frightful monster: believe me, you had better go back, and let me stay."

"No," answered Beauty firmly, "to this I will never consent; you must go home to-morrow morning."

They now wished each other a sorrowful good-night, and went to bed, thinking it would be impossible for them to close their eyes; but no sooner had they lain down, than they fell into a profound sleep, from which they did not awake till morning. Beauty dreamed that a lady approached her, who said:

"I am much pleased, Beauty, with the generous affection you have shown, in being willing to give your life to save that of your father; it shall not go unrewarded."

Beauty related this dream to her father; but though it afforded him some comfort, he could not take leave of his darling child without shedding bitter tears. When the merchant was out of sight, Beauty sat down in the large hall and began to cry also; but as she had a great deal of courage, she soon resolved not to make her unhappy condition still worse by useless sorrow. She determined on taking a view of the different parts of the palace, with which she was much delighted. What was her surprise, at coming to a door on which was written "Beauty's apartment"! She opened it hastily, and her eyes were dazzled by the splendour of everything it contained: but the things that more than all the rest excited her wonder, were a large library of books, a harpsichord, and music.

"The Beast is determined I shall not want amusement," said she. The thought then struck her, that it was not likely such provision should have been made for her, if she had but one day to live. She opened the library, and perceived a book, on which was written, in letters of gold:—

"Beauteous lady, dry your tears,
Here's no cause for sighs or fears;
Command as freely as you may,
Compliance still shall mark your sway".

"Alas!" thought she, "there is nothing I so much desire

as to see my poor father, and to know what he is this moment doing."

Great was her amazement, when, casting her eyes on a looking-glass that stood near, she saw her home, and her father riding up to the cottage in the deepest affliction. Her sisters had come out to meet him, who, notwithstanding all their endeavours to look sorry, could not help betraying their joy. In a short time this disappeared; but Beauty began to think that the Beast was very kind to her; and that she had nothing to fear. About noon she found a table prepared, and a delightful concert of music played all the time she was eating her dinner, without her seeing a single creature. At supper, when she was going to place herself at table, she heard the noise of the Beast, and could not help trembling with terror.

"Will you allow me, Beauty," said he, "the pleasure of seeing you sup?"

"That is as you please," answered she.

"Not in the least," said the Beast, "and the Beast you alone command in this place. If you dislike my company, you have only to say so, and I shall leave you. But tell me, Beauty, do you not think me very ugly?"

"Truly, yes," replied she, "for I cannot tell a falsehood; but I think you are very good."

"You are right," continued the Beast; "and, besides my ugliness, I am also ignorant; I know well enough that I am but a beast.

"Pray do not let me interrupt you eating," pursued he: "and be sure you do not want for anything, for all you see is yours, and I shall be grieved if you are not happy."

"You are very good," replied Beauty, "I must confess I think very highly of your disposition; and that makes me almost forget your ugliness."

"Yes, I trust I am good-tempered," said he, "but still I am a monster."

"Many men are more monsters than you," replied Beauty; "and I am better pleased with you in that form, ugly as it is, than with those who, under the form of men, conceal wicked hearts."

"If I had any understanding," resumed the Beast, "I would thank you for what you have said; but I am too stupid to say anything that could give you pleasure."

Beauty supped with an excellent appetite, and had nearly got the better of her dread of the monster; but was ready to sink with horror, when he said:

"Beauty, will you be my wife?"

She was afraid of putting him in a passion by refusing, and remained silent for a few moments before saying:

"No, Beast."

The Beast sighed deeply, and said, in a melancholy tone:

"Adieu, Beauty!" and left her, turning his head two or three times as he went, to look at her once more. Beauty, finding herself alone, began to feel the greatest compassion for the poor Beast.

"Alas!" said she, "what a pity it is he should be so very frightful, since he is good-tempered!"

Beauty lived three months in this palace, very contentedly: the Beast visited her every evening, and entertained her with his conversation while she supped, and though what he said was not very clever, yet, perceiving in him every day new virtues, instead of dreading the time of his coming, she continually looked at her watch, to see if it was almost nine o'clock; at which time he never failed to visit her. There was but one thing that made her uneasy; which was that the Beast, before he retired, constantly asked her if she would be his wife, and appeared extremely sorrowful at her refusals. Beauty one day said to him:

"You distress me exceedingly, Beast, in obliging me to refuse you so often: I wish I could prevail on myself to marry you, but I am too sincere to flatter you that this will ever happen."

"I love you exceedingly," replied the Beast; "however,

I think myself fortunate in your being pleased to stay with me; promise me, Beauty, that you will never leave me."

Beauty was quite confused when he said this, for she had seen in her glass that her father had fallen sick of grief for her absence, and pined to see her.

"I would willingly promise," said she, "never to leave you entirely; but I have such a longing desire to see my father, that if you refuse me this pleasure I shall die of grief."

"Rather would I die myself, Beauty," replied he, "than cause you affliction. I will send you to your father's cottage; you shall stay there, and your poor Beast shall die of grief."

"No," said Beauty, weeping, "I love you too well to be the cause of your death: I promise to return in a week; you have shown me that my sisters are married, and my brothers gone to the army; my father is therefore all alone. Allow me to pass one week with him."

"You shall find yourself with him to-morrow morning," answered the Beast, "but remember your promise. When you wish to return you have only to put your ring on a table when you go to bed. Adieu, Beauty!"

The Beast sighed, and Beauty went to bed extremely affected to

see him so distressed. When she awoke in the morning, she found herself in her father's cottage. Ringing a bell that was at her bedside, a servant entered, and on seeing her, gave a loud shriek; upon which the merchant ran upstairs, and, on beholding his daughter, was ready to die of joy. They embraced again and again; at length, Beauty began to recollect that she had no clothes to put on; but the servant told her she had just found a large chest filled with apparel, embroidered all over with gold, and ornamented with pearls and diamonds. Beauty thanked the kind Beast in her thoughts for his attention, and dressed herself in the plainest of the gowns, telling the servant to put away the others carefully, for she intended to present them to her sisters: but scarcely had she pronounced these words than the chest disappeared. Her father then observed, that no doubt the Beast intended she should keep the whole for herself; and immediately the chest returned to the same place.

While Beauty was dressing herself, notice was sent to her sisters of her arrival, and they lost no time in coming with their husbands to pay her a visit The husband of the eldest was extremely handsome; but so vain of his person, that he thought of nothing else from morning till night, and wholly disregarded the beauty of his wife. The second had married a man of excellent understanding; but he made no other use of it than to torment and affront all his acquaintances and his wife. The two sisters were ready to burst with envy when they saw Beauty dressed like a princess, and looking so very beautiful; not all the kindness she showed them produced the least effect; their jealousy was still increased, when she told them how happily she lived at the palace of the Beast. The envious creatures went secretly into the garden, where they cried with spite, to think of her good fortune.

"Sister," said the eldest, "let us try to keep her here beyond the week allowed by the Beast; who will then be so enraged, that ten to one but he eats her up in a moment."

Having determined on this, they joined her in the cottage, and showed her so much affection, that Beauty could not help crying for joy. When the week was ended, the two sisters began to tear their hair, and counterfeited so much affliction at the thoughts of her leaving them, that she consented to stay another week; during which Beauty could not help constantly reproaching herself for the unhappiness she knew she must occasion her poor Beast, whom she tenderly loved, and for whose company she much wished. The tenth night of her being at the cottage, she dreamed she was in the garden of the palace; and that the Beast lay expiring, and in a dying voice reproached her with ingratitude. Beauty awaked and burst into tears.

"Am I not very wicked," said she, "to act so unkindly to a Beast who has treated me with such kindness? It is not his fault that he is ugly and stupid; and then he is so good! which is far better than all the rest. Why do I refuse to marry him? I should certainly be happier with him than my sisters with their husbands, for it is neither the person nor understanding of a husband that makes his wife happy, but kindness, virtue, and obliging temper; and all these the Beast possesses in perfection. I do not love him, but I feel for him the sincerest friendship, esteem, and gratitude."

She put her ring on the table, and soon fell asleep again. In the morning she found herself in the palace of the Beast; dressed herself with great magnificence, that she might please him the better, and thought she had never passed so long a day. At length the clock struck nine, but no Beast appeared. Beauty imagined she had been the cause of his death; she ran from room to room all over the palace, calling in despair upon his name; but still no Beast came. After seeking for a long time, she recollected her dream, and instantly ran towards the grass plot on which she had seen him; and there she found the poor Beast extended senseless, and to all appearance dead. She threw herself upon his body, thinking nothing at all of his ugliness, and finding his heart still beat, she ran hastily and fetched some water, and threw it on his face. The Beast opened his eyes, and said:

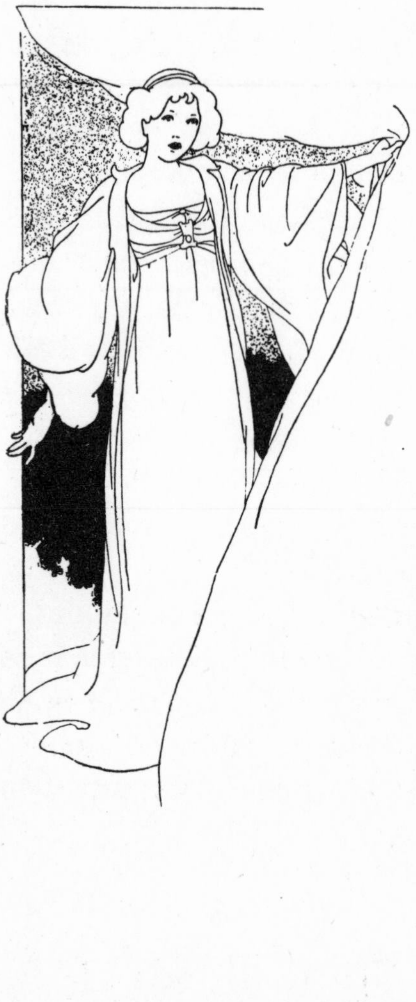

"You forgot your promise, Beauty. My grief for the loss of you made me resolve to starve

. . . and there she found the poor Beast extended senseless, and to all appearances dead. (PAGE 140)

Orson no sooner tasted the flavour of the fruit than he gave it to the bear.
(PAGE 153)

myself to death; at least I shall die content, since I have had the pleasure of seeing you once more."

"No, dear Beast," replied Beauty, "you shall not die; you shall live to become my husband; from this moment I offer you my hand, and swear to be only yours. Alas! I thought I felt only friendship for you; but the pain I feel convinces me that I could not live without seeing you."

Scarcely had Beauty pronounced these words, before the palace was suddenly illuminated, and music, fireworks, and all kinds of amusements announced the most splendid rejoicings. This, however, had no effect on Beauty, who watched over her dear Beast with the most tender anxiety. But what was her amazement, to see all at once at her feet the handsomest prince that was ever seen, who thanked her with the utmost tenderness for having broken his enchantment! Though this prince was deserving her whole attention, she could not refrain from asking him what was become of the Beast.

"You see him, Beauty, at your feet," answered the prince. "A wicked fairy had condemned me to keep the form of a beast till a beautiful young lady should consent to marry me, and had forbidden me on pain of death to show that I had any understanding. You alone, dearest Beauty, have had the generosity to judge of me by the goodness of my heart; and,

in offering you my crown, the recompense falls infinitely short of what I owe you."

Beauty, in the most pleasing surprise, assisted the handsome prince to rise, and they proceeded together to the palace; when her astonishment was very great, to find there her father and all her family, who had been conveyed thither by the beautiful lady she saw in her dream.

"Beauty," said the lady (for she was a great fairy), "receive the reward of the virtuous choice you have made. You have preferred goodness of heart to sense and beauty:

you therefore deserve to find these qualities united in the same person. You are going to be a great queen: I hope a crown will not destroy your virtue. As for you, ladies," said the fairy to the eldest sisters, "I have long been witness to the malice of your hearts, and the injustice you have committed. You shall become two statues; but under that form you shall preserve your reason as before, and shall be fixed at the gates of your sister's palace; nor will I inflict on you any greater punishment than that of witnessing her happiness. You will never recover your natural forms till you are fully sensible of your faults; and, to say the truth, I much fear you will ever remain statues. I have sometimes seen that pride, anger, and idleness may be conquered; but to amend a malignant and envious temper would be absolutely a miracle."

At the same instant the fairy, with a stroke of her wand, transported all who were present to the young prince's dominions, where he was received with transports of joy by his subjects. He married Beauty, and passed with her a long and happy life, because their actions were founded upon virtue.

Valentine and Orson

BELLISANT, the beautiful sister of the renowned Pepin, King of France, was married to Alexander, Emperor of Constantinople. Now the Emperor's chief minister was the high priest, a selfish and cruel man, who, observing the goodness of the new Empress, feared that she might acquire too much influence in her new country, and so wickedly resolved to seek her destruction.

The Emperor was a suspicious and credulous man, and one day when he was alone the High Priest entered the apartment saying:

"May your Majesty be ever guarded from the base attempts of the wicked and treacherous! I may not, being a priest, reveal the name of the criminal who has entrusted to me a dreadful secret; but, in the most solemn manner, I conjure your Majesty to beware of the designs of the Empress;

for that beautiful and dissembling lady is faithless and disloyal, and even now is planning your death."

The Emperor, believing the High Priest's tale, could not restrain his fury; but, still loving the Queen, could not bring himself to pronounce the sentence of her execution; yet he resolved to banish her from his dominions, and commanded her to leave Constantinople. At the same time he forbade all persons, on pain of death, to assist or succour the unfortunate lady, allowing her no other attendant than her servant Blandiman, whom she had brought with her from France. Thus with her one faithful attendant she left the city where she had been Empress.

"Alas!" cried she, "now all my happiness is fled. Instead of cloth of gold, I am clad in mean attire; my precious stones of inestimable value are all taken from me, and only pearls of tears adorn my garments. Ah! my brother, what shouldst thou do with such a woeful sister?"

As she was thus complaining and weeping, her servant said to her:

"Alas! be not discomforted, but trust in Providence, who will keep and defend you!"

Having thus spoken, he espied a fountain, towards which they took their way. After refreshing themselves they proceeded towards France. Arriving at the forest of Orleans, the disconsolate princess was so overcome with grief and fatigue, that she was unable to proceed farther. Her faithful attendant gathered fallen leaves and moss to make a couch for her, and then hastened away to seek some habitation where he might procure food and assistance.

During Blandiman's absence the royal lady became the mother of two beautiful sons. She pressed the lovely infants by turns to her bosom, and shed tears of joy over them; when suddenly a huge bear rushed upon her, and snatching up one of the babes in its mouth, hastened into the thickest part of the forest. The wretched mother, distracted at the fate of her child, pursued the bear with shrieks and lamentations; till overcome with anguish and terror, she fell into a swoon near the mouth of the cave into which the bear had borne her infant. It happened that King Pepin, accompanied by several great lords and barons of the court, was on that day hunting in the forest of Orleans, and chanced to pass near the tree where the son of Bellisant lay sleeping on its bed of moss. The King was astonished with the beauty of the child, who opened his eyes as the King stood gazing on him, and, smiling, stretched out its little arms.

"See," said King Pepin, "this lovely infant seems to solicit my favour."

The King little imagined it was his nephew, the son of his sister Bellisant, that he now delivered into the hands of one of his pages, who took the babe to Orleans to be nursed, and gave it, by the King's orders, the name of Valentine. Scarcely had the page ridden away with the child, than the King met Blandiman, and demanded with great surprise what news from Constantinople. Blandiman, bending one knee to the ground, began to relate the disasters of the Empress; but upon King Pepin's hearing that the High Priest had accused her of plotting the Emperor's death, he flew into the most violent rage against his innocent sister, and said:

"I cannot believe the loyal High Priest would bring a false accusation against anyone, and I blame the Emperor for sparing the life of his treacherous, disloyal Queen: but let her beware how she comes into my power; and hear me, nobles,

henceforth it is death for anyone that names her in my presence."

So saying, he proceeded towards Orleans. Blandiman, with a heavy heart, searched the forest for his injured mistress, and at length espied her on the ground tearing her hair, and uttering cries of grief.

"Ah! Blandiman," she exclaimed, "but an hour since I was the joyful mother of two beautiful babes. A ravenous bear snatched one, and some other cruel beast of prey has doubtless devoured the other. At the foot of yonder tree I left it when I pursued the bear; but no trace of either of my children remains. They are gone, gone for ever; and I, wretched mother, have nothing left but to die. Go, Blandiman, leave me to perish, and tell the mighty Emperor of Constantinople to what a horrible fate he has destined his innocent wife and children."

Blandiman would not leave the unfortunate Queen; and when she became more calm, prevailed on her to take shelter in a monastery on the borders of the forest of Orleans. After some time he told her of the unjust wrath of King Pepin against her; which renewed the sorrows of the hapless lady, and determined her to continue in the monastery.

The bear that had carried away the infant, bore it to her cave, and laid it down unhurt before her young ones. The cubs, however, did not devour it, but stroked it with their rough paws: and the old bear perceiving their kindness for the little babe, gave it suck, and nourished it in this manner for the space of a whole year. The child became hardy and robust, and as it grew in strength, began to range the forest, and attack the wild beasts with such fury, that they shunned the cave where he continued to live with the old bear. He passed this kind of life during eighteen years, until he was the terror of the neighbouring country. The name of Orson was given to him, because he was nurtured by a bear; and his renown spread over all France. King Pepin had a great desire to see the wild man of the woods; and one day rode with his retinue into the forest of Orleans, in hopes of meeting him. The King, leaving his train at some distance, rode on, and passed near the cave which Orson inhabited. On hearing the sound of horses' feet, the wild man rushed upon the King, and would have strangled him in an instant, but for a valiant knight, who galloped up and wounded Orson with his sword. Orson then left the King, and running furiously upon the knight, caught him and his horse, and overthrew both. The King, being quite unarmed, could not assist the knight, but rode away to call the attendants to his rescue. However, before they arrived on the spot, the unfortunate knight was torn to

pieces, and Orson had fled to the thickest part of the forest, where all their endeavours could not discover him. The noise of this adventure increased everyone's terror, and the neighbouring villages were nearly abandoned by their inhabitants.

Valentine, in the meanwhile, had been educated in all kinds of accomplishments, with the King's fair daughter, Eglantine. Nothing could exceed the fondness of the young people for each other: indeed, there never was a lovelier princess than Eglantine, or a braver and more accomplished knight than Valentine. Valentine soon distinguished himself above the other leaders in battle. He fought near the King's side; and when his Majesty was taken by a troop of Saracens, Valentine rushed through their ranks, slew hundreds of them, and replacing the King on his horse, led him off in triumph.

Valentine having conquered the pagans, returned to the court of King Pepin, and was received with loud acclamations by the people, and joyfully welcomed by the Princess Eglantine. The distinctions and favour showered on him raised the envy and hatred of Henry and Haufray, the King's sons.

It happened shortly after that a petition was presented to the King, praying relief against Orson, the wild man of the woods; the fear of whom was now become so great that the peasants dared not go out to till their fields, nor the shepherds to watch their flocks. The King issued a proclamation, saying, that if any man would undertake to bring Orson,

dead or alive, to the city, he should receive a thousand marks of gold.

"Sire," said Henry, "I think no person is so proper to undertake this enterprise as the foundling Valentine, on whom your Majesty lavishes such great favours. Perhaps if he conquers the naked savage with his sword, you will not think it too much to reward him with the hand of our sister Eglantine."

Valentine fixing a firm look on the malicious brother, said:

"You give this counsel to compass my death: be it so. Know that I will not fail of victory here also. I will go without delay, and alone, to conquer the savage man."

"No, Valentine," said the King, "you shall not rush into destruction to gratify the ill will of evil-minded persons."

"Pardon me, my liege," replied Valentine; "it concerns my honour that I go. I will encounter this danger, and every other, rather than not prove myself worthy of your Majesty's favour and protection. To-morrow I will depart for the forest at the break of day."

At dawn, Valentine arose; and putting on his armour, having his shield polished like a mirror, he departed; and being arrived at the forest he alighted, and tying his horse to a tree, penetrated into the thickest part of the wood in search of Orson. He long wandered in vain, and being come near the mouth of a large cave, thought that might be the hiding-place of the wild man. Valentine then climbed a high tree near the cave: and scarcely was he seated among the branches than he heard Orson's roar. Orson had been hunting, and came with a swift pace, bearing a buck he had killed upon his shoulders. Valentine could not help admiring the beauty of his person, the grace and freedom of his motions, and his appearance of strength and agility. He felt a species of affection for the wild man, and wished it were possible to tame him. Valentine tore off a branch of the tree; and threw it at Orson's feet, who, looking up, and espying him in the tree, uttered a growl of fury, and darted up the tree like lightning. Valentine quickly descended on the other side. Orson seeing him on the ground, leaped down, and opening his arms, prepared in his usual manner, to rush upon and overthrow his antagonist; but Valentine, holding up the polished steel, Orson suddenly beheld, instead of the person he meant to seize, his own wild figure. Upon Valentine's lowering the shield, he again saw his enemy, and with a cry of transport again prepared to grasp him in his arms. The strength of Orson was so very great, that Valentine was unable to defend himself without having recourse to his sword. When Orson received a wound from his sword, he uttered loud shrieks of anger and surprise, and instantly tearing up by the roots a large tree, furiously attacked Valentine. A dreadful fight now ensued between these two brothers, and the victory was for a long time doubtful: Orson receiving many dreadful wounds from the sword of Valentine, and Valentine with great difficulty escaping from being crushed to death beneath the weighty club of Orson. Just at this time, the bear who had nursed Orson, and who was now in the cave, hearing the cries of rage, came out to see what was the matter with her favourite. Valentine, perceiving her approach, aimed a blow at her with his sword, which would probably have killed her on the spot, had not Orson rushed forward; and throwing one arm round the neck of the bear, he with the other hand supplicated for mercy for his old and only friend. Valentine was greatly affected with this generous action, and, laying aside his sword, made signs that he would not hurt the bear, and, in token of kindness, brought some grapes and a bottle of wine he had deposited near for his own refreshment in case of need, and presented them to Orson.

Orson no sooner tasted the flavour of the fruit than he gave it to the bear, and afterwards let her drink the wine, with both of which she seemed much pleased; while Orson, delighted to see her make such a repast, threw his arms round her and embraced her; and the bear, desirous to gratify her affection for him, stroked him with her huge paw, and uttered a gentle growl, as if to express her satisfaction.

Valentine now made many signs to Orson, persuading him to go with him, where he should be fed and clothed, and treated with the greatest kindness; but

Orson rejected all his offers with anger and contempt, making signs that he never would quit his beloved bear, nor his wild life in the woods. But it happened that the wine which the bear had drunk so greedily from Valentine's bottle caused her death; and soon after, testifying her love for Orson in the manner we have described, she faintly howled, and fell dead on the ground. Orson stood for a few moments motionless with alarm and amazement; then supposing his ancient friend might be only asleep, he stooped and endeavoured to rouse her, but finding all his efforts ineffectual, his grief is scarcely to be described. He threw himself upon the body, and uttered piercing shrieks of distress. At length he suddenly sprang up from the ground, and approaching Valentine made signs that he would now be his; and while the tears ran down his cheeks for the loss of his bear, he suffered Valentine to bind his hands, and followed his conductor. Valentine took his way towards Orleans; but wherever he passed, the people, perceiving the wild man, ran into their houses and hid themselves. On arriving at an inn where Valentine intended resting during the night, the terrified inhabitants fastened the door, and would not suffer them to enter. Valentine made signs to Orson, who, placing his shoulder against the door, forced it open in an instant, upon which the people of the inn all ran out at the back, and would not venture to return. A great feast was in preparation, and there was plenty of fowls and good provisions roasting at the fire. Orson tore the meat off the spit with his hands, and devoured it greedily; and espying a cauldron of water, put his head into it, and drank like a horse.

In the morning, Valentine resumed his journey, leading Orson as before. On arriving at the city, the inhabitants shut their doors, and ran into the highest rooms to gaze upon the wild man. Being come to the outer court of King Pepin's palace, the porter in a great fright barred the gate with heavy chains and bars of iron, and could not be prevailed upon to open it. After soliciting admittance for some time, and being still denied, Valentine made a sign to Orson, who, tearing up one of the large stone posts that stood by, shattered the gate to pieces. The Queen, the Princess Eglantine, and all their attendants, fled to hide themselves when they heard that Orson was arrived; and Valentine had the greatest difficulty in persuading them to believe that Orson was no longer furious and savage as he had been in the woods. At length the King permitted him to be brought in; and the whole court gathered in the apartment, and were much amused by his wild actions and gestures, although very cautious not to come near him. On Valentine's making signs, he kissed the King's robe, and the hand of the Princess Eglantine; for Orson had now become so attached to Valentine that he would obey him in all things, and would suffer no other person to control him.

Very soon after the capture of Orson, a herald appeared at the court of King Pepin, from the Duke of Aquitaine, summoning all true knights to avenge the cause of the Lady Fezon, daughter to the noble duke who was held in cruel captivity by Agramont, the Green Knight: the herald proclaiming, that whoever should conquer the Green Knight should receive the hand of the Lady Fezon in marriage, together with a princely dowry. This Green Knight was so famous for his cruelty and his victories, that the young lords of the court all drew back, and seemed unwilling to enter the lists; for it was known that he was defended by enchantment, and it was his practice to hang upon a high tree all the knights whom he had defeated. Valentine, however, offered himself without hesitation, and engaged to get ready and depart the next morning. The Princess Eglantine secretly resolved, if possible, to prevent the destruction of her beloved Valentine, by combating the Green Knight herself. She contrived to steal away the armour of Valentine while he slept, and equipping herself in it, mounted a fiery courser; and attended only by her favourite maid, in quality of a page, proceeded to the castle which the Green Knight inhabited, and where he kept the Lady Fezon a prisoner.

Valentine, meanwhile, missing his armour when he arose, and learning that the Princess had taken it and was gone on the perilous enterprise, was almost distracted with terrors for her safety. He ordered his horse to be prepared, and, followed by Orson, set out in search of the Princess. Haufray and Henry, disappointed in their former purpose, now resolved to waylay and kill Valentine. Accordingly, in a narrow alley of a dark wood, they sprang upon him, and seized him before he had power to draw his sword. Orson chanced to be a little way behind, but, upon hearing Valentine's voice, he rushed upon Henry who was about to stab Valentine in the back, and seized him in his arms. Orson's grasp almost crushed Henry to death, and Valentine would have killed Haufray, but first tearing their masks from their faces, and seeing they were the King's sons, he left them to the shame and disgrace their base conduct would bring upon them. He had some difficulty in prevailing on Orson to let them live; but they left the wicked brothers in the wood, and continued their journey, fortunately arriving at the castle of the Green Knight, just as the Princess Eglantine was almost overpowered in the combat. Valentine rushed with dreadful fury upon the Green Knight, and the fight was long and equal. At length Agramont demanded a parley.

"Knight," said he to Valentine, "thou art brave and noble. Behold; yonder hang twenty knights whom I have subdued and executed: such will be thy fate; I give thee warning."

"Base traitor," replied Valentine, "I fear thee not; come on; I defy thee."

"First," rejoined the Green Knight, "fetch me yonder shield; for in pity to thy youth, I tell thee, unless thou canst remove that shield, thou never canst rescue the Lady Fezon, or conquer me."

Valentine approached the shield; but, in spite of all his efforts, he could not loosen it from the tree, though it appeared to hang but on a slender branch. Valentine, breathless with his exertions to pull down the shield, stood leaning against the tree, when Agramont with a loud laugh exclaimed:

"Fly and save thyself, fair knight; for since thou canst not move the shield, thou art not destined to be my victor. Further, know, there is no one living who can subdue me, unless he be the son of a mighty king, and yet was suckled by a wild beast."

Valentine started on hearing these latter words, and ran

to Orson, who had been all this time employed in gazing with looks of delight and admiration on the Lady Fezon. Valentine led him to the enchanted shield, which, on Orson's raising his arm towards it, dropped instantly from its place. The Green Knight trembled and turned pale; then, gnashing his teeth, seized his sword, and attacked Orson with desperate fury. At the first blow, Agramont's trusty sword broke in pieces upon the enchanted shield. Next he caught up a battleaxe, which snapped instantly in two. He then called for a lance, which shivered to atoms in the same manner. Furious with these defeats, he threw aside his weapons, and trusting to his wonderful strength, attempted to grasp Orson in his arms; but Orson, seizing him as if he had been a mere child dashed him on the ground, and would have instantly destroyed him, had not Valentine interposed to save his life. Orson continued to hold him down till some chains were brought, when, in despite of the furious struggles of the Green Knight, Orson bound him in strong fetters, to lead him away a prisoner.

Agramont addressed himself to Valentine, and said:

"This savage man is my conqueror; therefore there must be some mystery in his fate. Haste, then, to the castle of my brother Ferragus, where you will find a Brazen Head that will explain to you who he is."

Valentine, having dispatched a herald to acquaint the Duke of Aquitaine with the release of his daughter, sent the Lady Fezon, with the Princess Eglantine, to the court of King Pepin, while he and Orson proceeded to the castle of the giant Ferragus. This castle was guarded by two lions, who roared with rage against Valentine, but when Orson appeared, they lay down and crouched beneath his feet. On entering the castle, a dwarf approached, and conducted them to a chamber abounding with gold, rubies, and other precious stones; in the centre there were four pillars of jasper, two of which were as yellow as the finest gold, a third more green than grass, and a fourth more red than a flame of fire. Between these pillars was an emerald of amazing value; and in the midst the Brazen Head rested upon a rich pedestal. Before the pedestal stood an enormous giant, who lifted his club to forbid their approach, but Orson seized him by the middle, and bore him from the chamber to a dungeon, where he secured him. Valentine fixed his eyes upon the Brazen Head, anxious to hear what it would say concerning his birth. At length when Orson had returned it spake thus:

"Thou, O renowned knight, art called Valentine the brave, and art the man destined to be the husband of the Princess Eglantine of France. Thou art son to the Emperor of Greece, and thy mother is Bellisant, sister to King Pepin of France. She was unjustly banished from her throne, and took refuge in a monastery, where she has resided these twenty years. The wild man, who hath so long accompanied thee, is thy brother. You were both born in the forest of Orleans.

Thou wert found and brought up under the care of King Pepin thy uncle, but thy brother was stolen and nurtured by a bear. Proceed, Valentine, to France, where thou wilt find the innocent Empress, thy hapless mother; at the moment when she embraces thy brother, speech will be given to him. Away, and prosper! These are the last words I shall utter. Fate has decreed that, when Valentine and Orson enter this chamber my power ends."

Having thus spoken, the Brazen Head fell from its pedestal: thunder shook the foundations of the castle; they were surrounded with thick darkness; and when the light again burst upon them, they found themselves on an open plain, and no traces of the castle remained. The little dwarf, whose name was Pacolet, at the same time appeared before them on a winged horse and said:

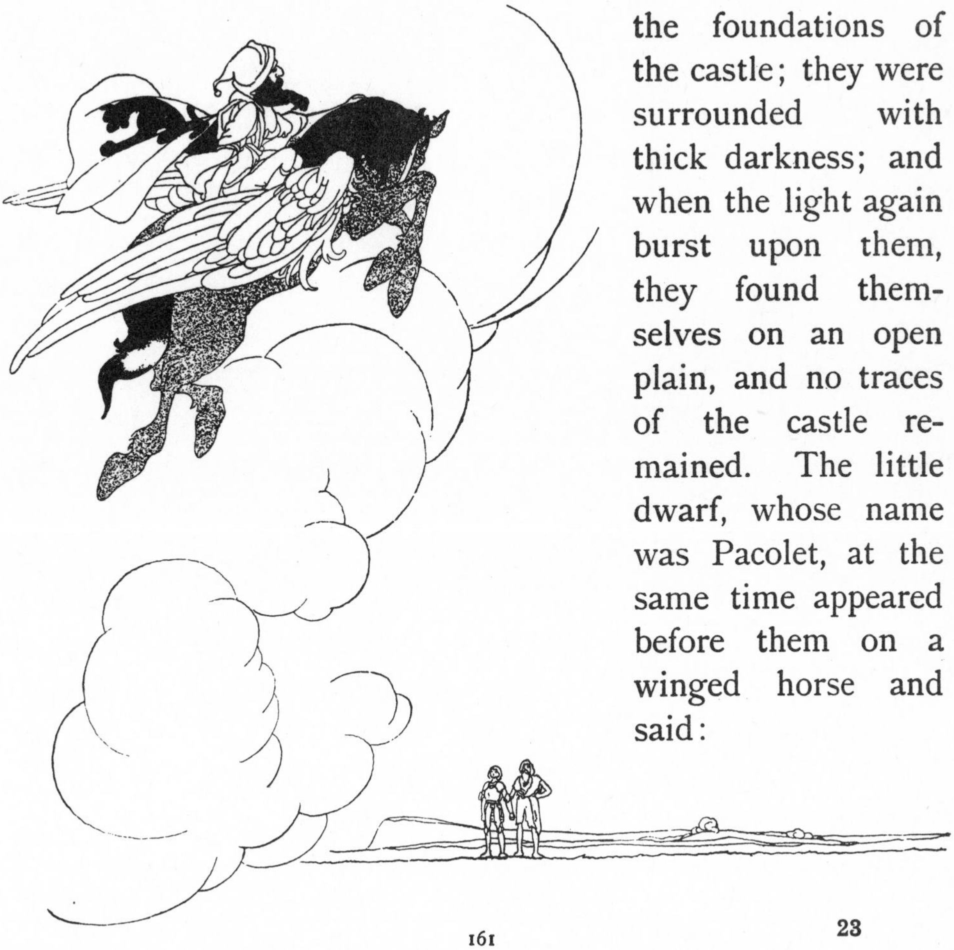

"Noble youths, I go before you to the court of King Pepin, to prepare your royal parents, who are already there, for your reception."

And instantly Pacolet mounted into the air, and was presently out of sight. Valentine now fell upon the bosom of his brother Orson, and Orson upon his; they embraced each other with the utmost affection, and joyfully proceeded towards France. While these transactions were passing, the Emperor of Constantinople had lived in great affliction for the loss of his Queen. The wicked High Priest had continued to represent her as the vilest of women, and to abuse the Emperor's confidence in him till he was on his deathbed; when, repenting of his treachery, he sent for the Emperor, and confessed before the whole court that he had basely slandered the princess. Nothing could exceed the Emperor's grief. He immediately set out with all his nobles for France, to implore King Pepin to assist him in searching for Bellisant. In every town on his journey he caused her innocence to be proclaimed, and offered an immense reward to anyone who should bring tidings of her to the court of King Pepin. It happened that Blandiman, who was buying provisions for the monastery at Orleans, as the Emperor passed through, heard the proclamation, and hastened with the tidings to his mistress. The Empress, overjoyed to have her innocence made known, quitted the monastery, and went to the palace of her brother, where she was received with shouts of triumph—King Pepin and the Emperor both falling at her feet to implore forgiveness. Scarcely had the reconciliation passed, and the Empress related her sorrowful history when the dwarf, Pacolet, appeared on the winged horse, to announce the wonderful declaration made by the Brazen Head, and the approach of

the royal brothers. The noble youths now presented themselves to their parents; and no sooner had the Empress Bellisant thrown her arms round the neck of her son Orson, than speech was given to him, and he expressed his duty and affection to his parents and uncle, in terms of such grace and propriety, as at once astonished and delighted the whole court. The Duke of Aquitaine, having already come to the palace of King Pepin, to congratulate his daughter, now took the hand of Orson, and presented him to the Lady Fezon as her future husband: King Pepin at the same time joined the hands of Valentine and the Princess Eglantine. Splendid preparations were immediately made for the celebration of the nuptials; and for a whole month nothing was to be heard of throughout France but tilts and tournaments, feasts and balls, fireworks and illuminations, with every other kind of splendid and magnificent entertainment.

Little Red Riding Hood

ONCE upon a time there lived a country girl, who was the sweetest little creature ever seen. Her grandmother had made for her a pretty red hood, which so became the child that everyone called her Little Red Riding-Hood. One day her mother, having made some cakes, said to her:

"Go, my child, and see how your grandmother does, for I hear she is ill; carry her some of these cakes, and a little pot of butter."

Little Red Riding-Hood, with a basket filled with the

cakes and the pot of butter, immediately set out for her grandmother's house, in a village a little distance away.

As she was crossing a wood she met a wolf, who had a mind to eat her up, but dared not do so because of some woodcutters at work near them in the forest. He ventured, however, to ask her whither she was going.

The little girl, not knowing how dangerous it was to talk to a wolf, replied:

"I am going to see my grandmother, and carry her these cakes and a pot of butter."

"Does she live far off?" said the wolf.

"Oh, yes," answered Little Red Riding-Hood, "beyond the mill you see yonder, at the first house in the village."

"Well," said the wolf, "I will go and see her too; I will take this way and you take that, and see which will be there the soonest."

The wolf set out, running as fast as he could, and taking the nearest way, while the little girl took the longest, and amused herself as she went along with gathering nuts, running after butterflies, and making nosegays of such flowers as she found within her reach.

The wolf soon arrived at the grandmother's cottage, and knocked at the door.

"Who is there?" asked a voice.

"It is your grandchild, Little Red Riding-Hood," said the wolf, counterfeiting her voice; "I have brought you some cakes and a little pot of butter, which Mother has sent you."

The good old woman, who was ill in bed, called out:

"Pull the bobbin, and the latch will go up."

The wolf pulled the bobbin, and the door opened. He sprang upon the poor old grandmother and ate her up in a moment.

The wolf then shut the door and laid himself down in the bed, and waited for Little Red Riding-Hood, who arrived soon after. Tap! Tap!

"Who is there?"

She was at first a little frightened at the hoarse voice of the wolf, but supposing that her grandmother had got a cold, answered:

"It is your grandchild, Little Red Riding-Hood. Mother has sent you some cakes and a little pot of butter." The wolf called out, softening his voice:

"Pull the bobbin, and the latch will go up."

Little Red Riding-Hood pulled the bobbin, and the door opened.

When she came into the room, the wolf, hiding himself under the bedclothes, said, trying all he could to speak in a feeble voice:

"Put the basket, my child, on the stool; take off your clothes, and come into bed with me."

The Wolf arrives at the Cottage

Little Red Riding-Hood accordingly undressed herself and stepped into bed, where, wondering to see how her grandmother looked in her nightclothes, she said:

"Grandmother, what great arms you have got."

"The better to hug thee, my child."

"Grandmother, what great ears you have got."

"The better to hear thee, my child."

"Grandmother, what great eyes you have got."

"The better to see thee, my child."

"Grandmother, what great teeth you have got."

"The better to eat thee up;" and saying these words, the wicked wolf fell upon poor Little Red Riding-Hood, and ate her up in a few mouthfuls.

Snowdrop

IT was the middle of winter when a certain queen sat working at a window the frame of which was made of fine black ebony; and as she was looking out upon the snow, she pricked her finger, and three drops of blood fell upon it. Then she gazed upon the red drops which sprinkled the white snow, and said: "Would that my little daughter may be as white as snow, as red as blood, and as black as ebony!" And so the little girl grew up: her skin was as white as snow, her cheeks as rosy as the blood, and her hair as black as ebony; and she was called Snowdrop.

But this queen died; and the king married another wife, who had a magical looking-glass, to which she used to go and gaze upon herself, and say:

"Tell me, glass, tell me true!
Of all the ladies in the land,
Who is the fairest? tell me who?"

And the glass answered:

"Thou, queen, art fairest in the land."

But when Snowdrop was seven years old, the glass one day answered the Queen:

> "Thou, queen, may'st fair and beauteous be,
> But Snowdrop is lovelier far than thee!"

When she heard this she turned pale with rage and envy; and called to one of her servants, and said:

"Take Snowdrop into the wide wood, that I may never see her more."

Then the servant led her away; but his heart melted when she begged him to spare her life, and he said:

"I will not hurt thee, thou pretty child."

So he left her by herself; and he felt as if a great weight were taken off his heart when he had made up his mind not to kill her.

Then poor Snowdrop wandered through the wood in fear. In the evening she came to a cottage, and went in to rest herself, for her little feet would carry her no farther. Everything was neat: on the table was spread a white cloth, and there were seven little plates with seven little loaves, and seven little glasses with wine in them; and knives and forks laid in order; and by the wall stood seven little beds. Then, as she was very hungry, she picked a little piece off each loaf, and drank a very little wine out of each glass; and after that she thought she would lie down and rest. So she tried all the little beds; one was too long, another was too short, till at last the seventh suited her; and there she laid herself down and went to sleep. Presently in came the masters of the cottage, seven little dwarfs who lived among the mountains, and dug and searched for gold. They lighted their seven lamps, and saw directly that all was not right.

The first said: "Who has been sitting on my stool?"

The second: "Who has been eating off my plate?"

The third: "Who has been picking my bread?"

The fourth: "Who has been meddling with my spoon?"

The fifth: "Who has been handling my fork?"

The sixth: "Who has been cutting with my knife?"

The seventh: "Who has been drinking my wine?"

Then the first looked round and said: "Who has been lying on my bed?"

And the rest came running to him, and everyone cried out that somebody had been upon his bed. But the seventh saw Snowdrop, and called all his brethren to come and see her; and they cried out with wonder and astonishment, and brought their lamps to look at her, and said:

"Good heavens! what a lovely child she is!"

And they were delighted to see her, and took care not to wake her; and the seventh dwarf slept an hour with each of the other dwarfs in turn, till the night was gone.

In the morning Snowdrop told them her story; and they pitied her, and said if she would keep all things in order, and cook and wash, and knit and spin for them, she might stay where she was, and they would take care of her. Then they went out all day long to their work, seeking for gold and silver in the mountains; and Snowdrop remained at home.

The Queen, now that she thought Snowdrop was dead, believed that she was certainly the handsomest lady in the land; and she went to the glass and said:

"Tell me, glass, tell me true!
  Of all the ladies in the land,
Who is fairest? tell me who?"

And the glass answered:

"Thou, queen, art the fairest in all this land;
But over the hills, in the greenwood shade,
Where the seven dwarfs their dwelling have made,
There Snowdrop is hiding her head; and she
Is lovelier far, O queen! than thee."

Then the Queen was alarmed; for she knew that the glass always spoke the truth, and was sure that the servant had betrayed her. She could not bear to think that anyone lived more beautiful than she was; so she disguised herself as an old pedlar, and went to the place where the dwarfs dwelt. Then she knocked at the door, and cried:

"Fine wares to sell!"

Snowdrop looked out at the window, and said:

"Good day, good-woman; what have you to sell?"

"Good wares, fine wares," said she; "laces and bobbins of all colours."

"I will let the old lady in; she seems to be a very good sort of body," thought Snowdrop, so she ran down, and unbolted the door.

"Bless me!" said the old woman, "how badly your stays are laced! Let me lace them up with one of my nice new laces."

Snowdrop did not dream of any mischief; so she stood up before the old woman; but she set to work so nimbly,

. . . and making nosegays of such flowers as she found within her reach.

(PAGE 166)

In the morning Snowdrop told them her story. (PAGE 171)

and pulled the lace so tight, that Snowdrop lost her breath, and fell down as if dead.

"There's an end of all thy beauty," said the spiteful Queen, and went away home.

In the evening the seven dwarfs returned, and were grieved to see their faithful Snowdrop stretched upon the ground motionless, as if dead. However, they lifted her up, and when they found what was the matter, they cut the lace; and in a little time she began to breathe, and soon came to life again. Then they said:

"The old woman was the Queen herself; take care another time, and let no one in when we are away."

When the Queen got home, she went straight to her glass, and spoke to it as usual; but it still said:

"Thou, queen, art the fairest in all this land;
But over the hills, in the greenwood shade,
Where the seven dwarfs their dwelling have made,
There Snowdrop is hiding her head; and she
Is lovelier far, O queen! than thee."

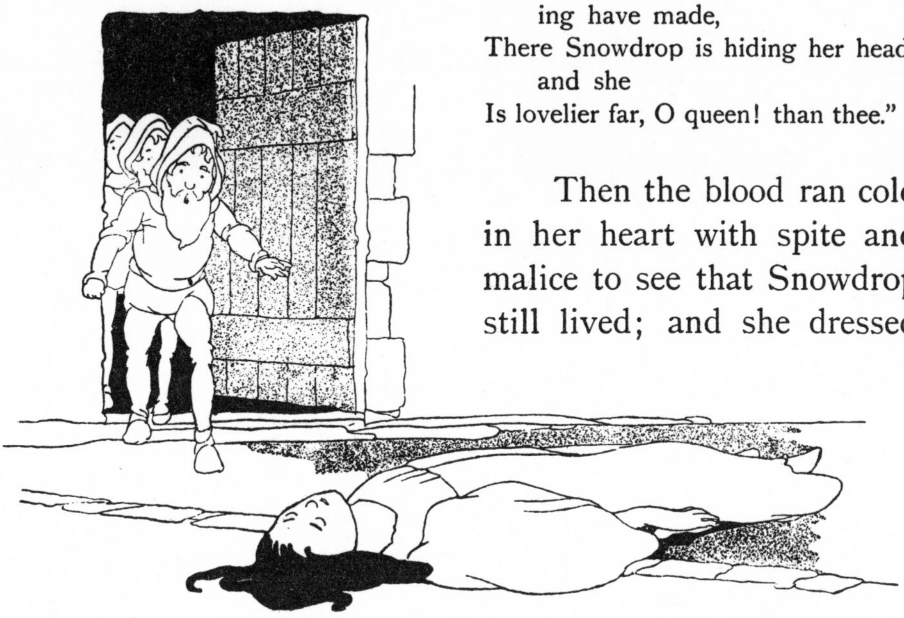

Then the blood ran cold in her heart with spite and malice to see that Snowdrop still lived; and she dressed

herself again in a very different disguise, and took with her a poisoned comb. When she reached the dwarfs' cottage, she knocked at the door, and cried:

"Fine wares to sell!"

But Snowdrop said: "I dare not let anyone in."

Then the Queen said: "Only look at my beautiful combs," and gave her the poisoned one. And it looked so pretty that she took it up and put it into her hair to try it, but the moment it touched her head the poison was so powerful that she fell down senseless.

"There you may lie," said the Queen, and went her way. By good luck the dwarfs returned early that evening, and when they saw Snowdrop lying on the ground, they thought what had happened, and soon found the poisoned comb. And when they took it away, she recovered; and they warned her once more not to open the door to anyone.

Meantime the Queen went home to her glass, and trembled with rage when she received the same answer as before. She went secretly into a chamber, and prepared a poisoned apple: the outside looked rosy and tempting, but whoever tasted it was sure to die. Then she dressed herself up as a peasant's wife, and travelled over the hills to the dwarfs' cottage, and knocked at the door; but Snowdrop put her head out of the window, and said:

"I dare not let anyone in."

"Do as you please," said the old woman, "but at any rate take this pretty apple; I will make you a present of it."

"No," said Snowdrop, "I dare not take it."

"You silly girl!" answered the other, "what are you afraid of? do you think it is poisoned? Come! do you eat one part, and I will eat the other."

Now the apple was so prepared that one side was good, though the other side was poisoned. Then Snowdrop was very much tempted to taste, for the apple looked exceedingly nice; and when she saw the old woman eat, she could refrain no longer. But she had scarcely put the piece into her mouth, when she fell down dead upon the ground.

"This time nothing will save thee," said the Queen; and she went home to her glass, and at last it said:

"Thou, queen, art the fairest
of all the fair."

And then her envious heart was glad, and as happy as such a heart could be.

When evening came, and the dwarfs returned

home, they found Snowdrop lying on the ground: no breath passed her lips, and they were afraid that she was dead. They lifted her up, and combed her hair, and washed her face with wine and water; but all was in vain, the little girl seemed quite dead. So they laid her upon a bier, and watched and bewailed her three whole days; then they proposed to bury her: but her cheeks were still rosy, and her face looked as it did while she was alive. So they made a coffin of glass that they might still look at her, and wrote her name upon it, in golden letters, and that she was a king's daughter. And the coffin was placed upon the hill, and one of the dwarfs sat by it and watched.

And thus Snowdrop lay for a long time, and still only looked as though she were asleep; for she was even now as white as snow, and as red as blood, and as black as ebony. At last a prince came and called at the dwarfs' house; and he saw Snowdrop, and read what was written in golden letters. Then he offered the dwarfs money, and earnestly prayed them to let him take her away; but they said:

"We will not part with her for all the gold in the world."

At last, however, they had pity on him, and gave him the coffin: but the moment he lifted it up to carry it home with him, the piece of apple fell from between her lips, and Snowdrop awoke, and said:

"Where am I?"

And the Prince answered: "Thou art safe with me."

Then he told her all that had happened, and said: "I love you better than all the world: come with me to my father's palace, and you shall be my wife."

And Snowdrop consented, and went home with the Prince: and everything was prepared with pomp and splendour for their wedding.

To the feast was invited, among the rest, Snowdrop's old enemy, the Queen; and as she was dressing herself in fine rich clothes, she looked in the glass and said:

"Tell me, glass, tell me true!
Of all the ladies in the land,
Who is fairest? tell me who?"

And the glass answered:

"Thou, lady, art loveliest *here*, I ween;
But lovelier far is the new-made queen."

When she heard this, she started with rage; but her envy and curiosity were so great, that she could not help setting out to see the bride. And when she arrived, and saw that it was no other than Snowdrop, who, as she thought, had been dead a long while, she choked with passion, and fell ill and died; but Snowdrop and the Prince lived and reigned happily over that land many years.

Puss in Boots

A MILLER died, having divided what he possessed among his three sons in the following manner: his mill to the eldest, his ass to the second, and his cat to the youngest. The poor young fellow who had only the cat, complained that he was hardly used.

"My brothers," said he, "by joining their stocks together, may do very well in the world; but for me, when I have eaten my cat, and made a fur cap of his skin, I may soon die of hunger!"

The cat, however, addressed him as follows:

"Do not thus afflict yourself, my good master: you have only to give me a bag, and get a pair of boots made for me, so that I may scamper through the dirt and the brambles, and you shall see that you are not so ill provided for as you imagine."

Though the cat's master did not much depend upon these promises, he did not despair.

PUSS IN BOOTS

Having obtained what he asked for, the cat began to equip himself: he drew on the boots, and putting the bag about his neck, took hold of the strings with his fore paws, and sallied forth. Puss first attempted to go into a warren, in which there were many rabbits. He put some bran and parsley into his bag; and, stretching himself out at full length as if he were dead, waited for some young rabbits, who as yet knew nothing of the cunning tricks of the world, to come and get into the bag, the better to feast upon the dainties.

Scarcely had he lain down before a giddy young rabbit crept into the bag, and the cat immediately drew the strings, and killed him without mercy.

Proud of his prey, Puss hastened to the palace, where he asked to speak to the King. On being shown in, he made a low bow, and said:

"I have brought you, Sire, this rabbit from the warren of my lord the Marquis of Carabas, who commanded me to present it to your Majesty with the assurance of his respect."

"Tell my Lord of Carabas," replied the King, "that I accept of his present with pleasure, and am greatly obliged to him."

Soon after the cat laid himself down in the same manner in a field of corn, and two fine partridges got into his bag, which he immediately killed and carried to the palace. The King received them as he had done the rabbit,

and ordered his servants to give the messenger something to drink. In this manner he continued to carry presents of game to the King from my Lord Marquis of Carabas, once at least every week.

One day, the cat having heard that the King intended to take a ride that morning by the river's side with his daughter, who was the most beautiful princess in the world, said to his master:

"If you will follow my advice, your fortune is made. Take off your clothes, and bathe yourself in the river, just in the place I shall show you, and leave the rest to me."

The Marquis of Carabas did exactly as he was desired, without being able to guess at what the cat intended. While he was bathing the King passed by, and Puss directly called out as loud as he could bawl:

"Help! help! My Lord Marquis of Carabas is in danger of drowning!"

The King put his head out of the carriage to see what was the matter: when, perceiving the very cat who had brought him so many presents, he ordered his attendants to go to the assistance of my Lord Marquis of Carabas.

While they were employed in taking the Marquis out of the river, the cat ran to the King's carriage, and told his Majesty that while his master was bathing, some thieves had run off with his clothes as they lay by the river's side; the cunning cat all the time having hidden them under a large stone. The King commanded the officers of his wardrobe to fetch one of the handsomest suits it contained, and present it to my Lord Marquis of Carabas. As the fine clothes they brought made him look like a gentleman, and set off his person, which was very comely, to the greatest advantage, the King's daughter was mightily taken with his appearance, and the Marquis of Carabas had no sooner cast upon her two or three respectful glances, than she became violently in love with him. The King insisted on his getting into the carriage, and taking a ride with them. The cat, enchanted to see how well his scheme was likely to succeed, ran before to a meadow, and said to the reapers:

"Good people, if you do not tell the King, who will soon pass this way, that the meadow you are reaping belongs to my Lord Marquis of Carabas, you shall be chopped as small as mincemeat."

The King did not fail to ask the reapers to whom the meadow belonged?

"To my Lord Marquis of Carabas," said they all at once; for the threats of the cat had frightened them terribly.

"You have here a very fine piece of land, my Lord Marquis," said the King.

"Truly, Sire," replied he, "it does not fail to bring every year a plentiful harvest."

The cat went on before, and came to a field where

labourers were making sheaves of the corn they had reaped, to whom he said as before:

"Good people, if you do not tell the King, who will presently pass this way, that the corn you have reaped in this field belongs to my Lord Marquis of Carabas, you shall be chopped as small as mincemeat."

The King passed a moment after, and enquired to whom the corn belonged?

"To my Lord Marquis of Carabas," answered they very glibly; upon which the King again complimented the Marquis on his noble possessions.

The cat still continued to go before, and gave the same charge to all the people he met; so that the King was greatly astonished at the splendid fortune of my Lord Marquis of Carabas.

Puss at length arrived at a stately castle, which belonged to a rich Ogre; all the lands the King had passed through and admired were his. The cat took care to learn every particular about the Ogre, and what he could do, and then asked to speak with him, saying, as he entered the room in which he was, that he could not pass so near his castle without doing himself the honour of enquiring as to his health.

The Ogre received him as civilly as an Ogre could do, and desired him to be seated.

"I have been informed," said the cat, "that you have the gift of changing yourself into all sorts of animals; into a lion, or an elephant for example."

"It is very true," replied the Ogre sternly, "and to convince you, I will directly take the form of a lion."

The cat was so much terrified at finding himself so

near to a lion, that he sprang from him, and climbed to the roof of the house, but not without much difficulty, as his boots were not very fit to walk upon the tiles.

Some minutes after, the cat perceiving that the Ogre had quitted the form of a lion, ventured to come down, and owned that he had been a good deal frightened.

"I have been further informed," continued the cat, "but I know not how to believe it, that you have the power of taking the form of the smallest animals also; for example, of changing yourself to a rat or a mouse: I confess I should think this must be impossible."

"Impossible! You shall see;" and at the same instant he changed himself into a mouse, and began to frisk about the room. The cat no sooner cast his eyes upon the Ogre in this form, than he sprang upon him and devoured him in an instant.

In the meantime the King, admiring the magnificent castle as he came near it, ordered his attendants to drive up to the gates. The cat, hearing the carriage on the drawbridge, immediately came out, saying:

"Your Majesty is welcome to the castle of my Lord Marquis of Carabas."

"And is this splendid castle yours also, my Lord Marquis of Carabas? No doubt it is no less magnificent within than without: pray, my Lord Marquis, indulge me with a sight of it."

The Marquis gave his hand to the young Princess as she alighted, and followed the King: they entered a spacious hall, where they found a splendid collation which the Ogre had prepared for some friends whom he had that day expected; but who, hearing that the King with the Princess and a great gentleman of the court were within, had not dared to enter. The King was so much charmed with the amiable qualities and noble fortune of the Marquis of Carabas, and the young Princess too had fallen so violently in love with him, that when the King had partaken of the collation, and drunk a few glasses of wine, he said to the Marquis:

"It will be your own fault, my Lord Marquis of Carabas, if you do not become my son-in-law."

The Marquis received the intelligence with a thousand respectful acknowledgments, accepted the honour conferred upon him, and married the Princess that very day.

The cat became a great lord, and never ran after rats and mice but for his amusement.

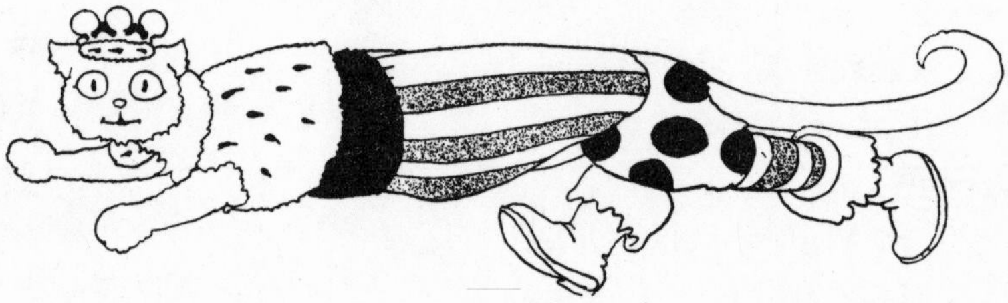

Hop o' my Thumb

ONCE upon a time there was a poor woodman who had seven children, all boys, the eldest no more than ten, the youngest only seven. This youngest was a puny little chap who rarely spoke a word; he was indeed the smallest person ever seen, being when born no bigger than a thumb, and thus he got the name of Hop o' my Thumb. Still he was by far cleverer than any of his brothers, and though he spoke but little he heard more than was imagined. The woodman and his wife at length became so poor that they could no longer give their children their usual food. One evening when the boys were in bed, the husband, sighing deeply, said:

"You see, dear wife, it is impossible for us to maintain our children any longer, and to see them die of hunger before my eyes is what I never could support. I am determined to take them to-morrow morning to the forest, and leave them in the thickest part of it, so that it will be impossible to find their way back."

"Ah!" cried the poor wife, "you cannot consent to be the death of your own children!" but at length, considering how dreadful it would be to see them die of hunger before her eyes, she consented to her husband's proposal, and went sobbing to bed.

Hop o' my Thumb had been all the time awake; and hearing his father talk more earnestly than usual, slipped away from his brothers, and crept under his father's bed to hear all that might be said without being seen. When his father and mother left off talking, he got back to his own place, and passed the night thinking what he should do. He rose early and ran to the river's side, filled his pockets with white pebbles, and returned home.

All set out, as their father and mother had agreed, and Hop o' my Thumb said not a word of what he had discovered. They reached a forest that was so thick, that at ten paces distant they could not see each other. The woodman set to work, cutting down wood, and the children began to gather all the twigs, and to make faggots of them. Then the father and mother, observing them all busy, slipped away without being perceived, and getting into a by-path, soon lost sight of the forest.

In a short time the children, finding themselves alone, began to cry as loud as they could. Hop o' my Thumb let them cry; for he knew how to conduct them safely home, having taken care to drop the white pebbles he had in his pocket the whole of the way by which they had come: he therefore only said:

"Never mind, my lads: father and mother have left us by ourselves; only take care to follow me, and I will lead you back again."

They followed Hop o' my Thumb, who soon brought them to their father's house, by the very same path by which they had come. Just as the woodman and his wife had returned home without their children, a gentleman of the village had sent to pay them two guineas, which had so long been owing for work they had done, that they never expected to receive it; this money quite rejoiced their hearts; for the poor creatures were exceedingly hungry, and had no means of getting anything to eat. The woodman sent his wife out to buy some meat; and as it was a long time since she had made a hearty meal, she bought enough for six or eight persons: but it might be that she had not yet learned to leave out her children, when she was thinking of what would be enough for dinner. She and her husband had no sooner eaten heartily than she cried out:

"Alas! where are our poor children? How they would feast on what we have left! It was all your fault. I told you over and over that we should repent the hour when we

left them to starve in the forest! Oh, mercy! they may perhaps be already eaten up by the wolves!"

The woodman grew angry with his wife, who repeated more than twenty times, that he would repent of what he had done, and that she had again and again told him so: he at last threatened to give her a good beating if she did not hold her tongue: not but that he was quite as sorry as his wife for what had happened, but that her scolding teased him.

"Alas!" repeated she, "what is become of my dear children?" and once she said this so loud that the children, who were listening at the door, cried out together:

"Here we are, mother, here we are!"

She flew to let them in, and kissed every one of them.

"How glad I am to see you, you little rogues!" said she. "Are you not tired and hungry? Ah, poor little Bobby! why, thou art dirt all over, my child! come hither, and let me wash thy face."

Bobby was the youngest excepting Hop o' my Thumb; and had always been his mother's favourite. The children

The cat became a great lord. (PAGE 184)

Hop o'my Thumb . . . crept under his father's bed to hear all that might be said without being seen. (PAGE 186)

sat down to dinner, and ate quite heartily. The parents were quite delighted at having their children again, and this continued till their money was all spent: then, finding themselves in the same condition as before, they, by degrees, again determined to leave them once more in the forest; and that they might not a second time be disappointed, they resolved to lead them a much greater distance than at first. They could not, however, consult with each other on this business so secretly but Hop o' my Thumb found means to overhear all that passed. It gave him no uneasiness, for he thought nothing could be easier than to do exactly the same as he had done before: but though he rose early to go to the river's side and get the pebbles, he could not get out, for the door was locked. Hop o' my Thumb was at a loss what to do; but his mother having given each of the children a piece of bread for breakfast, he thought he could make his share serve the same purpose as the pebbles. He accordingly put it carefully into his pocket.

It was not long before they set out, and their parents took care to lead them into the very thickest and darkest part of the forest, and then slipped away along a by-path as before. This did not give Hop o' my Thumb any concern, for he thought himself quite sure of getting back by means of the crumbs he had strewed by the way; but what was his surprise at finding that not a morsel was left! The birds had eaten it all up!

The poor children were in a terrible plight; for the further they went, the more they found it difficult to get out of the forest. At length night came on, and they mistook the whistling of the wind for the howling of wolves, and every moment expected to be devoured.

When it began to grow light, Hop o' my Thumb climbed to the top of a tree, and looked on all sides, to discover, if possible, some means of assistance: he saw a small light like that of a candle, but it was at a great distance beyond the forest: he came down thinking to find his way to it, but it had disappeared; and he was in perplexity what to do next. They continued walking in the direction in which he had seen the light, and at last, having reached the end of the forest, again got sight of it. They quickened their steps, and after great fatigue arrived at the house in which it was. They knocked at the door, which was opened by a good-natured-looking lady, who asked what brought them thither? Hop o' my Thumb answered, that they were poor children who had lost their way in the forest, and begged that she would give them a bed till morning.

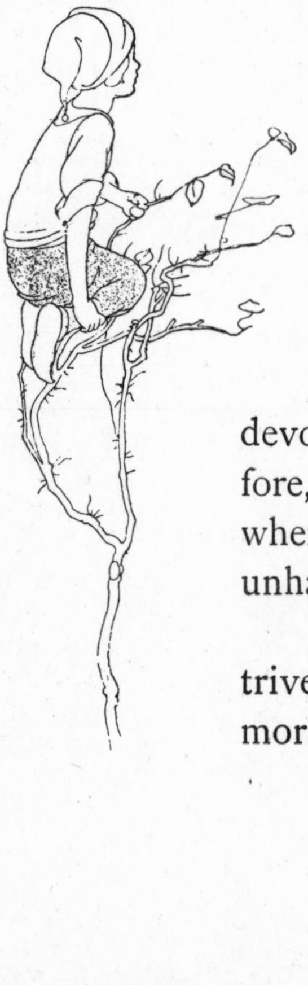

The lady, seeing they had such pretty faces, began to shed tears, and said:

"Ah! poor children, whither are you come? Do you not know that this is the house of an Ogre who eats little boys and girls?"

"Alas!" replied Hop o' my Thumb, "what shall we do? If we go back to the forest, it is certain that we shall be devoured by the wolves; we had rather, therefore, be eaten up by the gentleman; besides, when he sees us, he may perhaps pity our unhappy condition, and spare our lives."

The Ogre's wife, thinking she could contrive to hide them from her husband till the morning, let them in, and made them warm

HOP O' MY THUMB

themselves by a good fire, before which there was a whole sheep roasting for the Ogre's supper. When they had stood a short time by the fire, there came a loud knocking at the door. It was the Ogre! His wife hurried the children under the bed, telling them to lie still: she then let her husband in.

The Ogre immediately asked if the supper was ready, and if the wine was fetched from the cellar, and then sat down to table. Presently he began to sniff right and left, saying he smelled child's flesh.

"It must be this calf which has just been killed," answered his wife.

"I smell child's flesh," cried the Ogre. "I smell child's flesh; there is something going on I do not understand."

Saying this, he rose and went straight to the bed.

"Ah! ah! deceitful creature, is it thus you think to cheat me? Wretch! but that thou art old and tough, I would eat thee too! But come, what thou hast done is lucky enough, for the brats will make a nice dish for three ogres, my particular friends, who are to dine with me to-morrow."

He drew them out one by one from under the bed. The

poor children fell on their knees, begging his pardon as well as they could speak; but this Ogre was one of the cruellest of all the Ogres, and, far from feeling any pity, began to devour them already with his eyes, and told his wife "they would be delicious morsels if she served them up with a savoury sauce". He then fetched a large knife, and began to sharpen it on a long whetstone which he held in his left hand, approaching all the time nearer and nearer to the bed. The Ogre took up one of the children, and was going to set about cutting him to pieces, when his wife said to him:

"What in the world makes you take the trouble of killing them to-night? Will it not be time enough to-morrow morning?"

"Hold your prating," replied the Ogre, "they will be the tenderer for keeping."

"But you have so much meat in the house already," answered his wife; "here is a calf, two sheep, and half a pig."

"Right," said the Ogre; "give them a good supper, that they may not lose their plumpness, and send them to bed."

The good creature accordingly gave them a plentiful supper: but the poor children were much too frightened to eat. As for the Ogre, he sat down to his wine delighted with the thought of giving his friends so delicate a repast on the morrow, and, after drinking up all his wine, he at once went to bed.

The Ogre had seven daughters, all very young. They

had fair complexions, because they fed on raw meat like their father; but they had small grey eyes, quite round, and sunk in their heads, hooked noses, wide mouths, and very long sharp teeth standing at a great distance from each other. They were too young to have done a great deal of

mischief; but they gave signs of being, when older, as cruel as their father, for they already delighted in biting young children. These young ogresses had been put to bed early, all in one very large bed, and each had a crown of gold on her head. There was in the same chamber another bed of equal size, and in this the Ogre's wife put the seven little boys.

Hop o' my Thumb, having observed that the Ogresses had all crowns of gold upon their heads, and fearing the Ogre might awake and repent of not having killed him and his brothers, got out of bed about midnight, as softly as he could, and, taking off their nightcaps and his own, crept to the Ogre's daughters, took off their crowns, and put the nightcaps on their heads instead; he then put the crowns on himself and his brothers, and again got into bed.

Everything succeeded well. The Ogre, waking soon after midnight, was sorry he had deferred what he could have done that very night. He therefore hurried out of bed, and, taking up his large knife,—

"Let us see," said he, "what the young rogues are about, and do the job at once!" He stalked quietly to the room in which his daughters slept, and going up to the bed which held the boys, who, excepting Hop o' my Thumb, were all asleep, he felt their heads one by one.

HOP O' MY THUMB

The Ogre, feeling the crowns of gold, said to himself:

"I had like to have made a pretty mistake!" He went next to the bed which held his daughters, and feeling the nightcaps: "Ah, here you are, my lads!" said he; and instantly killed all his daughters, one by one. Well satisfied, he returned to bed.

As soon as Hop o' my Thumb heard him snoring, he awoke his brothers, and told them to put on their clothes quickly, and follow him. They stole down softly to the garden, and then jumped from the walls into the road. They ran with all their strength the whole night, but were all the time so terrified they scarcely knew which way to take.

When the Ogre awoke in the morning, he said to his wife:

"Prythee, go and dress the young rogues I saw last night."

The Ogress was surprised at her husband's kindness, not dreaming of the real meaning of his words. She went upstairs, and the first thing she beheld was her seven daughters all killed. The Ogre, fearing his wife might spend too much time in what he had set her about, went himself to help her, and was not less surprised than she had been at the shocking spectacle.

"Ah! what have I done!" cried he; "but the little varlets shall pay for it, I warrant them!"

He threw some water on his wife's face; and as soon as she recovered he said to her:

"Bring me quickly my seven-league boots, that I may go and catch the little vipers."

The Ogre set out with all speed, and after striding over different parts of the country, at last turned into the very road in which the poor children were journeying towards their father's house, which they had nearly reached. They had seen the Ogre striding from mountain to mountain, and crossing rivers at one step. Hop o' my Thumb perceiving a hollow place under a rock, made his brothers get into it, and then stepped in himself, keeping his eye fixed on the Ogre to see what he would do next.

The Ogre, finding himself tired with the journey he had made,—for seven-league boots are very fatiguing—began to think of resting himself, and happened to sit down on the very rock in which the poor children lay concealed. Being overcome with fatigue he fell asleep, and soon began to snore so terribly that the little fellows were as frightened as when the Ogre stood over them with a knife in his hand, intending to kill them. Hop o' my Thumb, seeing how much his brothers were terrified, said to them:

"Courage, my lads! You have nothing to do but to steal away while the Ogre is fast asleep, and leave me to shift for myself."

The brothers followed his advice, and were very soon at their father's house. In the meantime, Hop o' my Thumb went softly up to the Ogre, and gently pulled off the seven-league boots, and drew them on his own legs; for though the boots were very large, as they were fairies they could make themselves smaller, so as to fit any leg they pleased.

HOP O' MY THUMB

Hop o' my Thumb had no sooner made sure of the Ogre's seven-league boots, than he determined to go to the palace, and offer his services to carry orders from the king to his army, and bring His Majesty the earliest accounts of the battle in which it was at that time engaged.

He had not proceeded many strides before he heard a voice which desired him to stop. Hop o' my Thumb looked about him to discover whence it came, and the same voice continued:

"Listen, Hop o' my Thumb, to what I am about to say. Go not to the palace. Waste no time; the Ogre sleeps; he may awake. Know, Hop o' my Thumb, that the boots you took from the Ogre while asleep are two fairies; I am the eldest of them. We have observed the clever feats you have performed, and have resolved to bestow upon you the gift of riches, if you will once more employ your wits to good purpose, and be as brave as before. But fairies are not allowed to speak such matters as these. Break the shell of the largest nut you can find in your pocket, and in it is a paper which will tell you all that is necessary to be done."

Hop o' my Thumb, instead of wondering what had happened, instantly searched his pocket for the nut, and, having cracked it with his teeth, found in it a piece of paper, which he read as follows:—

"Hie thee to the Ogre's door,
These words speak, and no word more:
Ogress, Ogre cannot come;
Great key give to Hop o' my Thumb."

Hop o' my Thumb began to say the two last lines over and over again, that he might not forget them; and when he thought he had learned them by heart, he made two or three of his largest strides, and reached the Ogre's door. He knocked loudly, and for the second time was received by the Ogre's wife, who at sight of Hop o' my Thumb started back, as if she would have shut the door; but Hop o' my Thumb, knowing he had not a moment to lose, made as if he did not perceive how much she was afflicted at seeing the person who had caused her daughters to be killed by their own father.

Hop o' my Thumb accordingly began to talk as if he was in a great hurry, saying that matters were now changed; that the Ogre, having laid hold of him and his brothers as they were gathering nuts by the side of a hedge, was going to take them back to his house, when all at once the Ogre perceived a number of men who looked like lords, and were on the finest horses ever beheld, coming up to him at full speed; that he soon found they were sent by the king, with a message to borrow of the Ogre a large sum of money, the king believing him to be the richest of his subjects; that the lords finding themselves fatigued with the long journey they had made, the Ogre had desired them to proceed no farther, as he had with him a messenger who would not fail of doing cleverly whatever he was employed about; that the great lords had thanked the Ogre a thousand times, and, in the name of the king, had bestowed upon him the honourable title of Duke of Draggletail; that the Ogre had then taken off his boots, and helped to draw them on Hop o' my Thumb's legs, and charging him to make haste, gave him the following message:—

"Ogress, Ogre cannot come;
Great key give to Hop o' my Thumb."

The Ogress, seeing her husband's boots, and being mightily delighted with the thoughts of becoming Duchess of Draggletail, and living at Court, was ready to believe all that was told her. She

fetched the great key and gave it to Hop o' my Thumb, telling him where to find the chest of money and jewels to which it belonged. Hop o' my Thumb took as much of these treasures as he thought would be sufficient to maintain his father, mother, and brothers without the fatigue of hard labour, saying to himself all the time, that it was better that an honest woodman should have a small part of such vast riches, than that an Ogre should make no use of them whatever.

In a short time Hop o' my Thumb returned home, and was joyfully received by the whole family. The fame of his boots having been talked of at Court, the king sent for him, and, it is said, employed him on the most important affairs of his kingdom; so that he became one of the richest of his subjects.

As for the Ogre, he fell in his sleep from the corner of the rock, from which Hop o' my Thumb and his brothers had escaped, to the ground, and bruised himself so much that he could not stir; he therefore stretched himself out at full length, and waited for someone to come and assist him. But though several woodmen, passing near the place, and hearing the Ogre groan, went up to ask him what was the matter, yet the Ogre was so exceedingly big, that they could not have carried even one of his legs; so they were obliged to leave him; till at length the night came on, when a large serpent came out of a neighbouring wood, and stung him so that he died miserably.

As soon as Hop o' my Thumb, who was become the king's favourite, heard the news of the Ogre's death, he informed His Majesty of all that the good-natured Ogress had done to save the lives of him and his brothers. The king was so pleased that he asked Hop o' my Thumb if there was any favour he could bestow upon her.

Hop o' my Thumb thanked the king, and desired that the Ogress might obtain the honourable title of Duchess of Draggletail; which was no sooner asked than granted. The Ogress came to Court and lived happily for many years, enjoying the vast fortune she found in the Ogre's coffers.

As for Hop o' my Thumb, he every day grew more witty and brave; till at last the king made him the greatest lord in the kingdom, and put all affairs under his direction.

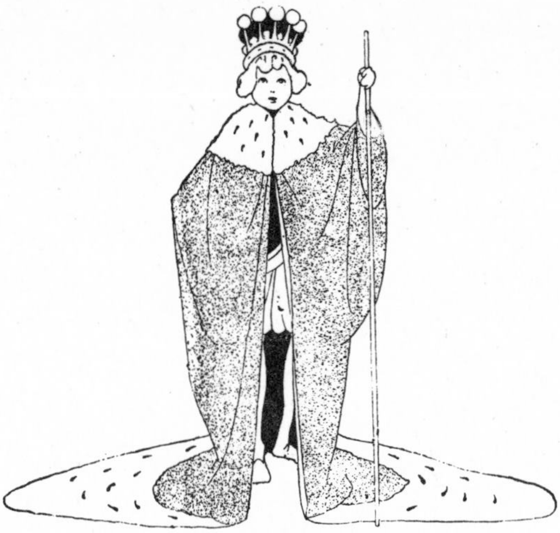

The Little Tin Soldier

THE soldiers were like each other to a hair—all but one, who had only one leg, because he had been made last, when there was not quite enough tin left; and it is this one-legged tin soldier's fortunes that seem worthy of being told.

On the table where they stood were other playthings, but the most charming of all was a pretty pasteboard castle. Through its little windows one could look into the rooms. In front stood some tiny trees, clustering round a little mirror representing a lake. Some waxen swans swam on the lake and were reflected in it.

All this was very pretty, but prettiest of all was a little lady standing in the doorway of the castle. She, too, was cut out of pasteboard, but she had on a frock of the softest muslin, and a narrow sky-blue riband was flung across her shoulders like a scarf, and in the middle of this scarf was set a glittering tinsel rose. The little lady was a dancer, and she stretched out both her arms, and raised one of her legs so high in the air that the tin soldier could not see it, and thought she had, like himself, only one leg.

"That would be just the wife for me," thought he, "but then she is of too high a rank. She lives in a castle, and I have only a box; and even that is not my own, for five and twenty men live in it. Still, I must make her acquaintance." Then he laid himself down at full length behind a snuff-box, so that he had a full view of the delicate little lady still standing on one leg without losing her balance.

When evening came, all the other tin soldiers were put into the box, and the people of the house went to bed. Then the playthings began to have their own games. The tin soldiers rattled in the box, for they wished to play too, but the lid would not open. The nutcrackers cut capers, and the slate pencil danced on the table. There was such a noise that the canary woke and began to talk too; but he always talked in verse. The only two who did not move from their places were the tin soldier and the dancer. She remained standing on the very tip of her toe, with outstretched arms; and he stood just as firmly on his one leg, never for a moment taking his eyes off her.

Twelve o'clock struck, and with a crash the lid of the snuff-box sprang open—there was no snuff in it, it was only a toy puzzle—and out jumped a little black conjurer. "Tin soldier!" said the conjurer, "please keep your eyes to yourself!"

But the tin soldier pretended not to hear.

"Well, just wait till to-morrow!" said the conjurer.

When the children got up next morning, the tin soldier

was placed on the window ledge, and, whether the conjurer or the wind caused it, all at once the window flew open, and out fell the tin soldier, head foremost, from the third story to the ground. It was a dreadful fall, for he fell headfirst into the street, and at last rested with his cap and bayonet stuck between two paving stones, and his one leg in the air.

The servant-maid and the little boy came downstairs directly to look for him; but though they nearly trod on him, they could not see him. If the tin soldier had but called out, "Here I am!" they might easily have found him; but he thought it would not be becoming to cry out, as he was in uniform.

Presently it began to rain a perfect downpour. When it was over, two little street arabs came by.

"Look!" said one, "there is a tin soldier. Let him have a sail."

So they made a boat out of newspaper, and put the tin soldier into it. Away he sailed down the gutter, both children running along by the side, clapping their hands. The paper boat rocked to and fro, and every now and then was whirled round so quickly that the tin

'That would be just the wife for me,' thought he, 'but then she is of too high a rank.' (PAGE 203)

Mr Whittington and his lady lived in great splendour and were very happy. (PAGE 220)

soldier became quite giddy. Still he did not move a muscle, but looked straight before him, and held his musket tightly clasped.

All at once the boat was carried into a long drain, where the tin soldier found it as dark as in his own box.

"Where can I be going now?" thought he. "It is all that conjurer's doing. Ah! if only the little maiden were sailing with me, I would not mind its being twice as dark."

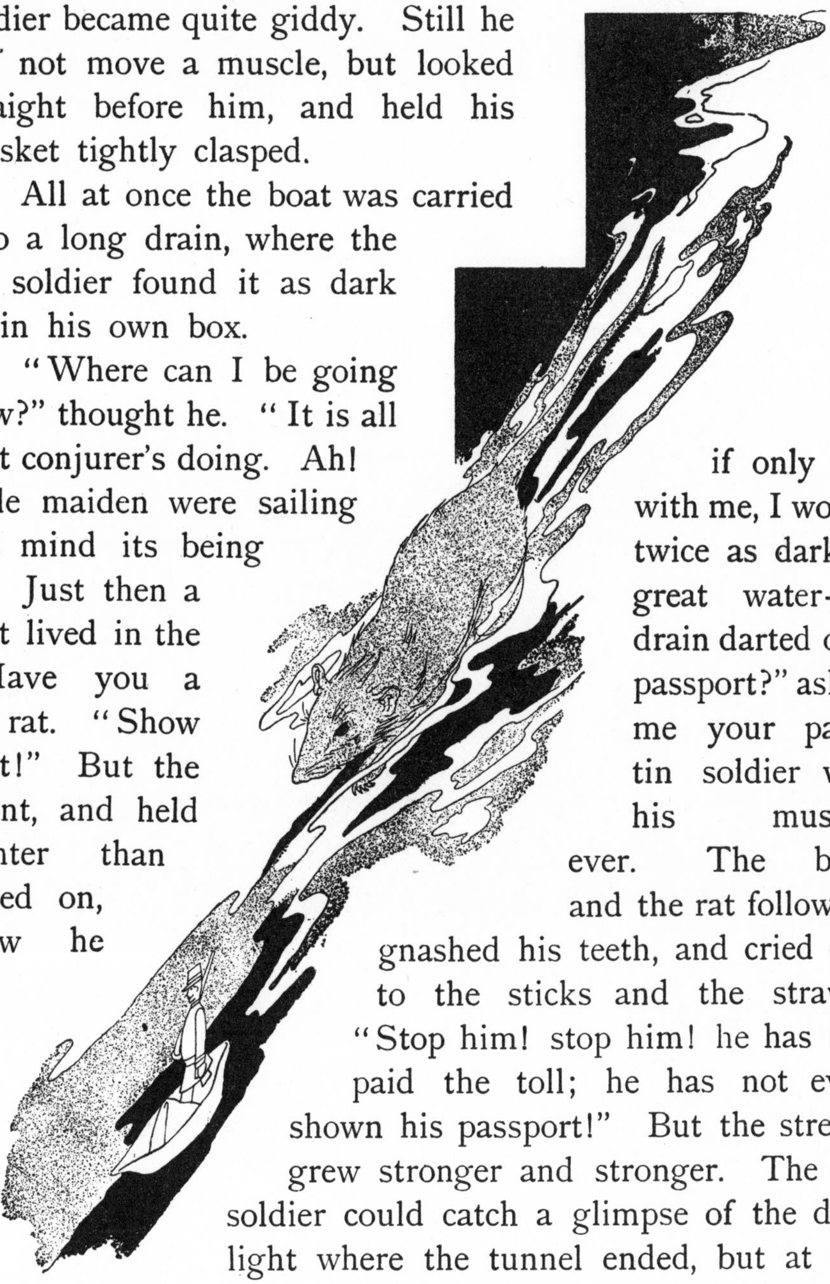

Just then a great water-rat that lived in the drain darted out. "Have you a passport?" asked the rat. "Show me your passport!" But the tin soldier was silent, and held his musket tighter than ever. The boat sailed on, and the rat followed. How he gnashed his teeth, and cried out to the sticks and the straws: "Stop him! stop him! he has not paid the toll; he has not even shown his passport!" But the stream grew stronger and stronger. The tin soldier could catch a glimpse of the daylight where the tunnel ended, but at the same time he heard a roaring noise that might have made the boldest tremble. Where the tunnel ended, the water of the gutter fell into a great canal. This was as dangerous for the tin soldier as a waterfall would be for us.

The fall was now so close that he could no longer stand upright. The boat darted forwards; the poor tin soldier held himself as stiffly as possible, so that no one could accuse him of having even blinked. The boat span round three or four times, and was filled with water to the brim; it must sink now!

The tin soldier stood up to his neck in water; but deeper and deeper sank the boat, and softer and softer grew the paper, till the water was over the soldier's head. He thought of the pretty little dancer whom he should never see again, and these words rang in his ears:—

Fare on, thou soldier brave!
Life must end in the grave.

The paper split in two, and the tin soldier fell through the rent, and was at once swallowed by a large fish. Oh, how dark it was! darker even than in the tunnel, and much narrower too. But the tin soldier was as constant as ever, and lay there at full length, still shouldering his arms.

The fish swam to and fro, and made the strangest movements, but at last he became quite still. After a while, a flash of lightning seemed to dart through him, and the daylight shone brightly, and someone cried out: "I declare! here is the tin soldier!" The fish had been caught, taken to the market, sold, and brought into the kitchen, where the servant-girl was cutting him up with a large knife. She seized the tin soldier by the middle with two of her fingers,

and took him into the parlour, where everyone was eager to see the wonderful man who had travelled in a fish.

They set him on the table, and the tin soldier was in the very room in which he had been before. He saw the same children, the same playthings on the table—among them the beautiful castle with the pretty little dancing maiden, still standing upon one leg, while she held the other high in the air; she too was constant. It quite touched the tin soldier. He looked at her, and she looked at him, but neither spoke a word.

And now one of the boys took the soldier and threw him into the stove. He gave no reason for doing so; but no doubt it was the fault of the conjurer in the snuff-box.

The tin soldier now stood in a blaze of light. He felt extremely hot, but whether from the fire, or from the flames of love, he did not know. He had entirely lost his colour. Whether this was the result of his travels, or the effect of strong feeling, I know not. He looked at the little lady, and she looked at him, and he felt that he was melting; but, constant as ever, he still stood shouldering his arms. A door opened, and the draught caught the dancer; and, like a sylph, she flew straightway into the stove to the tin soldier. Instantly she was in a blaze and was gone. The soldier was melted and dripped down among the ashes; and when the maid cleaned out the fireplace the next day, she found his remains in the shape of a little tin heart. Of the dancer, all that was left was the tinsel rose, and that was burnt as black as coal.

Dick Whittington and His Cat

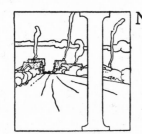

IN the reign of Edward the Third there was a poor orphan boy, named Dick Whittington, living in a country village a long way from London. He was a sharp little lad, and the stories that he heard, of London being paved with gold, made him long to visit that city.

One day, a large wagon and eight horses, with bells at their heads, drove through the village. Dick thought it must be going to London, so he asked the wagoner to let him walk by the side of the wagon. As soon as the wagoner heard that poor Dick had neither father nor mother, and saw by his ragged clothes that he could not be worse off than he was, he told him he might go if he would; so they set off together.

Dick got safely to London, and was in such a hurry to see the fine streets paved with gold, that he ran through many of them, thinking every moment to come to those that were paved with gold; for Dick had seen a guinea three times in his own little village, and remembered what a deal of money it brought in change; so he thought he had nothing to do but to take up some little bits of the pavement, and he would then have as much money as he could wish for. Poor Dick ran till he was tired, and had quite forgotten his friend the wagoner. At last, finding it grow dark, and that every way he turned he saw nothing but dirt instead of gold, he sat down in a dark corner, and cried himself to sleep. Next morning, being very hungry, he got up and walked about, and asked everybody he met to give him a halfpenny to keep him from starving. At last, a good-natured-looking gentleman saw how hungry he looked.

"Why don't you go to work, my lad?" said he.

"I would," answered Dick, "but I do not know how to get any."

"If you are willing," said the gentleman, "come with me;" and so saying, he took him to a hayfield, where Dick worked briskly, and lived merrily till the hay was all made. After this, he found himself as badly off as before; and being almost starved again, he laid himself down at the door of Mr. Fitzwarren, a rich merchant. Here the cook-maid, an ill-tempered creature, called out to poor Dick:

"What business have you there, you lazy rogue? If you do not take yourself away, we will see how you will like a sousing of some dish-water I have here, that is hot enough to make you jump."

At this time, Mr. Fitzwarren himself came home to dinner; and when he saw a dirty ragged boy lying at the door, he said:

"Why do you lie there, my lad? you seem old enough to work; I am afraid you are lazy."

"No, sir," said Dick to him. "I would work with all my heart; but I do not know anybody, and I am sick for want of food."

"Poor fellow!" answered Mr. Fitzwarren; "get up, and let me see what ails you."

Dick tried to rise, but was too weak to stand, for he had not eaten anything for three days. So the kind merchant ordered him to be taken into the house, and have a good dinner given to him; and to be kept to do what dirty work he could for the cook. Dick would have lived happily in this good family, if it had not been for the ill-natured cook, who was finding fault and scolding him from morning till night; and besides, she was so fond of basting, that, when she had no roast meat to baste, she would be basting poor Dick. But though the cook was so ill-tempered, the footman was quite different. He had lived in the family many years, and was an elderly man, and very kind-hearted. He had once a little son of his own, who died when about the age of Dick; so he could not help feeling pity for the poor boy, and sometimes gave him a halfpenny to buy gingerbread or a top. The footman was fond of reading, and used often in the evening to entertain the other servants with some amusing book. Little Dick took pleasure in hearing this good man, which made him wish very much to learn to read too; so the next time the footman gave him a halfpenny, he bought a little book with it; and with the footman's help, Dick soon learnt his letters, and afterwards to read.

About this time, Miss Alice, Mr. Fitzwarren's daughter, was going out one morning for a walk, and Dick was told to put on a suit of good clothes that Mr. Fitzwarren gave him, and walk behind her. As they went, Miss Alice saw a poor woman with one child in her arms, and another on her back. She pulled out her purse and gave the woman some money; but as she was putting it into her pocket again, she dropped it on the ground, and walked on. It was lucky that Dick was behind, and saw what she had done; so he picked up the purse, and gave it to her again. Another time, when Miss Alice was sitting with the window open and amusing herself with a favourite parrot, it suddenly flew away to the branch of a high tree, where all the servants were afraid to venture after it. As soon as Dick heard of this, he pulled off his coat, and climbed up the tree as nimbly as a squirrel; and after a great deal of trouble, caught her and brought her down safely to his mistress. Miss Alice thanked him, and liked him ever after for this. The ill-humoured cook was now a little kinder; but, besides this, Dick had another hardship to get over. His bed stood in a garret, where there were so many holes in the floor and the walls, that every night he was waked in his sleep by the rats and mice, which ran over his face, and made such a noise that he sometimes thought the walls were tumbling down about him. One day, a gentleman who came to see

Mr. Fitzwarren required his shoes to be cleaned; Dick took great pains to make them shine, and the gentleman gave him a penny. With this he thought he would buy a cat; so the next day, seeing a little girl with a cat under her arm, he went up to her, and asked if she would let him have it for a penny. The girl said she would, and that it was a very good mouser. Dick hid the cat in the garret, and always took care to carry a part of his dinner to her; and in a short time he had no more trouble from the rats and mice. Soon after, his master had a ship ready to sail; and as he thought it right all his servants should have some chance for good fortune as well as himself, he called them into the parlour, and asked them what they would send out. They all had something that they were willing to venture, except poor Dick, who had neither money nor goods. For this reason he did not come into the parlour with the rest; but Miss Alice guessed what was the matter, and ordered him to be called in. She then said she would lay down some money for him from her own purse; but her father told her this would not do, for Dick must send something of his own. When poor Dick heard this, he said he had nothing but a cat.

"Fetch your cat then, my good boy," said Mr. Fitzwarren, "and let her go."

Dick went upstairs and brought down poor puss, and gave her to the captain, with tears in his eyes. All the company laughed at Dick's odd venture; and Miss Alice, who felt pity for the poor boy, gave him some halfpence to buy another cat.

This, and other marks of kindness shown him by Miss Alice, made the ill-tempered cook jealous of poor Dick; and she began to use him more cruelly than ever, and always made game of him for sending his cat to sea. She asked if he thought his cat would sell for as much money as would buy a stick to beat him. At last, poor Dick could not bear this any longer, and thought he would run away from his place; so he packed up his few things, and set out very early in the morning on the first of November. He walked as far as Highgate, and there sat down on a stone, which to this day is called Whittington's stone, and began to think which road he should take farther. While he was thinking what he should do, the bells of Bow Church began to ring, and he fancied their sounds seemed to say:

"Turn again, Whittington,
Lord Mayor of London."

"Lord Mayor of London!" said he to himself. "Why, to be sure I would put up with almost anything now, to be Lord Mayor of London, and ride in a fine coach, when I grow to be a man! I will go back and think nothing of the cuffing and scolding of the old cook, if I am to be Lord Mayor of London at last."

Dick went back, and was lucky enough to get into the house and set about his work before the cook came down.

The ship, with the cat on board, was a long time at sea; and was at last driven by the winds on a part of the coast of Barbary. The people came in great numbers to see the sailors, and treated them very civilly; and when they became better acquainted, were eager to buy the fine things with which the ship was laden. When the captain saw this, he sent patterns of the best things he had to the king of the country; who was so much pleased with them, that he sent for the captain and the chief mate to the palace. Here they were placed, as is the custom of the country, on rich carpets, marked with gold and silver flowers. The King and Queen were seated at the upper end of the room; and a number of dishes, of the greatest rarities, were brought in for dinner; but, before they had been on the table a minute, a vast number of rats and mice rushed in, and helped themselves from every dish. The captain wondered at this, and asked if these vermin were not very unpleasant.

"Oh, yes!" they said, "and the King would give half his riches to get rid of them; for they not only waste his dinner, as you see, but disturb him in his bedroom, so that he is obliged to be watched while he is asleep."

The captain was ready to jump for joy when he heard this. He thought of poor Dick's cat, and told the King he had a creature on board his ship that would kill all the rats and mice. The King was still more glad than the captain.

"Bring this creature to me," said he, "and if it can do what you say, I will give you your ship full of gold for her."

The captain, to make quite sure of his good luck, answered, that she was such a clever cat for catching rats and mice, that he could hardly bear to part with her; but that to oblige His Majesty he would fetch her.

"Run, run!" said the Queen, "for I long to see the creature that will do such a service."

Away went the captain to the ship, while another dinner was got ready. He came back to the palace soon enough to see the table full of rats and mice again, and the second dinner likely to be lost in the same way as the first. The cat did not wait for bidding, but jumped out of the captain's arm, and in a few moments laid almost all the rats and mice dead at her feet. The rest, in a fright, scampered away to their holes.

The King and Queen were charmed to get so easily rid of such a plague. They desired that the creature might be brought for them to look at. On this, the captain called out: "Puss, puss!" and the cat ran and jumped upon his knee. He then held her out to the Queen, who was afraid to touch a creature that was able to kill so many rats and mice; but when she saw how gentle the cat seemed, and how glad she was at being stroked by the captain, she ventured to touch her too, saying all the time: "Poot, poot," for she could not speak English. At last the Queen took puss on her lap, and by degrees became quite free with her, till puss purred herself to sleep. When the King had seen the actions of mistress puss, and was told that she would soon have young ones, which might in time kill all the rats and mice in his country, he bought the captain's whole ship's cargo; and afterwards gave him a great deal of gold besides, which was worth still more, for the cat. The captain then took leave, and set sail with a fair wind, and arrived safe at London.

One morning, when Mr. Fitzwarren had come into the counting house, and seated himself at the desk, somebody came tap, tap, tap, at the door.

"Who is there?" asked Mr. Fitzwarren.

"A friend," answered someone; and who should it be but the captain, followed by several men carrying vast lumps of gold, that had been paid him by the King of Barbary for the ship's cargo. They then told the story of the cat, and showed the rich present that the King had sent to Dick for her; upon which the merchant called out to his servants:

"Go fetch him, we will tell him of the same;
Pray call him Mr. Whittington by name."

Mr. Fitzwarren now showed himself a really good man, for while some of his clerks said so great a treasure was too much for such a boy as Dick, he answered:

"God forbid that I should keep the value of a single penny from him! It is all his own, and he shall have every farthing's worth of it."

He sent for Dick, who happened to be scouring the cook's kettles, and was quite dirty; so that he wanted to excuse himself from going to his master. Mr. Fitzwarren, however, made him come in, and ordered a chair to be set for him, so that poor Dick thought they were making game of him, and began to beg his master not to play tricks with a poor boy, but to let him go again to his work.

"Indeed, Mr. Whittington," said the merchant, "we are all in earnest with you; and I heartily rejoice in the news these gentlemen have brought you; for the captain has sold your cat to the King of Barbary, and brought you, in return for her, more riches than I possess; and I wish you may long enjoy them!"

Mr. Fitzwarren then told the men to open the great treasure they had brought with them, and said:

"Mr. Whittington has now nothing to do but to put it in some place of safety."

Poor Dick hardly knew how to behave himself for joy. He begged his master to take what part of it he pleased, since he owed it all to his kindness.

"No, no," answered Mr. Fitzwarren, "this is all your own; and I have no doubt you will use it well."

Dick next asked his mistress, and then Miss Alice, to accept a part of his good fortune, but they would not; and at the same time told him that his success afforded them great pleasure. But the poor fellow was too kind-hearted to keep it all to himself; so he made a handsome present to the captain, the mate, and every one of the sailors, and afterwards to his good friend the footman, and the rest of Mr. Fitzwarren's servants; and even to the ill-natured cook. After this, Mr. Fitzwarren advised him to get himself dressed like a gentleman; and told him he was welcome to live in his house till he could provide himself with a better.

When Whittington's face was washed, his hair curled, his hat cocked, and he was dressed in a nice suit of clothes, he was as handsome and genteel as any young man who visited at Mr. Fitzwarren's; so that Miss Alice, who had been so kind to him, and thought of him with pity, now looked upon him as fit to be her sweetheart; and the more so, no doubt, because Whittington was now always thinking what he could do to oblige her, and making her the prettiest presents that could be. Mr. Fitzwarren soon saw their love for each other, and proposed to join them in marriage; and to this they both readily agreed. A day for the wedding was soon fixed; and they were attended to church by the Lord Mayor, the Court of Aldermen, the Sheriffs, and a great number of the richest merchants in London, whom they afterwards treated with a very fine feast.

History tells us that Mr. Whittington and his lady lived in great splendour, and were very happy. They had several children. He was Sheriff of London in the year 1360, and several times afterwards Lord Mayor: the last time, he entertained King Henry the Fifth, on His Majesty's return from the famous Battle of Agincourt. In this company, the King, on account of Whittington's gallantry, said:

"Never had prince such a subject;" and when Whittington was told this at the table, he answered:

"Never had subject such a king."

Going with an address from the city, on one of the King's victories, he received the honour of knighthood. Sir Richard Whittington supported many poor; he built a church, and also a college, with a yearly allowance to poor scholars, and near it raised a hospital. The figure of Sir Richard Whittington, with his cat in his arms, carved in stone, was to be seen till the year 1780, over the archway of the old prison of Newgate, that stood across Newgate Street.

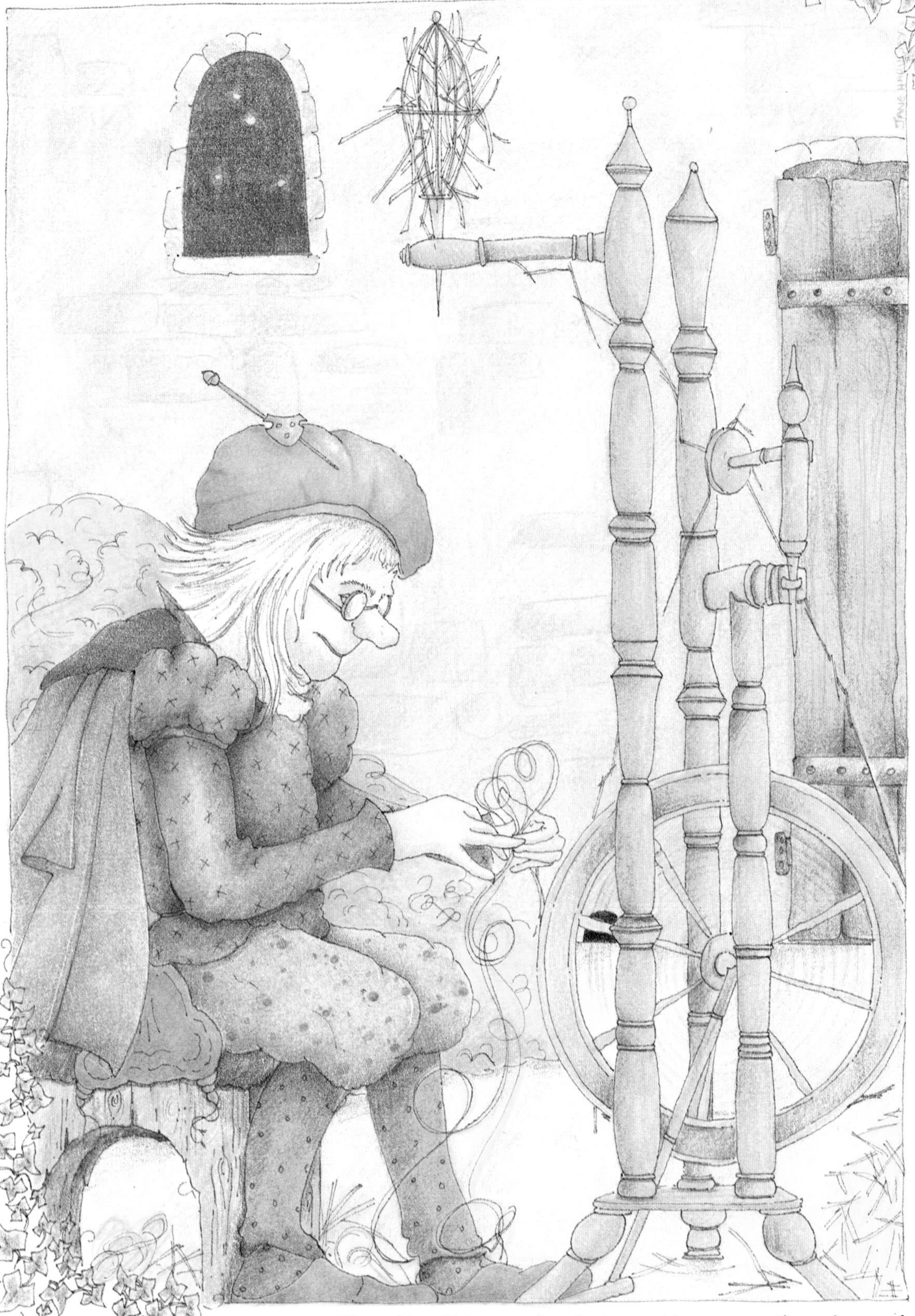

He set himself down to the wheel; round it went merrily, and presently the work was done and the gold all spun. (PAGE 222)

She went to her great gallery of looking-glasses, to see if anything was wanting. (PAGE 238)

Rumpel-Stilts-Kin

ONCE a poor miller who had a very beautiful daughter was so vain and proud of her, that he told the King that she could spin gold out of straw. When the King heard the miller's boast, he ordered the girl to be brought before him. Then he led her to a chamber where there was a great quantity of straw, gave her a spinning-wheel, and said: "All this must be spun into gold before morning, as you value your life." It was in vain that the poor maiden declared that she could do no such thing; the chamber was locked and she remained alone.

She was lamenting over her hard fate, when the door opened, and a little man hobbled in, and said:

"Good-morrow, my good lass; what are you weeping for?"

"Alas!" answered she, "I must spin this straw into gold, and I know not how."

"What will you give me," said the little man, "to do it for you?"

"My necklace," replied the maiden. He set himself down to the wheel; round it went merrily, and presently the work was done and the gold all spun.

When the King came, he was greatly astonished and pleased; but he shut up the poor miller's daughter with a fresh task. Then she knew not what to do, and sat down once more to weep; but the little man presently opened the door, and said:

"What will you give me to do your task?"

"The ring on my finger," replied she. So he took the ring, and began to work, till by the morning all was finished.

The King was delighted; but still he was not satisfied, and took the miller's daughter into a larger room, and said:

"All this must be spun to-night; and if you succeed, you shall be my queen."

As soon as she was alone the dwarf came in, and said:

"What will you give me to spin gold for you this third time?"

"I have nothing left," said she.

"Then promise me," said the little man, "your first little child when you are queen."

"That may never be," thought the miller's daughter; but as she knew no other way to get her task done, she promised him what he asked, and he spun once more the whole heap of gold. The King came in the morning, and finding all he wanted, married her, and so the miller's daughter became Queen.

At the birth of her first child the Queen rejoiced very

The Little Man and the Miller's Daughter

much, and forgot the little man and her promise; but one day he came into her chamber and reminded her of it. Then she was grieved at her misfortune, and offered him all the treasures of the kingdom in exchange; but in vain, till at last her tears softened him, and he said:

"I will give you three days' grace, and if during that time you tell me my name, you shall keep your child."

Now the Queen lay awake all night, thinking of all the odd names that she had ever heard, and dispatched messengers all over the land to enquire after new ones. The next day the little man came, and she began with Timothy, Benjamin, Jeremiah, and all the names she could remember; but to all of them he said: "That's not my name."

The second day she began with all the comical names she could hear of, Bandy-legs, Hunch-back, Crook-shanks, and so on; but the little man still said to every one of them: "That's not my name."

The third day came back one of the messengers, and said: "I can hear of no other name; but yesterday, as I was climbing a hill among the trees of the forest, where the fox and the hare bid each other good-night, I saw a little hut, and before the hut burnt a fire, and round about the fire danced a funny little man upon one leg, and sung:

"'Merrily the feast I'll make,
To-day I'll brew, to-morrow bake;
Merrily I'll dance and sing,
For next day will a stranger bring:
Little does my lady dream
Rumpel-Stilts-Kin is my name!'"

When the Queen heard this, she jumped for joy, and as soon as her little visitor came, and said:

"Now, lady, what is my name?"

"Is it John?" asked she.

"No!"

"Is it Tom?"

"No!"

"Can your name be—Rumpel-Stilts-Kin?"

"Some witch told you that! Some witch told you that!" cried the little man; and dashed his right foot in a rage so deep into the floor, that he was forced to lay hold of it with both hands to pull it out. Then he made the best of his way off, while everybody laughed at him for having had all his trouble for nothing.

Blanch and Rosalinda

THERE once lived a widow, Goody Hearty, with two pretty daughters, the eldest, on account of the fairness of her complexion, named Blanch, and the other Rosalinda, because her cheeks were like roses, and her lips like coral. One day while spinning at the door, the mother saw a poor old woman going by, leaning on a stick.

"You seem tired, dame," said she to the old woman; "sit down, and rest a little." At the same time she bid her daughters fetch a chair. They both went, but Rosalinda ran fastest, and brought one.

"Will you please to drink?" said Goody Hearty.

"Thank you," answered the old woman; "and methinks if you had anything *nice* that I liked, I could eat a bit."

"You are welcome to the best I have in my house," said Goody Hearty; "it is but homely fare."

She then ordered her daughters to spread a clean cloth on the table, while she went to the cupboard, whence she took some brown bread and cheese, to which she added a mug of cider. As soon as the old woman was seated,

Goody Hearty desired her eldest daughter to go and gather some plums off her own plum tree. Blanch, instead of obeying readily, grumbled and muttered as she went.

"Surely," said she to herself, "I did not take all this care and pains with my plum tree for that old greedy creature."

However, she durst not refuse gathering a few plums, but gave them with a very ill will, and very ungraciously.

"As for you, Rosalinda," said her mother, "you have no fruit to offer this good dame, for your grapes are not ripe."

"That's true," replied Rosalinda; "but my hen has just laid, and if the gentlewoman likes a new-laid egg, 'tis very much at her service;" and, without staying for an answer, she ran to the hen-roost, and brought the egg; but just as she was presenting it, the old woman turned into a fine beautiful lady!

"Good woman," said she to Goody Hearty, "I have long seen your industry, perseverance, and pious resignation, and I will reward your daughters according to their merits: the eldest shall be a great queen, the other shall have a country farm." With this she struck the house with her stick. It immediately disappeared, and in its room up came a pretty little snug farm.

"This, Rosalinda," said she, "is your lot; I know I have given each of you what you like best."

Having said this, the fairy went away, leaving mother and daughters greatly astonished. They went into the farm-house, and were charmed with the neatness of the furniture; the chairs were only wood, but so bright you might see your face in them. The beds were of linen, as white as snow.

There were forty sheep in the sheep-pen; four oxen, and four cows, in their stalls; and in the yard all sorts of poultry, hens, ducks, and pigeons. There was also a pretty garden, well stocked with flowers, fruit, and vegetables.

Blanch saw the fairy's gift to her sister without being jealous, and was wholly taken up with the thoughts of being a queen; when, all of a sudden, she heard some hunters riding by, and going to the gate to see them, she appeared so charming in the King's eyes, that he resolved to marry her.

When Blanch was a queen, she said to her sister:

"I do not care that you should be a farmer. Come with me, sister, and I will match you to some great lord."

"I am much obliged to you, sister," replied Rosalinda, "but I am used to a country life, and I choose to stay where I am."

Queen Blanch arrived at her palace, and was delighted. The first three months her thoughts were engrossed by dress, balls, and plays. She was soon accustomed to all this, and found a great deal of trouble. The ladies of the Court were all very respectful in her presence; but she knew well that they did not love her, and when out of her sight, would often say to one another: "See what airs this little country girl gives herself! Sure His Majesty must have a very mean fancy to make choice of such a consort."

These discourses reached the King's ears, and made him reflect on what he had done. He began to think he was wrong, and repented his marriage. The courtiers saw this, and accordingly paid her little or no respect. She was very unhappy, for she had not a single friend to whom she could declare her griefs. All the time there was a physician to inspect whatever she ate or drank; not a grain of salt was allowed to be put in her soup, nor was she permitted to take a walk, though she had ever so much a mind to it. She had several children, but governesses were appointed to them, who brought them up contrary to her wishes; yet she had not the liberty to find fault. Poor Queen Blanch grew so thin, that it was a pity to see her. She had not seen her sister for three years, because she imagined it would disgrace a person of her rank and dignity to pay a visit to a farmer's wife. Her melancholy made her very ill, and her physicians ordered change of air. She therefore resolved to spend a few days in the country. Accordingly, she asked the King leave to go, who very readily granted it, because he thought he should be rid of her for some time. She set out, and soon arrived at the village. As she drew near Rosalinda's house, she beheld, at a little distance from the door, a company of shepherds and shepherdesses, dancing and making merry.

"Alas!" said the Queen, sighing; "there was a time when I used to divert myself like those poor people, and no one found fault with me."

The moment Rosalinda perceived her sister, she ran to embrace her. The Queen ordered her carriage to stop, and, alighting, rushed into her sister's arms; but Rosalinda was grown so plump, and had such an air of content, that the Queen, as she looked on her, could not forbear bursting into tears.

Rosalinda was married to a farmer's son, who had no fortune of his own; but then he ever remembered that he was indebted to his wife for everything he had, and he strove to show his gratitude by his obliging behaviour. Rosalinda had not many servants; but those she had, loved her as though she had been their mother, because she used them kindly. She was beloved by all her neighbours, and they all endeavoured to show it. She neither had, nor wanted, much money. Corn, wine, and oil were the growth of her farm; her cows supplied her with milk, butter, and cheese. The wool of her sheep was spun to clothe herself, her husband, and the two children they had. All enjoyed perfect health, and when the work of the day was over, they spent the evening in all sorts of pastimes.

"Alas!" cried the Queen, "the fairy made me a sad present in giving me a crown. Content is not found in magnificent palaces, but in an innocent country life."

Scarce had she done speaking, before the fairy appeared.

"In making you a queen," said the fairy, "I did not intend to reward, but to punish you for giving me your plums with an ill will. To be contented and happy, you must, like your sister, possess only what is necessary, and wish for nothing else."

"Ah, madam!" cried Blanch, "you are sufficiently revenged; pray put an end to my distress."

"It is at an end," said the fairy. "The King, who loves you no longer, has just married another wife, and to-morrow his officers will come to forbid you returning any more to the palace."

It happened just as the fairy had foretold, and Blanch passed the remainder of her days with her sister Rosalinda, in all manner of happiness and content, and never thought again of Court, unless it was to thank the fairy for having brought her back to her native village.

The Fair One with Golden Locks

THERE was once a Princess so fair that she was called the Fair One with Golden Locks: for her hair shone brighter than gold, and flowed in curls almost to her feet. These ringlets were always encircled by a wreath of the sweetest flowers, and her garments were adorned with pearls and diamonds; so that it was impossible to behold her without admiration.

A rich and handsome young Prince, whose territories joined hers, and was not married, resolved to demand her in marriage. Accordingly he ordered a sumptuous coach to be made for his ambassador; allowed him a hundred horses, and a hundred lackeys, and conjured him, if possible, to bring the Princess back with him.

When the ambassador had taken his leave, and departed the kingdom, the whole discourse of the court was of nothing but this match; and the King, who made no question but the Fair One with Golden Locks would consent to his wishes, began to make preparations of rich apparel and royal furniture. The ambassador in the meantime arrived where he was sent; and having his audience of the Fair One with Golden Locks, delivered the subject of his embassy. But whether it was that she was not that day in a good humour, or that she did not like the compliment, she thanked the ambassador for the honour his master did her, and said she had no inclination to marry.

The ambassador left the Princess's court very sad and pensive, because she had refused to go with him; he also carried back all the presents which he had brought from the King: for she would accept none of his diamonds or other curiosities: but that she might not seem to despise or affront the King, she took a thousand of English pins.

When the ambassador arrived at the King's city, where he was expected with great impatience, the people were afflicted to see him return without the Fair One with Golden Locks; and the King wept like a child; nor could his courtiers give him any consolation.

There was a youth at court called Avenant. The King loved him, and indeed everybody, except the envious, who could not bear that the King should be kind to him, and entrust him as he did with all his affairs. Being one day in company with some persons, who, speaking of the ambassador's return, said he had not been able to prevail with the lady, Avenant inconsiderately said:

"If the King had sent me to the Fair One with Golden Locks, I dare say I could have prevailed on her."

The enviers of Avenant's prosperity immediately ran to the King, saying:

"Sir, what does your Majesty think Avenant says? He boasts that if you had sent him to the Fair One with the

Golden Hair, he could have brought her with him; which shows he is so vain as to think himself handsomer than your Majesty, and that her love for him would have made her follow him wherever he went."

This put the King in a rage, and his passion was so great that he hardly knew what he did.

"What!" said he, "does this youngster make a jest at my misfortune, and pretend to set himself above me? Go, and put him in my great tower, and there let him starve to death."

The King's guards went and seized Avenant, dragged him to prison, and used him in the most cruel manner. The unfortunate youth had only straw to lie upon, and must soon have died, but for a small stream that ran by the foot of the tower, of which he drank a little sometimes to moisten his mouth, which was almost dried up by hunger. One day, when almost spent, he said to himself, fetching a deep sigh:

"Wherein can I have offended the King? He has not a more faithful subject; nor have I ever done anything to displease him."

The King happened at that time to pass by the tower; and hearing the voice of the person he had once loved so well, stopped to hear him.

Being greatly moved by his sufferings the tears trickled down his cheeks:

he opened the door of the tower, and called him by his name. Upon which Avenant came forth in a pitiful condition, and, throwing himself at the King's feet,

"What have I done, Sire," said he, "that your Majesty should use me thus?"

"Thou hast ridiculed me and my ambassador," replied the King; "and hast said that if I had sent thee to the Fair One with Golden Locks, thou couldst have brought her with thee."

"It is true, Sire," replied Avenant, "for I would have so thoroughly convinced her of your transcending qualities, that it should not have been in her power to have denied me; and in this, surely, I said nothing offensive to your Majesty."

The King, casting an angry look on those who had spoken ill of his favourite, took him away with him, repenting heartily of the wrong he had done him.

"Avenant," says the King after supper, "I still love the Fair One with Golden Locks; I have a mind to send thee to her, to try whether thou canst succeed."

Avenant replied that he was ready to depart the very next morning.

"Hold," said the King, "I will provide thee first with a most sumptuous equipage."

"There is no necessity for that," answered Avenant, "I need only a good horse, and your letters of credence."

Upon this the King embraced him; being overjoyed to see him so soon ready. He took leave of the King and proceeded on his embassy all alone, without any pomp or noise: and thought of nothing as he went, but how to engage the Fair One with Golden Locks to marry the King. He had a table-book in his pocket, and when any good thought came into his head, fit to be made use of in his speech, he alighted, and sitting under the shade of some tree, wrote it down in his book, that he might forget nothing. One morning, being upon his journey by break of day, and entering into a spacious meadow, a fine thought came into his head. He alighted, and seated himself by the bank of a little stream. After he had done writing he looked about him, and suddenly perceived a large gilded carp, which stirred a little, and that was all it could do, for having attempted to catch some flies, it had leaped so far out of the water as to throw itself on the grass, where it was almost dead, not being able to recover its natural element. Avenant took pity on the poor creature, put it again gently into the river, where the carp began to rejoice, and sunk to the bottom; but soon rising up again, brisk and gay, to the side of the river.

"Avenant," said the carp, "I thank you for the kindness you have done me; had it not been for you, I had died; but you have saved my life, and I will reward you."

After this short compliment, the carp darted itself to the bottom of the water, leaving Avenant not a little surprised at its great civility. Another day he saw a crow being pursued by a huge eagle, which would have seized and swallowed it had not Avenant taken compassion on the unfortunate bird. Thus, said he: "do the stronger oppress the weaker; for what right has the eagle to devour the crow?" Saying this, he took his bow, and aiming at the eagle, let fly an arrow, which pierced him, so that he fell down dead; which the crow seeing, came in joy, and perched upon a tree, saying:

"Avenant, you have been extremely generous to succour

me, who am but a poor wretched crow; but I am not ungrateful, and will do you as good a turn."

Avenant admired the wit of the crow, and continuing his journey, entered into a wood so early one morning, that he could hardly see his way, where he heard an owl crying in despair. Surely, said he to himself, this owl, wherever it is, is in deep distress; and may perhaps be caught in some fowler's net. So, looking about everywhere, he at length came to a place where certain fowlers had spread their nets to catch little birds.

"What pity 'tis," said he, "men are only made to torment one another, or else to persecute poor animals who never do them any harm!"

So saying, he drew his knife, cut the cords, and set the owl at liberty; who, before it took wing, said:

"Avenant, it is not necessary I should say much to make you sensible how greatly I am indebted to you: the action speaks for itself. The fowlers are coming, I should have been taken, and must have died, without your assistance: I have a grateful heart, and will remember it."

These were three remarkable adventures that befell Avenant in his journey to the palace of the Fair One with Golden Locks. When he arrived, everything was surprising: diamonds lay in heaps like common stones; and the treasury was so amazingly rich, and the wardrobe so wonderfully fine, that he thought, if the mistress of it should marry his master, he would be a happy man. He washed himself, combed and powdered his hair, and put on a suit of cloth of gold; which having done, he put a rich embroidered scarf about his neck, with a small basket, wherein was a little dog of which he was very fond. And Avenant was so amiable, and did everything with so good a grace, that when he presented himself at the gate of the palace, all the guards paid him great respect, and everyone strove who should first give notice to the Fair One with Golden Locks, that Avenant, the neighbouring King's ambassador, demanded audience.

The Princess hearing the name of Avenant, said:

"It has a pleasing sound, and I dare say he is agreeable and pleases everybody. Go, fetch me my rich embroidered gown of blue satin, dress my hair, and bring my wreaths of fresh flowers: let me have my high shoes, and my fan, and let my audience chamber and throne be clean, and richly adorned; for I would have him everywhere with truth say, that I am really the Fair One with Golden Locks."

At length she went to her great gallery of looking-glasses, to see if anything was wanting; after which she ascended her throne of gold, ivory, and ebony.

Avenant was conducted into the chamber of audience,

where he stood so transported with admiration, that he had scarce power to open his lips. At length, however, he took courage, and made his speech wonderfully well; wherein he prayed the Princess not to let him be so unfortunate as to return without her.

"Gentle Avenant," said she, "I assure you, I would rather favour you than any other: but you must know, about a month since, I went to take the air by the side of a river, with my maids of honour; as I was pulling off my glove, I pulled a ring from my finger, which by accident fell into the river: this ring I valued more than my own kingdom. I have made a vow never to hearken to any proposals of marriage, unless the ambassador who makes them shall also bring me my ring."

When Avenant returned to his lodgings, he went to bed supperless; and his little dog, who was called Cabriole, made a fasting night of it too, and went and lay down by his master, who did nothing all night but sigh and lament, saying:

"How can I find a ring that fell into a great river a month ago? It would be folly to attempt it. The Princess enjoined me this task, merely because she knew it was impossible."

He continued to be greatly afflicted, when Cabriole said:

"My dear master, do not despair of your good fortune; for you are too good to be unhappy; therefore, when it is day, let us go to the riverside."

Avenant made no answer, but gave his dog two little cuffs with his hand, and being overwhelmed with grief, fell asleep. But when Cabriole perceived it was day, he barked so loud that he waked his master.

"Rise, Sir," said he, "put on your clothes, and let us go and try our fortune."

Avenant took his little dog's advice, and having dressed himself, went to the riverside, when all on a sudden he heard a voice call: "Avenant! Avenant!" upon which he looked around him, but seeing nothing, was proceeding in his walk. Presently he heard himself called again.

"Who calls?" said he.

Cabriole, who was very little, and looked closely into the water, cried out:

"It is a gilded carp!"

Immediately the carp appeared, and said:

"Avenant, you saved my life, and now I am come to requite your kindness: here, my dear Avenant, here is the ring which the Fair One with Golden Locks dropped into the river."

Upon which he stooped and took it out of the carp's mouth, to whom he returned a thousand thanks. And instead of returning home, he went directly to the palace with little Cabriole, who skipped about, and wagged his tail for joy.

"Alas," said the Princess, on being told that Avenant desired an audience, "the poor youth is come to take his leave!"

Avenant, being admitted, presented her the ring, saying:

"Madam, I have executed your command; and now, I hope, you will receive my master for your royal consort."

When she saw her ring, and that it was no ways injured, she was so amazed, she could hardly believe her eyes.

"Surely," said she, "you must be favoured by some fairy."

"Madam," said he, "I am acquainted with no fairy; but I was willing to obey your command."

"Well," continued she, "you must do me another service, without which I will never marry. There is a prince who lives not far hence, whose name is Galifron, and whom nothing would serve but that he must needs marry me. He declared that if I denied him, he would enter my kingdom with fire and sword. He is a giant, as high as a steeple; he devours men as an ape eats chestnuts; when he goes into the country, he carries cannons in his pocket, to use instead of pistols; and when he speaks aloud he deafens the ears of those that stand near him. I answered that I did not choose to marry. Nevertheless, he has not ceased to persecute me, and has put an infinite number of my subjects to the sword: therefore you must fight him, and bring me his head."

"Well, Madam," said Avenant, "I will fight this Galifron. I believe I shall be vanquished; but I will die like a man of courage."

The Princess, astonished at his intrepidity, said a thousand things to dissuade him, but all in vain; and he retired to provide himself with proper weapons, and all things necessary. Then he put Cabriole in his little basket, mounted his courser, and arriving in Galifron's kingdom, demanded of all he met where he might meet with him; and everybody told him he was such a demon that nobody durst come near him; and the more this was confirmed to him, the greater were his fears. But Cabriole encouraged him, saying:

"My dear master, when you are fighting, I will bite

him by the legs; and while he looks behind, to drive me away, you may take that opportunity to kill him."

Avenant admired the ingenuity of his dog; but feared his assistance would not avail. At length he arrived at Galifron's castle, the roads all the way being strewed with the bones of men, which the giant had devoured. It was not long before he saw him stalking through a wood, taller than the highest trees, and with a dreadful voice uttering these words:

"Oh, for a meal of children's flesh,
Tender, young, new-killed, and fresh;
My teeth are sharp, and half a score
Would serve—till I could get some more".

In answer to which, Avenant immediately sang the following:

"Approach and see your conqueror here,
Who from thy jaws thy teeth will tear;
Your barbarous deeds I will requite,
And send your soul to endless night".

When the caitiff heard this, he looked about, and at last perceived Avenant with his sword drawn. Being in a most dreadful passion, he lifted up his iron mace, and had certainly beat out Avenant's brains at the first blow, had not a crow at that instant perched upon the giant's head, and with his bill pecked out both his eyes. The blood trickled down his face, whereat he grew desperate, and laid about him on every side; but Avenant took care to avoid his blows, and gave him great wounds with his sword, which he pushed up to the very hilt; so that the giant fell. Avenant immediately cut off his head, while the crow, perched upon a tree, said:

"Avenant, I did not forget the kindness I received at your hands, when you killed the eagle that pursued me; I promised to make you amends, and now I have been as good as my word."

"I acknowledge your kindness, Mr. Crow," replied Avenant; "I am still your debtor, and your servant."

So saying, he mounted his courser, and rode away with the giant's horrid head.

When he arrived at the city, everybody crowded after him, crying:

"Long live the valiant Avenant, who has slain the cruel monster."

The Princess heard the noise, and trembled for fear she should hear of Avenant's death. But presently she saw Avenant enter with the giant's head, at the sight of which she trembled, though there was nothing to fear.

"Madam," said he, "behold your enemy is dead; and now, I hope, you will no longer refuse the King, my master."

"Alas!" replied the Fair One with Golden Locks, "I must still refuse him, unless you can find means to bring me some of the water of the gloomy cave. Not far hence there is a very deep cave, about six leagues in compass, the entrance into which is guarded by dragons which dart fire from their mouths and eyes; in this cave is a very deep hole, full of toads, adders, and serpents. At the bottom of this hole is a kind of cellar, through which runs the fountain of beauty and health. This is the water I must have; its virtues are wonderful: for the fair, by washing in it, preserve their beauty; and the deformed it renders beautiful; if they are young, it preserves them always youthful; and if old, it makes them young again. Now judge you, Avenant, whether I will ever leave my kingdom, without carrying some of this water along with me."

"Madam," said he, "you are so beautiful, that this water will be of no use; but I am an unfortunate ambassador, whose death you seek. I will go in search of what you desire, though I am certain never to return."

The Fair One with Golden Locks did not alter her resolution; so Avenant departed. At length he arrived at the top of a mountain, where he sat down to rest, giving his horse liberty to feed, and Cabriole to run after the flies. He knew the gloomy cave was not far off, and at length he perceived a horrid rock as black as ink, whence issued a thick smoke. Immediately after he spied one of the dragons casting forth fire from his jaws and eyes, his skin all yellow and green, with prodigious claws, and a long tail, rolled in a hundred folds. Cabriole saw it also, and knew not where to hide himself for fear. Avenant, with resolution, drew his sword, and with the phial which the Fair One with Golden Locks had given him to fill with the water of beauty, went towards the cave, saying:

"Cabriole, here is an end of me; I never shall be able to get this water, it is so well guarded by the dragons; therefore, when I am dead, fill this phial with my blood, and carry it to the Princess, that she may see what her severity has cost me. Then go to the King, my master, and give him an account of my misfortunes."

While he was saying this, he heard a voice call "Avenant, Avenant!"

"Who calls me?" said he; and presently he spied an owl in the hole of an old hollow tree, who, calling again, said:

"You rescued me out of the fowler's net, where I had been assuredly taken, had not you saved my life: I promised to make you amends. Give me your phial, I will go and fetch you the water of beauty."

Avenant gladly gave the phial, and the owl, entering into the cave, in less than a quarter of an hour returned with it well filled. Avenant was overjoyed, gave the owl a thousand thanks, and returned with a merry heart to the

city. Arrived at the palace, he presented the phial to the Fair One with Golden Locks, who had then nothing further to say. She returned Avenant thanks, and gave orders for everything that was requisite for her departure, after which she set forward with him. The Fair One with Golden Locks said to him sometimes upon the road:

"If you had been willing, I could have made you a king; and then we need not have left my kingdom."

But Avenant replied:

"I would not be guilty of such a piece of treachery to my master for all the kingdoms of the earth, though I must acknowledge your beauties are more resplendent than the sun."

At length they reached the King's chief city, who, understanding that the Fair One with Golden Locks was arrived, went forth to meet her with many rich presents. The nuptials were solemnized with demonstrations of joy. But the Fair One with Golden Locks, who loved Avenant in her heart, was never pleased but when she was in his company, and would be always speaking in his praise.

"I had never come hither," said she to the King, "had it not been for Avenant, who, to serve me, has conquered impossibilities. You are infinitely obliged to him; he procured me the water of beauty and health, by which I shall never grow old, and shall always preserve my health and beauty."

The enviers of Avenant's happiness, who heard the Queen's words, went to the King, saying:

"Were your Majesty jealous, you have reason enough to be so, for the Queen is desperately in love with Avenant."

"Indeed," said the King, "I am sensible of the truth of what you tell me; let him be put in the great tower, with fetters upon his feet and hands."

Avenant was seized and confined in the great tower, where he saw nobody but the jailer, who at times brought him a little black bread and water, which he gave him through a lattice. However, his little dog Cabriole never forsook him, but cheered him the best he could, and brought him all the news of the court.

When the Fair One with Golden Locks was informed of his misfortune, she threw herself at the King's feet, and in tears besought him to release Avenant. But the more she besought him, the more was he incensed, believing it was her affection that made her so zealous a suppliant in his behalf. Finding she could not prevail, she grew very melancholy. The King thought she did not consider him handsome enough, so he resolved to wash his face with the water of beauty, in hopes the Queen would then conceive a greater affection for him than she had. This water stood in a phial upon a table in the Queen's chamber, where she had put it, that it might not be out of her sight. But one of the chambermaids going to kill a spider with her besom, by accident threw down the phial and broke it, so that all the water was lost. She dried it up with all the speed she could, and not knowing what to do, bethought herself that she had seen a phial of clear water in the King's cabinet very like that which she had broken; without more ado therefore, she went and fetched that phial, and set it upon the table in place of the other.

This water the King made use of to poison the lords and princes of the court when they were convicted of any great crime, to which purpose, instead of cutting off their heads, or hanging them, he caused their faces to be rubbed with this water, which cast them into so profound a sleep that they never waked again. Now the King one evening took this phial, and rubbed his face well with the water, after which he fell asleep and died. Cabriole was one of the first that came to the knowledge of this accident, and immediately ran to inform Avenant, who bid him go to the Fair One with Golden Locks, and remind her of the poor prisoner.

Cabriole slipped unperceived through the crowd, for there was a great noise and hurry at court upon the King's death; and getting to the Queen, "Madam," said he, "remember poor Avenant."

She presently called to mind the afflictions he had suffered for her sake, and his fidelity. Without speaking a word she went directly to the great tower and took off the fetters from Avenant's feet and hands herself; after which, putting the crown upon his head, and the royal mantle upon his shoulders,

"Amiable Avenant," said she, "I will make you a sovereign prince, and take you for my consort."

Avenant threw himself at her feet and in passionate and respectful terms returned her thanks. Everybody was overjoyed to have him for king. The nuptials were the most splendid in the world, and the Fair One with Golden Locks lived a long time with her beloved Avenant.

Sindbad the Sailor

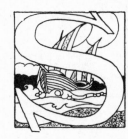

SINDBAD THE SAILOR, after all his adventures and wanderings, settled down in happiness and prosperity in Bagdad. Here are the accounts which he told to his friends of his seven marvellous voyages.

THE FIRST VOYAGE

My father died while I was young and left me a fortune. Having no one to restrain my conduct, I fell into a state of dissipation, by which I not only wasted my time, but injured my health, and destroyed my property.

When I recovered, I collected together the remains of my fortune, and purchased merchandise, with which I embarked on board a vessel for the port of Balsora.

During the voyage we touched at several islands, where we sold or exchanged our goods. We were one day becalmed near a small island. As its appearance was inviting, we determined to dine upon it. But while we were laughing and preparing for dinner, the island began to move, and at the same moment the people in the ship called out that we were on the back of a monstrous whale. Some jumped into the boat, and others swam to the ship; but before I could get off the animal dived into the sea, and I had only time to catch hold of a piece of wood that had been brought from the ship to serve as a table. Upon this piece of timber I was carried away by the current, the others having reached the vessel; and a gale having sprung up, the ship sailed without me.

I floated during that and the succeeding night, but the following morning was thrown on a small island.

I found fresh water and fruit. I looked about for some place of habitation, but found none. There were a number of colts grazing together, but no traces of other animals. When evening approached I took some more fruit, and climbed into a tree as a resting-place. About midnight the sounds of trumpets and drums seemed to pass around the island, which continued until morning, when again it seemed to be uninhabited. On the next day I found that the island was small, and that no other land was in sight. I therefore gave myself up as lost. Nor were my apprehensions diminished, when I found that the shore abounded with enormous serpents and other sea monsters. I found, however, that they were timid, and that the rattling of sticks would induce them to dive into the water.

I climbed the tree next night, and the drums and trumpets returned as before. On the third day, I had the satisfaction of perceiving a body of men, who, on landing, were astonished to find me there. Having related to them how I came hither, they told me they were grooms of King Mihrage; that the island belonged to genii, who visited it every night with drums and trumpets; that the genii had allowed their sovereign to train his colts upon the island; and that they, being sent every six months to select some, had arrived for that purpose.

The grooms carried me to King Mihrage, who allowed me apartments in his palace.

One day I saw men unloading a ship in the harbour, and perceived that some of the bales were those which I had embarked for Balsora. Going up to the captain, I said:

"Captain, I am Sindbad."

"Surely," said he, "I and the passengers saw Sindbad swallowed in the waves many hundred miles away."

Some others, however, coming up, I was recognized; and the captain then restored me the bales, with many congratulations. I made a valuable present to King Mihrage, who bestowed a rich gift on me in return; and, having made some advantageous purchases, I arrived at Balsora, where, after I had sold my goods, I found myself possessed of a hundred thousand sequins.

THE SECOND VOYAGE

Becoming weary of a quiet life in Balsora, and having purchased commodities, I again went to sea with some merchants. After having touched at several places, we landed at an uninhabited island. We amused ourselves in different ways, but I, having taken my wine and provisions, sat down and fell asleep. When I awoke, I found that my companions were gone, and that the ship had sailed. I climbed to the top of a very high tree, and perceived at a distance an object that was very large and white. I descended to the ground, and ran towards this strange-looking object. When I approached it I found it was about fifty paces in circumference, quite round, and as smooth as ivory, but had no sort of opening. It was now almost sunset, and suddenly the sky became darkened. I looked up and beheld a bird of enormous size, moving like a prodigious cloud towards me. I recollected that I had heard of a bird called the roc, so large that it could carry away young elephants, and I therefore conjectured that the large object I had been looking at was the egg of this bird.

As the bird approached I crept close to the egg, so that I had one of the legs of this winged animal before me; this limb being as large as the trunk of a tree, I tied myself firmly to it with my turban.

The next morning the bird flew away, and carried me from this desert island. I was borne so high that I could not see the earth, and then carried downwards so swiftly that I lost my senses. When I recovered, finding myself

C 165

SINDBAD FINDS THE SERPENTS

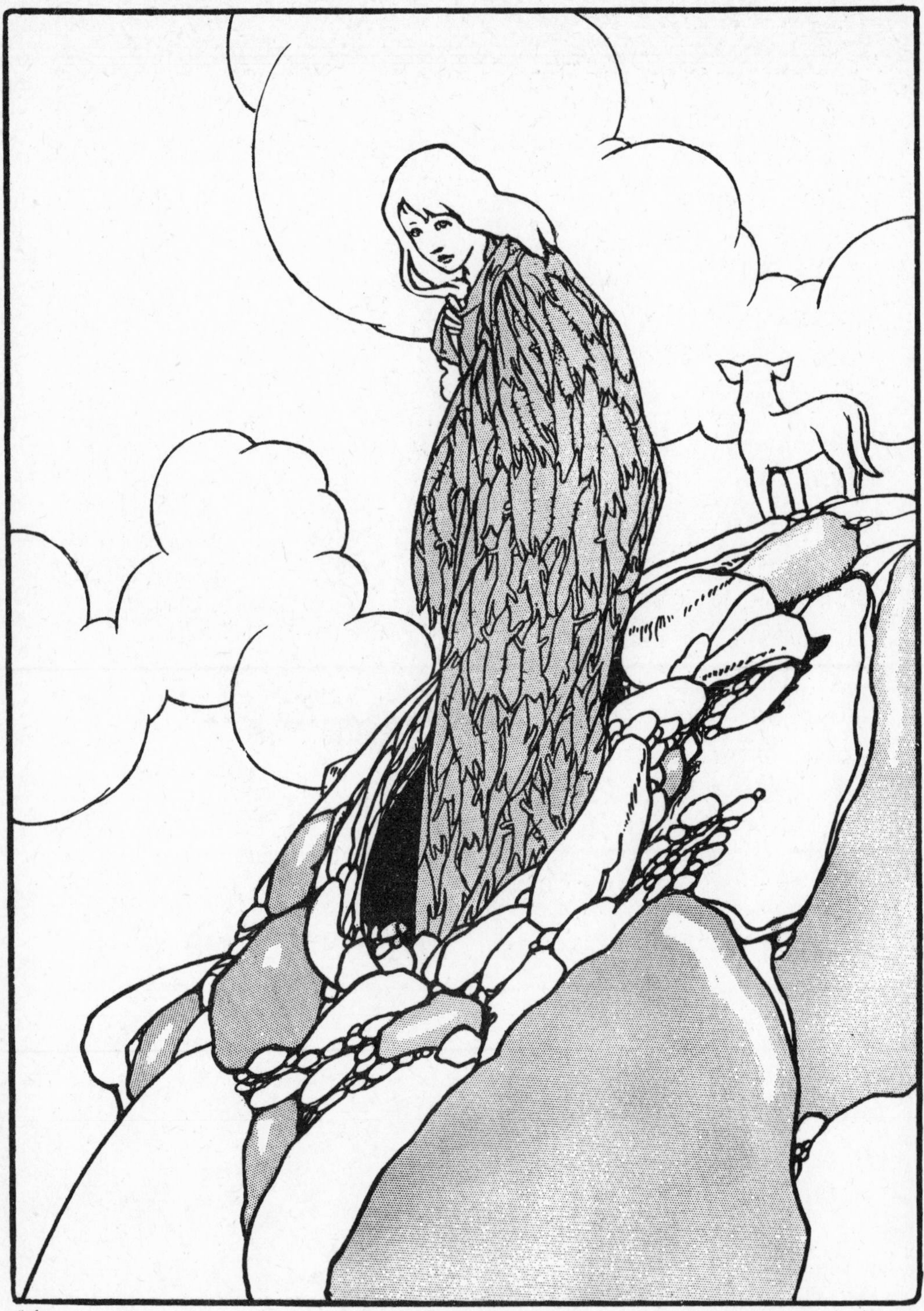

C 165

THE MOUSESKIN CLOAK

on the ground, I quickly untied the cloth that bound me, and scarcely was I free, when the bird, having taken up a large serpent, again flew away. I found myself in a deep valley, the sides of which were too steep to be ascended. As I walked up and down in despair, I perceived that the valley was strewed with diamonds of surprising magnitude. But I soon saw other objects of much less inviting appearance. Serpents of the most terrific size were peeping out of holes on every side. When night came, I took shelter in a cave, the entrance of which I guarded with the largest stones I could find, but the hissing of the serpents entirely deprived me of sleep. When day returned, the serpents retired to their holes; and I came out of my cave, but with extreme fear. I walked heedless of the serpents until I became weary, and then

sat down and fell asleep. I was awakened by something which fell near me. It was a large piece of fresh meat, and presently I saw several other pieces.

I was now convinced that I must be in the famous valley of diamonds, and that the pieces of meat were thrown in by merchants, who expected eagles to pounce upon the flesh, to which diamonds were almost sure to adhere. I hastened to pick up some of the largest diamonds I could find, which I put into a little bag, and fastened it to my girdle. I then selected the largest piece of flesh in the valley, which I tied to my waist with the cloth of my turban, and then lay down upon my face to wait for the eagles. Very soon one of the strongest pounced upon the meat on my back, and flew with me to its nest on the top of the mountain. The merchants began shouting to frighten the eagles, and when they had obliged the birds to quit their prey, one of them came to the nest where I was. At first the man was frightened when he saw me there, but having recovered himself, asked me how

I came hither. I told him and the rest of the merchants my story. I then opened my bag, and they declared that they had never seen diamonds of equal lustre and size with mine. The merchants having gathered their diamonds together, we left the place the next morning; and crossed the mountains until we reached a port. We there took shipping and proceeded to the island of Roha. There I exchanged some of my diamonds for other merchandise, and we proceeded to Balsora. From Balsora I proceeded to my native city, Bagdad, in which I lived in ease upon the vast riches I had acquired.

THE THIRD VOYAGE

I soon resolved upon a third voyage, and once more took shipping at Balsora. After we had been at sea a few weeks, we were overtaken by a dreadful storm, and were obliged to cast anchor near an island which the captain had endeavoured to avoid; for he assured us that it was inhabited by pigmy savages, covered with hair, who would speedily attack us in great numbers. Soon an innumerable multitude of frightful savages, about two feet high, boarded the ship. Resistance was useless. They took down our sails, cut our cable, towed the ship to land, and made us all go on shore. We went towards the interior of the island and discovered a large building. It was a lofty palace, having a gate of ebony, which we pushed open, and soon discovered an apartment in which were human bones and roasting spits. Presently there appeared a hideous black man, who was as tall as a palm tree. He had but one eye, his teeth were long and sharp, and his nails like the talons of a bird. He took me up as I would a kitten, but finding I was little better than skin and bone, put me down with disdain. The captain, being the fattest of the party, was sacrificed to his appetite. When the monster had finished his meal he stretched himself upon a great stone bench in the portico, and fell asleep, snoring louder than thunder. In this manner he slept till morning. In the morning he went out. I said to my companions:

"Do not waste time in useless sorrow; let us hasten to look for timber to make rafts."

We found some timber on the seashore, and laboured hard; but having no tools, it was evening before we had finished; and whilst we were on the point of pushing the raft off the beach, our hideous tyrant returned and drove us to his palace, as if we had been a flock of sheep. We saw another of our companions sacrificed, and the giant lay down to sleep as before. Our desperate condition gave us courage; nine of us got up very softly, and held the points of the roasting spits in the fire until we made them red-hot; we then thrust them at once into the monster's eye. He uttered a frightful scream, and having endeavoured in vain to find us, opened the ebony gate and left the palace. We did not stay long behind him, but hastened to the seashore, and having got our rafts ready, only waited for daylight to embark. But at dawn we beheld our monstrous enemy, led by two giants of equal size, and followed by many others. We jumped upon our rafts, and pushed them from the shore, the tide assisting us. The giants seeing us likely to escape, tore great pieces of rock, and wading in the water up to their waists, hurled them at us with all their might. They sunk every one of the rafts but that on which I was; thus all my companions, excepting two, were drowned. We rowed as fast as we could, and got out of the reach of these monsters. We were at sea two days, but at last found a pleasant island. Having eaten some fruit, we lay down to sleep, but were soon awakened by the hissing of an enormous serpent. One of my comrades was instantly devoured by this terrific creature. I climbed up a tree as fast as I could, and reached the topmost branches; my remaining companion was following me, but the dreadful reptile entwined itself round the tree and caught him. The serpent then descended and glided away. I waited until late the next day before I ventured to descend. Evening again approached, and I gathered together a great quantity of small wood, brambles, and thorns. Having made them into faggots, I formed a circle round the tree, and fastened the uppermost to the branches of the tree. I then ascended to the highest branches. At night the serpent came again, but could not reach the tree; and having ineffectually gone round and round my little fortification until daylight, he went away. The next day I beheld a ship in full sail at a considerable distance. With the linen of my turban I made a signal, which was perceived. I was taken on board the ship and there related

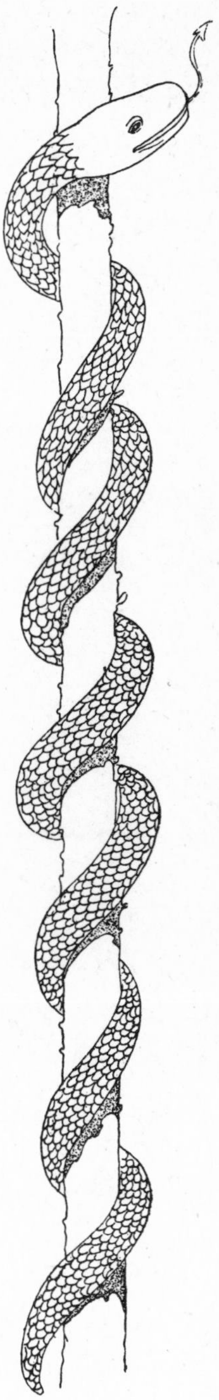

my adventures. The captain was kind in the extreme, and told me that he had some bales of goods which had belonged to a merchant who had unintentionally left him some time ago on an uninhabited island; and who, being unavoidably dead, he intended to sell the goods for the benefit of his relatives, and that I should have the profit of selling them. I now recollected this was the captain with whom I had sailed on my second voyage. I soon convinced him that I was really Sindbad, whom he supposed to have been lost. He was delighted at the discovery, and eagerly acknowledged that the property was mine. I continued my voyage, sold my goods to great advantage, and returned to Bagdad.

THE FOURTH VOYAGE

My desire of seeing foreign countries rendered my pleasures at home perfectly unsatisfactory. I therefore arranged my affairs, commenced a voyage overland to Persia, and, having bought a large stock of goods, loaded a ship and again embarked. The ship struck upon a rock, and the cargo was lost. A few others and myself were borne by the current to an island, in which we were surrounded by black savages, and carried to their habitations. The savages offered us herbs; my companions eagerly took them, for they were hungry. Grief would not allow me to eat; and presently I perceived that the herbs had deprived my comrades of their senses. Rice, mixed with oil of cocoanuts, was then offered to us, of which my companions ate greedily. My unhappy friends were devoured one after another, having by these means become desirable to the cannibals. But I languished so much, that they did not think me fit to be eaten. They left me to the care of an old man, from whom I contrived to escape; and taking care to pursue a contrary way from that which the savages had gone I never stopped till night. At the end of seven days, on the seashore I found a number of white persons gathering pepper. They asked me in Arabic who I was, and whence I came; and I gave them an account of the shipwreck, and of my escape. They treated me kindly and presented me to their King, who behaved to me with great liberality. During my stay with them, I observed that when the King and his nobles went hunting, they rode their horses without bridle or saddle. With the assistance of some workmen I made a bridle and saddle, and having put them upon one of the King's horses, presented the animal thus accoutred to His Majesty. He was so delighted, that he instantly mounted and rode about the grounds almost the whole day. All the ministers of state and the nobility induced me to make saddles and bridles for them, for which they made me such magnificent presents that I soon became extremely rich. The King at last re-

quested that I would marry, and become one of his nation. From a variety of circumstances I could not refuse, and he therefore gave me one of the ladies of his Court, who was young, rich, beautiful, and virtuous. We lived in the greatest harmony in a palace belonging to my wife. I had contracted a great intimacy with a very worthy man who lived in this place. Having heard one day that his wife had just died, I hastened to condole with him on this unexpected calamity. We were alone together, and he appeared to be in the deepest grief. After I had remonstrated with him some time on the inutility of so much sorrow, he told me that it was an established law that the living husband should be buried with the deceased wife, and that within an hour he must submit. I shuddered at the dreadful custom. In a short time the woman was attired in her most costly dress and jewels, and placed in an open coffin. The procession then began, the husband following the corpse. They ascended to the top of an exceedingly high mountain, and a great stone was removed, which covered the mouth of a deep pit. The corpse was let down, and the husband, having taken leave of his friends, was put into another open coffin, with a pot of water and seven small loaves, and he was let down. The stone was replaced, and they all returned. The horror of this was still fresh upon my mind, when my wife fell sick and died. The King and the whole Court, out of respect to me, instantly prepared to assist at a similar ceremony with me. I restrained the feeling of despair until we arrived at the top of the mountain, when I fell at the feet of the King and besought him to spare my life. All I said was ineffectual, and after my wife was interred, I also was put down into the deep pit, all being totally indifferent to my cries and lamentations. I made the cave echo with my unavailing complaints. I lived some days on the bread and water which had been put into my coffin, but this supply was at length exhausted. I then wandered to a remote part of this frightful cave, and lay down to prepare for death. I was thus wishing only for a speedy termination to my misery, when I heard something walking and panting. I started up, upon which the thing panted still more, and then ran away. I pursued it, and sometimes it seemed to stop, but on my approach continued to go on before me. I pursued it, until at last I saw a glimmering light like a star. This redoubled my eagerness, until at last I discovered a hole large enough to allow my escape. I crept through the aperture, and found myself on the seashore, and discovered that the creature was a sea monster which had been accustomed to enter at that hole to feed upon the dead bodies. Having eaten some shellfish, I returned to the cave, where I collected all the jewels I could find in the dark. These I carried to the seashore, and having tied them up very neatly into bales with the cords that let down the coffins, I laid them on the beach, waiting till some ship should pass. In two days a ship came out of the harbour, and passed by that part of the coast. I made a signal, and a boat took me on board. I was obliged to say that I had been wrecked; for, had they known my real story, I should have been carried back, as the captain was a native of this country, We touched at several islands, and at the port of Kela, where I found a ship ready to sail for Balsora; and having presented some jewels to the captain who had brought me to Kela, I sailed, and at last arrived at Bagdad.

THE FIFTH VOYAGE

Having forgotten my former perils, I built a ship at my own expense, loaded it with a rich cargo, and, taking with me other merchants, once more set sail. After having been much driven about by a storm, we landed upon a desert island to search for fresh water; we there found a roc's egg, equal in size to that which I had seen before. The merchants and sailors gathered round it, and though I advised them not to meddle with it, they nevertheless made a hole in it with their hatchets, and picked out the young roc, piece after piece, and roasted it. They had scarcely finished when two of the old birds appeared in the air. We hastened on board ship and set sail. We had not proceeded far before we saw the immense birds approaching us, and soon after they hovered over the ship. One of them let fall an enormous fragment of stone, which fell into the sea close beside the ship, but the other let fall a fragment which split our ship. I caught hold of a piece of the wreck, on which I was borne by the wind and tide to an island, the shore of which was very steep. I reached the dry land, and having found the most delicious fruits and excellent water, became refreshed. Farther in the island I saw a feeble old man sitting near a rivulet. When I enquired of him how he came thither, he only answered by signs for me to carry him over the rivulet, that he might eat some fruit. I took him on my back, and crossed the brook, but instead of getting down, he clasped his legs so firmly round my throat, that I thought he would have strangled me, so that with pain and fright I soon fainted. When I recovered, the old fellow was still in his former position, and he quickly made me rise up and walk under the trees, while he gathered the fruit at his ease. This lasted a considerable time. One day, while carrying him about, I picked up a large gourd called a calabash, and, having cleared out the inside, I pressed into it the juice of grapes. Having filled it, I left it for several days, and at length found that it became excellent wine. I drank of this, and for a while forgot my sorrows, so that I began to sing with cheerfulness. The old man made me give him the calabash, and liking the flavour of the wine, he drank it off, soon became intoxicated, fell from my

shoulders, and died in convulsions. I hastened to the seaside, and soon found the crew of a ship. They told me I had fallen into the hands of the Old Man of the Sea, and was the first person that had ever escaped. I sailed with them, and the captain, when we landed, took me to some persons whose employment was to gather cocoanuts. We all took up stones and pelted the monkeys that were at the very top of the cocoanut trees, and these animals in return pelted us with cocoanuts. When we had obtained as many as we could carry, we returned to the town. I soon obtained a considerable sum by the cocoanuts I thus obtained, and at length sailed for my native land.

THE SIXTH VOYAGE

At the expiration of another year, I prepared ıor a sixth voyage. This proved very long and unfortunate, for the pilot lost his course and knew not where to steer. At length he told us we must inevitably be dashed to pieces against a rock which we were fast approaching. In a few moments the vessel was a complete wreck. We saved our lives, our provisions, and our goods.

The shore on which we were cast was at the foot of a mountain which it was impossible to climb, so that I shortly beheld my companions die one after another. There was a frightful cavern in the rock, through which flowed a river. To this, in a fit of desperation, I resolved to trust myself. I went to work and made a long raft. I loaded it with bales of rich stuffs, and large pieces of rock crystal, of which the mountain was in a great measure formed. I went on board the raft, and the current carried me along. I was carried

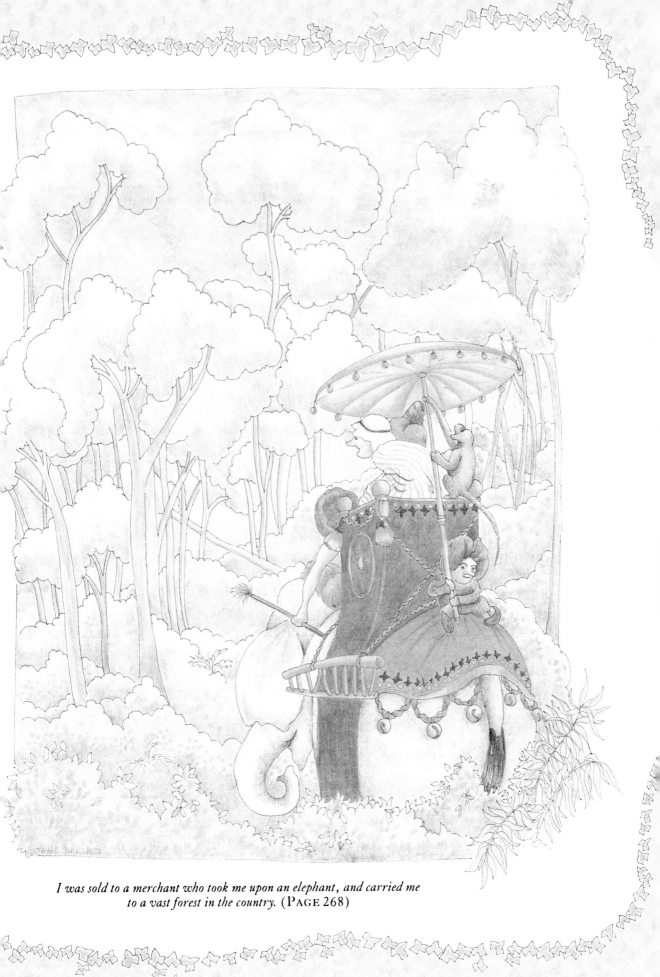

I was sold to a merchant who took me upon an elephant, and carried me to a vast forest in the country. (Page 268)

'This is my house', said the swallow. (PAGE 302)

in darkness during many days, and at last fell asleep. When I awoke, I found myself in a pleasant country. My raft was tied up, and some blacks, who were near me, said that they had found me floating in the river which waters their land. They took me to their king, and carefully conducted my cargo with me. When we came to the city of Serindib, I related my story to the monarch, who ordered it to be written

in letters of gold. I presented the King with some of the most beautiful pieces of rock crystal, and entreated him to let me return to my own country, which he readily agreed to, and even gave me a letter and a present to my sovereign, the Caliph Haroun Alraschid. The present consisted of a ruby made into a cup, and decorated with pearls; the skin of a serpent, which appeared like burnished gold, and which could repel disease; some aloe-wood, camphire, and a female slave of excessive beauty. I returned to my native country, delivered the present to the Caliph, and received his thanks, with a reward.

THE SEVENTH AND LAST VOYAGE

The Caliph Haroun Alraschid one day sent for me, and told me I must bear a present to the King of Serindib. I ventured to expostulate with him on account of my age, but I could not prevail on him to forgo his request. I arrived at Serindib, and prayed an audience with the King. I was conducted to the palace with great respect, and delivered to the monarch the Caliph's letter and present. The present consisted of the most ingenious and valuable works of art, with which the King was exceedingly delighted, and he was also pleased to acknowledge how much he esteemed my services. When I departed, the monarch bestowed on me some rich gifts; but the ship had not long been at sea, before it was attacked by corsairs, who seized the vessel, and carried us away as slaves. I was sold to a merchant, who, having found that I could use the bow and arrow with skill, took me upon an elephant, and carried me to a vast forest in the country. My master desired me to climb an exceedingly high tree, and wait there until I saw a troop of elephants pass by. I was then to shoot at them, and if one of them fell, I was to go to the city and give the merchant notice. Having given me these directions, and a bag of provisions, he left me. On the morning of the second day, I saw a great number of elephants. I succeeded in shooting one of them, upon which the others went away, and I returned to the city and told my employer; he commended my diligence and caressed me. We went back to the forest and dug a hole, in which the elephant was to remain until it decayed and left the teeth. I continued this trade nearly two months, and killed an elephant almost every day. One morning all the elephants came up to the tree in which I was; they howled dreadfully. One of them fastened his trunk round the tree and tore it up by the roots. I fell with the tree; the animal took me up with his trunk, and placed me on his back, and then, at the head of his troop, he brought me to a place where he gently laid me on the ground, and they all went away. I discovered that I was upon a large broad hill, covered all over with the bones and teeth of elephants, and was soon convinced that this was their burying-place. I reached the city once more; my master thought I was lost, for he had seen the torn tree, and found my bow and arrows. I told him what had happened, and conducted him to the hill. We loaded the elephant on which we had come, and thus collected more teeth than a man could have obtained in his whole life.

The merchant told me that not only he himself, but the whole city, was indebted to me, and that I should return to my own country with sufficient wealth to make me happy. My patron loaded a ship with ivory, and the other merchants made me valuable presents. I reached Balsora and landed my ivory, which I found to be much more valuable than I had expected. I set out with caravans to travel overland, and at last reached Bagdad, where I presented myself to the Caliph, and gave an account of my embassy. He was so astonished at my adventure with the elephants that he ordered the narrative of it to be written in letters of gold and to be deposited in his treasury.

Mouse-skin

ONCE a nobleman had an only daughter, whom he placed in a mount, there to remain as long as there was war in the country. The father had secretly caused a room to be built in the mount, and had laid in provisions, and wood enough to last for seven years; and she was not to come out until he fetched her; but if at the end of seven years he did not come for her, she might conclude that he was dead, and might then leave the mount. A little dog was her only companion.

The damsel occupied herself with spinning, weaving, and sewing; and thus one year passed after another. She made a number of fine clothes, some of which were embroidered with gold, and others with silver; but when she had no longer anything to spin or otherwise employ her, the time began to be tedious. Her stock of food was nearly exhausted, and she was fearful that her father would not return. As the time that she was to remain had nearly expired, and he had not come to fetch her, she concluded that he was dead. She now began to dig her way out, but this was very slow work, and no easy task.

In the meantime all her provisions were consumed. But the mount was full of mice, and her little dog destroyed a great many every day; these she skinned, roasted, and ate the meat, and gave the bones to her little dog. She stitched all the skins together, and made herself a cloak or garment, which was so large that she could quite wrap herself up in it. Every day she laboured, and at length succeeded so as to be able once more to see the light of day. When she had made an opening large enough, she went out, accompanied by her faithful dog. She then closed up the opening, and left the hill with her dog, and went through the wood, and there was much she found had changed in the seven years she had lived underground. She had her silver and her gold dresses on, and over them she wore the mouseskin cloak, which quite covered her, so that she had more the appearance of a poor man's child than of a young lady of rank. At the first house she came to she enquired who lived at the manor. She was told it was the young lord, who had inherited it after the death of the former proprietor.

"How then did he die?" asked she, hardly able to conceal her feelings.

She received for answer, that he was a brave soldier, and drove the enemy out of the country, but was killed in the last battle; that his only child was a daughter who had been carried off before that time, and no one had since ever heard anything of her.

The young maiden asked, if they could tell her where she could be employed, as she wanted to work.

"Our young master is soon to be married," said the people; "his bride, and her father and mother, are arrived at the mansion to make preparations for the wedding; if you go up there, you will surely find something to do."

The young girl then went up to her father's abode, and her little dog was so happy, for it knew the place again; but its mistress wept with grief, as she humbly knocked at the door. When the people heard that she wished to be employed, they gladly engaged her, and set her to sweep the yard, and do other menial work.

The day before the wedding the bride sent for her, and told her that she had a great favour to ask: "Thou art of the same height as I am," said she; "thou must to-morrow put on my bridal dress and veil, and drive to the church, and be wedded to the bridegroom, instead of me." The young girl could not imagine why the other objected to be wedded to the handsome young lord. The bride then told her, that there was another lover, to whom she had previously betrothed herself; but that her parents wanted to force her to marry this rich young lord; that she was afraid of disobeying them, but that she had agreed with her beloved, that on the wedding day she would elope with him. This she could not do if she were wedded at the altar to another; but if she sent someone in her place, everything might end well. The young maiden promised to do all requested of her.

The next day the bride was attired in the most costly dress, and all the people in the house came into her chamber to look at her; at length she said: "Now call that poor young girl that sweeps the yard, and let her also see me." The girl in the mouseskin dress came accordingly, and, when they were alone together, the bride locked the door, dressed her in the beautiful clothes, with the bridal veil over her head, and wrapped herself in the young girl's large mouseskin cloak.

The late lord's daughter was then conducted to a chariot, in which was the bridegroom, and they drove to church, accompanied by all the bridal guests. On the road they passed the mount, where she had live so long concealed. She sighed beneath her veil, and said:

"Yonder stands yet every pin,
With every little mouse's skin,
Where seven long years I pined in sadness
In the dark mount, and knew no gladness."

"What sayest thou, dearest?" asked the bride-groom.

"Oh, I am only talking to myself!" answered the bride.

When she entered the church, she saw the portraits of her parents on each side of the altar; but it appeared to her as if they turned from her, as she wept beneath her veil, gazing on them; she then said:

"Turn, turn again, ye pictures dear; dear father and mother, turn again";

and then the pictures turned again.

"What sayest thou, my dear bride?" asked the bride-groom.

"Oh, I am only talking to myself!" answered she.

They were then wedded in the church, the young lord put a ring upon her finger, and they drove home. As soon as the bride alighted from the carriage she hurried up into the lady's chamber, as they had agreed, where they changed dresses once more; but the wedding ring which she had on her finger she kept.

In the evening there was dancing, and the young lord danced with her whom he thought his bride; but when he took her hand, he said: "Where is the ring I put on your finger in the church?"

The bride was at first embarrassed, but said quickly: "I took it off and left it in my chamber, but now I will run and fetch it."

She then ran out of the room, called the real bride, and demanded the ring.

"No," answered the maiden, "the ring I will not part with; it belongs to the hand that was given away at the altar. But I will go with you to the door, then you can call him, and we will both stand in the passage; when he comes we will extinguish the light that is there, and I will stretch my hand in at the door, so that he can see the ring." Thus it was arranged.

The bridegroom was standing near the door, when the bride called him into the passage, and said: "See, here is the ring." At the same moment as the one damsel extinguished the light, the other stretched forth her hand with the ring.

But the bridegroom was not satisfied with merely seeing the ring, he seized the hand, and drew the young girl into the room, and then, to his astonishment, saw it was the damsel in the mouseskin dress. All the guests flocked round them, and were eager to know how it had all happened.

She then threw off her mouseskin dress, and stood clad in her beautiful gold embroidery, and was more lovely to look at than the other bride. Everyone was impatient to hear her story; and she was obliged to relate to them how long she had remained in the mount, and that her father had been their former lord. The little dog was fetched from her miserable room, and many of the neighbours knew it again.

Hereupon there was great joy and wonder. Everybody revered her father, who had fought so bravely for his country, and all were unanimous that the estate belonged to her. Her sorrow was turned into joy, and, as she wished everyone to be as happy as herself, she bestowed land and money on the other bride, that she might marry the man of her choice, to whom she had secretly given her heart. The parents were contented with this arrangement, and now the marriage feast was gay, when the young lord danced with his true bride, to whom he had been wedded in the church, and to whom he had given the ring.

Bushy Bride

ONCE there was a widower who had a son and daughter by his first marriage. They were good children, and loved each other dearly. Some time after, the man married a widow who had a daughter by her first husband, and she was ugly and bad, like her mother. From the day the new wife came there was no peace for her stepchildren, and at last the lad thought he'd best go out into the world and earn his own bread. When he had wandered a while he came to a king's palace, and got a place under the coachman, and so quick and willing was he, that the horses he looked after were so sleek and clean that their coats shone again.

The sister, who stayed at home, was treated worse than ever. Her stepmother and stepsister scolded so that the poor lassie hadn't an hour's peace. All the hard work she was forced to do, and early and late got nothing but bad words, and little food besides.

"UP POPPED AN UGLY HEAD OUT OF THE POOL"

C 165

"THEY MET A LARGE POODLE"

One day they had sent her to fetch water, when up popped an ugly head out of the pool, and said:

"Wash me, lassie."

"With all my heart," said the lassie.

So she began to wash and scrub the ugly head; but, truth to say, she thought it nasty work.

As soon as she had done washing it, up popped another head, and this was uglier still.

"Brush me, lassie," said the head.

"With all my heart."

With that she took in hand the matted locks, and hadn't very pleasant work with them.

When she had got over that, if a third head didn't pop out, and this was far more ugly and loathsome than both the others put together.

"Kiss me, lassie."

"Yes, I'll kiss you," said the lassie, and she did, though she thought it the worst work she had ever had to do in her life.

Then the heads began to chatter, and each asked what they should do for the lassie who was so kind and gentle.

"That she be the prettiest lassie in the world, and as fair as the day," said the first.

"That gold shall drop from her hair every time she brushes it," said the second.

"That gold shall fall from her mouth every time she speaks," said the third.

When the lassie came home, looking lovely, and beaming as the day itself, her stepmother and her stepsister got more and more cross, and worse still when she began to talk, and they saw golden guineas fall from her mouth. As

for the stepmother, she got so mad with rage she chased the lassie into the pig sty.

Well, it wasn't long before the stepmother wished her own daughter to go to fetch water. When she came to the water's edge, up popped the first head.

"Wash me, lassie," it said.

"Catch me wash you!" said the stepdaughter.

So the second head popped up.

"Brush me, lassie," it said.

"Catch me brush you!" said the stepdaughter.

So down it went, and the third head popped up.

"Kiss me, lassie," said the head.

"Catch me kiss you, pig's-snout!" said the girl.

Then the heads chattered together, and asked what they should do to the girl who was so spiteful and cross-grained, and they all agreed she should have a nose four ells long, and a snout three ells long, and a pine bush right in the midst of her forehead, and every time she spoke ashes were to fall out of her mouth.

So, when she got home with her buckets, she bawled out:

"Open the door!"

"Open it yourself, my darling child," said the mother.

"I can't reach it because of my nose," said the daughter.

When the mother came out and saw her, you may fancy

The Princess set off on her journey. (PAGE 305)

The frog put his head down, and dived deep under the water.
(PAGE 341)

how she screamed and groaned; but, for all that, there were the nose and the snout and the pine bush, and they got no smaller for all her grief.

Now, the brother who had got the place in the King's stable had taken a little sketch of his sister, which he carried away with him, and every morning and every evening he knelt down before the picture and prayed for his sister, whom he loved dearly. The other grooms had peeped through the keyhole of his room, and there they saw him on his knees. So they went about saying how the lad prayed to an idol which he had, and at last they went to the King and begged him only to peep through the keyhole, and then His Majesty would see the lad and what things he did. At first the King wouldn't believe it, but at last he crept on tiptoe and peeped in.

"Open the door!" called out the King; but the lad didn't hear him.

So the King called in a louder voice; but the lad was so deep in his prayers he couldn't hear him.

"OPEN THE DOOR, I SAY!" roared out the King. "It's I, the King, who want to come in!"

Up jumped the lad and ran to the door and unlocked it; but in his hurry he forgot to hide the picture.

When the King came in, and saw the picture, he stood there as if he couldn't stir from the spot.

"So lovely a woman there isn't in the wide world," said the King.

But the lad told him she was his sister whom he had drawn, and if she wasn't prettier than that, at least she wasn't uglier.

"Well, if she's so lovely," said the King, "I'll have

her for my Queen;" and then he ordered the lad to set off home that minute, and not be long on the road either. So the lad promised to make haste, and started off.

When the brother came to fetch his sister, the stepmother and stepsister said they must go too. So they all set out, and the good lassie had a casket in which she kept her gold, and a little dog whose name was "Little Flo": those two things were all her mother left her. And when they had gone a while they came to a lake which they had to cross.

At last they caught sight of land.

"There," said the brother at the helm, "where you see the white strand yonder, there's where we're to land."

"What is it my brother says?" asked the good lassie.

"He says you must throw your casket overboard," said the stepmother.

"Well, when my brother says it, I must do it," said the lassie, and overboard went the casket.

When they had sailed a bit farther the brother pointed again across the lake.

"There you see the castle we're going to."

"What is it my brother says?" asked the lassie.

"He says now you must throw your little dog overboard," said the stepmother.

Then the lassie wept and was sore grieved, for Little Flo was the dearest thing she had in the world; but at last she threw him overboard.

"When my brother says it, I must do it; but Heaven knows how it hurts me to throw you over, Little Flo," she said.

So they sailed on a good bit still.

"'There you see the King coming to meet us," said the brother, pointing towards the strand.

"What is it my brother says?" asked the lassie.

"He says you must make haste and throw yourself overboard," said the stepmother.

Well, the lassie wept and moaned; but when her brother told her to do that, she thought she ought to do it, and so she leapt down into the lake.

But when they came to the palace, and the King saw the bride, with a nose four ells long, and a snout three ells long, and a pine bush in the midst of her forehead, he was scared out of his wits. But the wedding was all ready, and there sat all the wedding guests waiting for the bride; so the King couldn't help himself, but was forced to take

her for better for worse. But so angry he was, that he had the brother thrown into a pit full of snakes.

Well, the first Thursday evening after the wedding, about midnight, in came a lovely lady into the palace kitchen, and begged the kitchen maid, who slept there, to lend her a brush. That she got, and then she brushed her hair, and as she brushed, down dropped gold.

A little dog was at her heel, and to him she said:

"Run out, Little Flo, and see if it will soon be day."

This she said three times, and the third time she sent the dog it was just about the time dawn begins.

Then she had to go; but as she went, she sang:

"Out on you, ugly Bushy Bride,
Lying so warm by the King's left side;
While I on sand and gravel sleep,
And over my brother adders creep,
And all without a tear.

"Now I come twice more, and then never again."

Next morning the kitchen maid told what she had seen and heard, and the King said he'd watch himself next Thursday night; and as soon as it got dark, out he went into the kitchen to the kitchen maid. But all he could do, and however much he rubbed his eyes and tried to keep himself awake, it was no good; for the Bushy Bride chaunted and sung till his eyes closed, and so, when the lovely lady came, he slept and snored. This time, as before, she borrowed a brush, and brushed her hair till the gold dropped, and sent her dog out three times; and as soon as it was grey dawn, away she went singing the same words, and adding:

"Now I come once more, and then never again."

The third Thursday evening the King said he would watch again, and he set two men to hold him, one under each arm, who were to shake and jog him every time he wanted to fall asleep; and two men he set to watch his Bushy Bride.

But when the night wore on, the Bushy Bride began to chaunt and sing, so that his eyes began to wink, and his head hung down on his shoulders. Then in came the

lovely lady, and got the brush and brushed her hair till the gold dropped from it. After that she sent Little Flo out again to see if it would soon be day, and this she did three times.

The third time it began to get grey in the east; then she sang:

"Out on you, ugly Bushy Bride,
Lying so warm by the King's
left side;
While I on sand and gravel
sleep,
And over my brother adders
creep,
And all without a tear.

"Now I come back never more," she said, and went towards the door. But the two men who held the King under the arms clenched his hands together, and put a knife into his grasp, and so, somehow or other, they got him to cut her in her little finger, and drew blood.

Then the true bride was freed, and the King woke up, and she told him now the whole story, and how her stepmother and sister had deceived her. The King sent at once and took her brother out of the pit of snakes, and the adders hadn't done him the least harm, but the wicked stepmother and her ugly daughter were thrown into it in his stead.

And no one can tell how glad the King was to be rid of that ugly Bushy Bride, and to get a Queen who was as lovely and bright as the day itself. So the true wedding was held with great state and pomp, and everyone talked of it over seven kingdoms; and then the King and his beautiful bride drove to church in their coach, and Little Flo went inside with them too, and when the blessing was given they drove back again, and after that I saw nothing more of them.

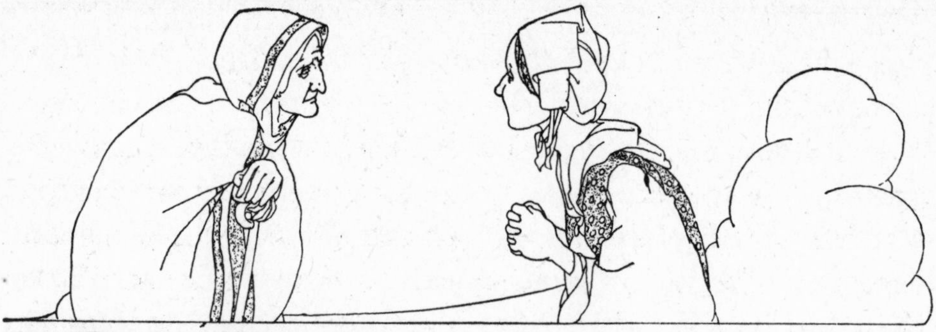

Thumbeline

ONCE upon a time there was a woman who wished very much for a child, but did not know where to find one. At last she went to a witch and said to her: "I do so much wish to have a little child; can you tell me where I can find one?"

"Here is a barley corn," said the witch. "Put it into a flower pot and wait and see what takes place."

"Thank you," said the woman, giving the witch the twelve shillings which she asked for her barley corn. She went straight home and planted the barley corn, and at once a large handsome flower sprang up. It looked like a tulip, but its leaves were as tightly closed as if they were the leaves of a bud. "What a lovely flower!" said the woman, kissing its red and golden coloured leaves. At her kiss the leaves burst open with a crack, and she saw that it was really a tulip such as one can see almost anywhere. But in the very centre of the blossom, on one of the green velvet stamens, sat a tiny maiden, a delicate and graceful little creature, scarcely half as long as a thumb;

and when the woman saw her she called her Thumbeline, because she was so small.

A finely polished walnut shell formed her cradle, and therein, on a bed of violets, under a rose-leaf coverlet, Thumbeline slept soundly. During the day she amused herself by floating across a plate full of water in a large tulip leaf, which served her for a boat. The woman had placed the plate of water on a table, and put a wreath of flowers round the edge of it, and from side to side of the plate the little maiden rowed herself with oars made of horse hair.

One night, as she lay asleep, a large toad crept through a broken pane in the window and leapt up on the table. "What a lovely little creature this is!" she thought; "what a charming wife she would make for my son!" So she took up the walnut shell in which the little maiden lay under her coverlet of rose leaf, and leapt with it through the window, and hopped back into the garden.

Through the garden a broad stream flowed, and in its marshy banks the old toad lived with her son. He was uglier even than his mother, and when he saw the pretty little maiden in her beautiful bed he was able only to cry: "Croak, croak, croak."

"Don't make such a noise," said the old toad, "or you will wake her, and then she may fly away, for she is as light as thistledown. We will put her on one of the large water-lily leaves that grow in the middle of the stream. It will seem an island to her; she is so small. She will not be able to get away from it, and we shall have plenty of time to get ready the state room under the marsh, where you are to live when you are married."

Out in the middle of the stream grew a number of water lilies, with broad green leaves that floated on the top of the water. The largest of these leaves seemed much farther off than any of the rest, and thither the old toad swam, carrying with her the walnut shell in which Thumbeline lay asleep.

Early in the morning, the little creature awoke, and, when she saw where she was, began to cry bitterly, for all round the leaf there was water, and she could see no way of reaching the land.

Meanwhile, down in the marsh the old toad was as busy as possible decking out her room with sedge and yellow rushes, so as to make it pretty and comfortable for her new daughter-in-law. When she had finished she swam out with her ugly son to the leaf where she had placed Thumbeline. She wished to carry off the pretty bed, that she might put it in the bridal chamber to be ready for the bride. To the little maiden the old toad in the water bowed low and said: "Here is my son. He is to be your husband, and you will have a very happy life together in the fine house I have prepared for you down in the marsh by the stream."

"Croak, croak, croak," was all the ugly son could say.

So the old toad and her son took up the pretty little cradle and swam away with it, leaving Thumbeline weeping alone on the lily leaf. She could not bear to think of living with the old toad, and of having her ugly son for a husband.

Now the little fishes, who had been swimming about in the water, and had seen the old toad, and had heard every word she said, leaped up till their heads were above the water, so that they might see the little girl; and when they caught sight of her,

they saw that she was very pretty, and felt very sorry that anyone so pretty should have to go and live with the ugly toads.

"No!" said they. "Such a thing must never be allowed."

So all the little fishes gathered together in the water round the leaf on which the little maiden stood, and they bit the stalk with their teeth until at last they bit it through. Then away went the leaf, sailing down the stream, carrying Thumbeline far away.

Past many towns she sailed, and when the birds in the bushes saw her they sang: "What a lovely little girl!"

On floated the leaf, until at last she came to another land. Round her head a pretty white butterfly kept fluttering, till at last it settled on the leaf. He was greatly pleased with Thumbeline, and she was glad of it, for it was not possible now that the ugly toad could ever reach her, and the land through which she was sailing was very beautiful, and the sun shone on the water till it sparkled like silver. So Thumbeline took off her sash and tied one end of it round the butterfly, and the other end to the leaf, which now sped on faster than before.

Presently a great cockchafer flew past. The moment he caught sight of the maiden he seized her, and away he flew with her into a tree. But the green leaf floated on, and the butterfly flew with it; for he was tied to the leaf, and could not get away.

Oh, how frightened Thumbeline was when the cockchafer flew away with her into the tree! She was sorry, too, for the pretty white butterfly which she had tied to the leaf; for, if he could not free himself, he would certainly die of hunger. But the cockchafer sat down beside her on one of the leaves of the tree, and gave her some honey from a flower to eat, and told her that she was very pretty, though not at all like a cockchafer. In a little all the cockchafers that lived in the tree came to visit her. They stared their hardest at Thumbeline, and one cockchafer said: "Why, she has only two legs! How ugly that looks!"

"She has no feelers," said another; "how stupid she must be!"

"How slender her waist is!" said a third. "Pooh! she looks just like a human being."

"How ugly she is!" said all the lady cockchafers. Thumbeline was really very lovely, and the cockchafer who had carried her off thought so; but when they all said she was ugly, he began to think that it must be true. So he would have nothing more to say to Thumbeline, but told her that she might go where she pleased. Then the cockchafers flew down with her from the tree, and placed her on a daisy, and Thumbeline wept because she thought she was so ugly that the cockchafers would have nothing to say to her. And all the time she was in reality one of the loveliest creatures in the world, and as tender and delicate as a rose petal.

All the summer poor Thumbeline lived alone in the forest. She wove a little bed with blades of grass, and hung it up under a clover leaf so that she might be sheltered from the rain. For food she sucked the honey from the flowers, and from the leaves every morning she drank the dew. So the summer and autumn passed away, and then came the winter. The birds that had sung to her so sweetly had flown away; the trees had lost their leaves, and the flowers were withered. The great clover leaf under whose shelter she had lived was shrivelled up, and nothing was left but a withered stalk.

Poor Thumbeline felt very cold, for her clothes were torn, and she was such a delicate little thing that she nearly died. The snow began to fall, and each flake, as it fell on her, was like a whole shovelful falling on one of us; for she was only about an inch high. Then she rolled herself up in a dry leaf; but it cracked in the middle, and there was no warmth in it, so she shivered with cold. Very near the wood in which she had been living there was a large corn-field; but the corn had been cut long before this, and there was nothing left but the hard, dry stubble standing out of the frozen ground. To Thumbeline, going through it, it was like struggling through another forest; and, oh, how cold it was! At last she came to the door of the house of a field-mouse, who lived in a hole under the stubble. It was a warm, cosy house, and the mouse was very happy, for she had a roomful of corn, besides a kitchen and a fine dining-room. Poor little Thumbeline stood before the door, just like a beggar girl, and prayed the mouse for a small bit of barley corn, because she was starving.

"Poor thing!" said the field-mouse, who was a kind-hearted creature; "come into my warm room and have dinner." The mouse was greatly pleased with Thumbeline, so she said: "If you like, you can spend the winter with me: of course you will keep my rooms tidy and tell me stories."

Thumbeline did all the kind old mouse asked, and was well treated and very comfortable. "We shall have a visitor soon," said the field-mouse one day; "my neighbour pays me a visit once a week. He is much richer than I am; he has fine large rooms and wears a beautiful black velvet fur. If you could get him for a husband you would indeed be well off. He is blind though, poor man! so you must tell him some of your prettiest stories." Thumbeline knew that the neighbour was only a mole, and she did not mean to trouble herself about him.

The mole came and paid his visit. He was dressed in his black velvet coat.

" He is very learned and rich," whispered the field-mouse to Thumbeline, "and his house is twenty times larger than mine."

Rich no doubt he was, and learned; but never having seen the sun or the beautiful flowers, he always spoke slightingly regarding them. Thumbeline had to sing to him; so she sang "Lady-bird, lady-bird, fly away home", and "As I was going along, long, long", and other songs, and the mole fell deeply in love with her because she had such a sweet voice.

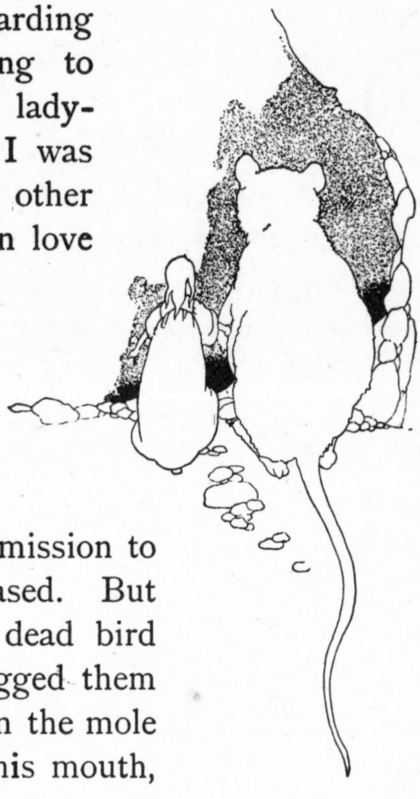

A short time before, the mole had dug a long underground passage between the two houses, and he gave the field-mouse and Thumbeline permission to walk in this whenever they pleased. But he told them that there was a dead bird lying in the passage, and he begged them not to be frightened by it. Then the mole took a piece of rotten wood in his mouth, and it shone like fire in the darkness, and he went before them to light them through the passage. When they came to where the dead bird lay, the mole pushed his broad nose through the ceiling so as to make a hole.

The daylight fell through the hole and shone on the body of the dead swallow. Its pretty wings were folded, and its head and claws hidden under its feathers. It made the little girl very sad to see it, for she dearly loved the birds. But the unfeeling mole thrust the swallow aside with his crooked legs, and said: "He will sing no more. What a wretched thing it must be to be a bird."

"Indeed you may well say so," cried the field-mouse. Thumbeline did not speak; but when the other two turned their backs on the dead bird, she stooped down and smoothed aside the feathers that covered the head, and kissed the closed eyelids.

"Perhaps t was you who sang so sweetly to me in the summer," she said; "how much pleasure you gave me, you dear pretty bird!"

The mole then stopped up the hole through which the daylight came, and walked home with the ladies. But at night Thumbeline could not sleep; so she got out of bed, and wove a fine large rug of soft hay. When she had finished it, she gathered together some soft flower down that she found in the field-mouse's sitting-room, and carried the rug and the down to the dead bird. The down was soft and warm like wool, and she put it carefully round him, and spread the coverlet over him, that he might lie warm in the cold earth.

"Goodbye! you dear, pretty bird," said she. "Thank you for all the sweet songs you sang in the summer, when the trees were green and the sun shone warmly." Saying this she laid her head on the breast of the bird; but almost at once she raised it in surprise. It seemed as if something inside the bird was going "thump, thump". It was the swallow's heart. The swallow had not been really dead, but only numbed with the cold, and when the warmth again stole over him his life came back.

Thumbeline trembled with fear, for the bird seemed very large in comparison with a little thing only an inch long. But her pity was stronger than her fear, and, being brave, she covered the poor swallow more thickly with the down, and ran and brought a balsam leaf that she herself had used as a coverlet, and spread it over the bird's head.

Next night she again stole into the passage to see him. He was still alive, but he was very weak, and could only open his eyes to look for a moment at his kind nurse, who stood over him, holding in her hand a rotten piece of wood, for she had no other light.

"Thank you, pretty maiden," whispered the sick swallow; "I am nice and warm now; I shall soon get back my strength, and be able to fly about again in the sunshine."

"Alas!" said she. "You must wait for some time. It is too cold out-of-doors just now; it snows and freezes. You

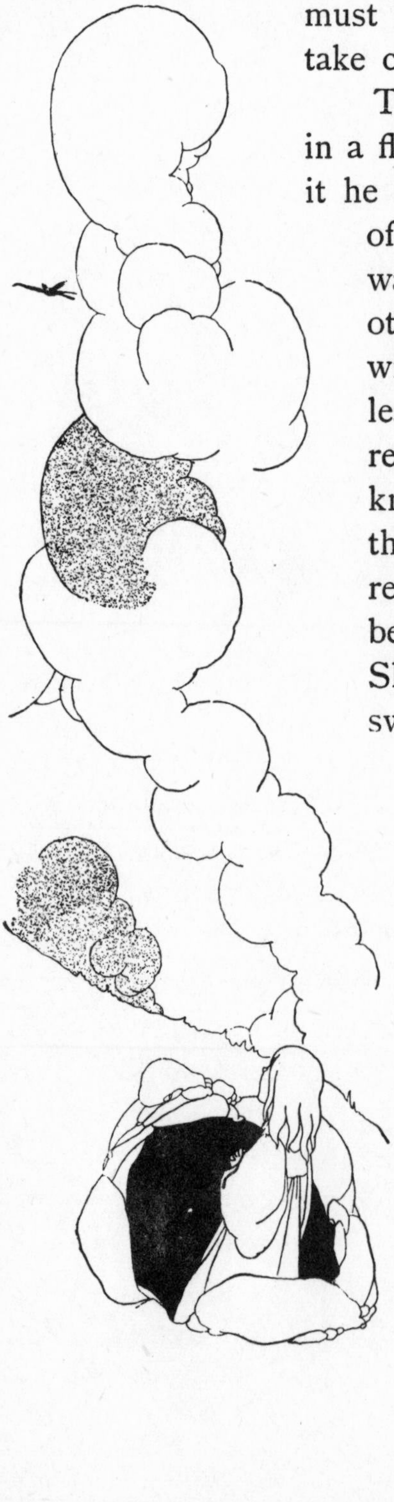

must stay in your warm bed, and I will take care of you."

Then she brought him some water in a flower leaf; and when he had drunk it he told her how he had wounded one of his wings in a thorn bush, and was not able to fly as fast as the other swallows; how they flew away without him; and how he fell senseless to the ground. He could not remember any more, and did not know how he came to be where he then lay. All the winter the swallow remained underground, and Thumbeline nursed him with tender care. She did not say a word about the swallow to the mole or field-mouse, for they did not like birds. Soon the spring came, and the sun warmed the earth, and the swallow said goodbye to his kind little nurse. She opened the hole in the ceiling which the mole had made, and the glorious sunshine poured into the passage, and the swallow begged her to go away with him. "She could sit on his back," he said; "and he would fly away with her into the green woods." But the little maiden knew that it would vex the field-mouse if she left her in that way, so she said: "No, I cannot come."

"Goodbye, then, goodbye, you little darling," said the swallow; and away he flew. Thumbeline gazed after him, and tears filled her eyes. She dearly loved the pretty swallow, whose life she had saved.

"Joy, joy!" sang the bird as he flew away, But poor Thumbeline was very sorrowful. She was not able to get out into the warm sunshine; for the corn which the farmer had sown in the field over the house of the field-mouse had grown up so high that it seemed a lofty and pathless wood to the maiden who was only an inch high.

"Now," said the field-mouse to her one day, "you are going to be married, Thumbeline. My neighbour, the mole, has proposed for you. You must begin to get your wedding clothes ready. You must have both woollen and linen, for nothing must be wanting in the wedding outfit of a mole's bride."

Thumbeline had to set to work with the spindle, and the field-mouse hired four spiders who had to weave day and night. Every evening the mole came, and he always spoke of the time when the summer would be over. Then he said they would be married. Just now the sun was so hot that it burned up the ground and made it as hard as a stone. But the little maiden was not at all happy. She thought the mole tiresome, and did not like him. In the morning when the sun rose, and in the evening when he set, she used to creep out at the door, and when the wind blew aside the ears of corn so that she could catch a glimpse of the blue sky, she used to think how lovely it was in the light, and long to see her dear swallow once more. When the autumn came, Thumbeline had her wedding outfit ready; and the field-mouse said to her: "Well, Thumbeline, in a month you shall be married." But the girl cried, and said she would never marry the tiresome mole.

"Nonsense!" said the mouse. "Don't be foolish, or I shall bite you. The mole will make you a handsome husband. The queen herself does not wear such a black velvet coat. He has, besides, a full kitchen and cellar. You ought to be thankful for your good fortune."

At length the wedding-day arrived. The mole came to fetch his bride. Thumbeline would have to go away and live with him under the earth, and never see the warm sun, because he did not like it. The poor little maid was very sad at the thought of saying farewell to the beautiful sun; and as the field-mouse had permitted her to stand at the door, she went out to look at it once more, and to say farewell to it.

"Farewell, dear bright sun!" she cried, stretching out her arms towards it. Then she walked a little away from the house, for the corn had been cut, and there was only the dry stubble left. "Farewell!" she said again, throwing her arms round a little red flower that grew close beside her. "Give my love to the swallow, if you should ever see him again."

Suddenly "Tweet, tweet" sounded over her head. She looked up, and there was the swallow flying past. As soon as he spied Thumbeline he flew to her with delight, and she told him her story, how unwilling she was to marry the stupid mole, and to live always under the earth, and never again see the bright sun. As she told him she could not help weeping.

THUMBELINE

"Then she sat down on the bird's back"

"The cold winter is coming," said the swallow, "and I am going to fly to a warmer land. Will you come with me? Tie yourself on my back. Then we will fly far away over the hills to warmer lands—where the sunshine is brighter than it is here, where there are lovely flowers, and it is always summer. Fly away with me, dear little Thumbeline."

"Yes, I will come with you," said the little maiden. Then she sat down on the bird's back with her feet resting on his outspread wings; and she fastened her girdle to one of his stronger feathers. And the swallow rose high into the air, and flew over forest and lake, and over snow-capped mountains. Poor Thumbeline would have been frozen, but she crept under the bird's warm feathers, peeping out from time to time so that she might catch a glimpse of the beautiful lands over which they were passing. At last they reached the warm countries. There by the wayside, and on the hedges, grew purple and green and white grapes, and pale lemons and golden oranges hung from the trees in the woods. The air was fragrant with the scent of myrtle and balm, and along the country lanes ran beautiful children, playing with large gay butterflies. The farther the swallow flew the more beautiful every place seemed to grow. At last they came to a lovely blue lake, and by the side of it, shaded by stately green trees, stood a pure white marble castle. It was an old building, and the vine leaves twined round its lofty columns. At the top of these there were many swallows' nests, and one of these was the nest of the swallow who carried Thumbeline.

"This is my house," said the swallow; "but it would not do for you to live here. Will you choose for yourself

one of those beautiful flowers?—and I will put you down on it, and then you shall have everything you can wish to make you happy."

"That will be charming," cried the little maiden, and clapped her tiny hands.

On the ground lay a large marble pillar, which had fallen and been broken into three pieces. Between the pieces grew the most beautiful large white flowers. The swallow flew down with Thumbeline and set her on one of the broad leaves. How surprised she was to see, in the middle of the flower, a tiny little man as white and transparent as glass! On his head was a graceful golden crown, and at his shoulders a pair of delicate wings. He was not much larger than the little maid herself. He was the flower-elf. An elf-man and an elf-maid live in every flower, and this was the King of all the flower-elves.

"How beautiful he is!" whispered Thumbeline.

The little flower-king was at first quite frightened at the bird. Compared to such a little thing as himself it was a giant. But when he saw Thumbeline he was charmed. Never had he seen such a pretty girl. He took the gold crown from his head and placed it on hers; he asked her name, and begged her to marry him, and become as she should the Queen of all the flowers.

This was certainly a different kind of husband from the son of the toad or from the mole with his black velvet coat; so she said "Yes" to this handsome prince, her new suitor. Then all the flowers opened, and out of each came a tiny lady and gentleman. They each brought Thumbeline a present; but the present she loved most of all was a pair of lovely white wings from a big white fly. When these were fastened to her shoulders she could fly from flower to flower.

Then there were great rejoicings, and the swallow, who sat in his nest overhead, was asked to sing a wedding song. He sang as well as he could; but his heart was sad, for he was very fond of the little maiden, and had hoped never again to part from her.

"You must no longer be called Thumbeline," said the flower-elf to her. "It's an ugly name, and you are very beautiful. We will call you Maia."

"Goodbye," sang the swallow, sad at heart, as he left the warm lands and flew away to the colder North. There he had a nest outside the window of a man who could tell fairy tales. For him the swallow sang "Tweet, tweet", and that's how we came to hear the whole story.

The Goose Girl

AN old widowed Queen had a beautiful daughter betrothed to a Prince who lived far away. As the time drew near for her to be married, she got ready to set off on her journey to his country. The Queen packed up many costly things—jewels, and gold, and silver; trinkets, fine dresses, everything that became a royal bride, for she loved her child very dearly; and she gave her a waiting-maid to ride with her, and each had a horse for the journey. The Princess's horse was called Falada, and it could speak.

When the time came for them to set out, the old Queen went into her bedchamber, and took a little knife, and cut off a lock of her hair, and gave it to her daughter, and said: "Take care of it, dear child; it is a charm that may be of use to you." Then they took sorrowful leave of each other, and the Princess set off on her journey. As they were riding along by the side of a brook, she felt very thirsty, and said to her maid: "Pray get down and fetch me some water in my golden cup."

"Nay," said the maid, "if you are thirsty, get down yourself, and lie down by the water and drink; I shall not be your waiting-maid any longer."

She was so thirsty that she got down, and knelt over the little brook and drank, for she was frightened, and dared not bring out her golden cup; and then she wept, and said: "Alas! what will become of me?" And the lock of hair answered her, and said:

> "Alas! alas! if thy mother knew it,
> Sadly, sadly her heart would rue it."

The Princess said nothing to her maid's ill behaviour, but got upon her horse again.

They rode farther, till the day grew so warm that the bride began to feel very thirsty again; and at last, when they came to a river, she forgot her maid's rude speech, and said: "Pray get down and fetch me some water to drink in my golden cup."

But the maid answered her even more haughtily than before: "Drink if you will, but I shall not be your waiting-maid." The Princess was so thirsty that she got off her horse and lay down, and held her head over the running stream, and cried, and said: "What will become of me?" And the lock of hair answered her again:

"Alas! alas! if thy mother knew it,
Sadly, sadly her heart would rue it."

And as she leaned down to drink, the lock of hair fell from her bosom and floated away, without her seeing it. But her maid saw it, and was very glad, for she knew the charm, and saw that the poor bride would be in her power, now that she had lost the hair. So when the bride had done, and would have got upon Falada again, the maid said: "I shall ride upon Falada, and you may have my horse instead:" so she was forced to give up her horse, and soon afterwards to take off her royal clothes, and put on her maid's shabby ones.

As they drew near the end of their journey, this treacherous servant threatened to kill her mistress if she ever told anyone what had happened. But Falada saw it all and marked it well. Then the waiting-maid got upon Falada, and the real bride was set upon the other horse, and they went on till at last they came to the royal Court. There was great joy at their coming, and the Prince flew to meet them, and lifted the maid from her horse, thinking she

was the one who was to be his wife. She was led to the royal chamber, but the true Princess was told to stay in the court below.

The old King happened to be looking out of the window, and saw her; and as she looked very pretty, and too delicate for a waiting-maid, he went into the royal chamber to ask the bride who it was she had brought with her, that was left standing in the court below. "I brought her with me for the sake of her company on the road," said she; "pray give the girl some work to do, that she may not be idle."

The old King could not for some time think of any work for her; but at last he said: "I have a lad who takes care of my geese; she may go and help him." Now the name of this lad, that the real bride was to help, was Curdken.

Soon after, the false bride said to the Prince: "Dear husband, pray do me one piece of kindness."

"That I will," said the Prince. "Then tell one of your slaughterers to cut off the head of the horse I rode upon, for it was very unruly, and plagued me sadly on the road:" but the truth was, she was much afraid lest Falada should tell all she had done to the Princess. She carried her point, and the faithful Falada was killed; but when the true Princess heard of it she wept, and begged the man to nail up Falada's head against a large dark gate in the city, through which she had to pass every morning and evening, that there she might still see him sometimes. Then the slaughterer said he would do as she wished, cut off the head, and nailed it under the dark gate.

Early the next morning, as she and Curdken went through the gate, she said sorrowfully:

"Falada, Falada, there thou art hanging!"

and the head answered:

"Bride, bride, there thou art ganging!
Alas! alas! if thy mother knew it,
Sadly, sadly her heart would rue it."

Then they drove the geese on. And when she came to the meadow, she sat down upon a bank, and let down her waving locks of hair, which were all

of pure silver. And when Curdken saw it glitter in the sun, he ran up, and would have pulled some of the locks out; but she cried:

"Blow, breezes, blow!
Let Curdken's hat go!
Blow, breezes, blow!
Let him after it go!
O'er hills, dales, and rocks,
Away be it whirl'd,
Till the silvery locks
Are all comb'd and curl'd!"

Then there came a wind, that blew off Curdken's hat; and away it flew, and he after it; till, by the time he came back, she had done combing and curling her hair, and put it up again. Then he was angry and sulky, and would not speak to her; but they watched the geese until evening, and then drove them homewards.

The next morning, as they were going through the dark gate, the poor girl looked up at Falada's head, and cried:

"Falada, Falada, there thou art hanging!"

and it answered:

"Bride, bride, there thou art ganging!
Alas! alas! if thy mother knew it,
Sadly, sadly her heart would rue it."

Then she drove on the geese, and sat down again in the meadow, and began to comb out her hair as before; and Curdken ran up to her, and wanted to take hold of it; but she cried quickly:

"Blow, breezes, blow!
Let Curdken's hat go!
Blow, breezes, blow!
Let him after it go!
O'er hills, dales, and rocks,
Away be it whirl'd,
Till the silvery locks
Are all comb'd and curl'd!"

Then the wind came and blew his hat far away, so that he had to run after it; and when he came back, she had done up her hair, and all was safe.

THE GOOSE GIRL

After they came home, Curdken went to the old King and said: "I cannot have that strange girl to help me to keep the geese any longer."

"Why?" asked the King.

"Because she does nothing but tease me all day long." Then the King made him tell all that had passed.

And Curdken said: "When we go in the morning through the dark gate with our flock of geese, she weeps, and talks with the head of a horse that hangs upon the wall, and says:

"'Falada, Falada, there thou art hanging!"

and the head answers:

"'Bride, bride, there thou art ganging!
Alas! alas! if thy mother knew it,
Sadly, sadly her heart would rue it.'"

And Curdken went on telling what had happened where the geese fed; and how his hat was blown away, and he was forced to run after it, and leave his flock. The old King told him to go out again as usual the next day; and when morning came, he placed himself behind the dark gate, and heard how she spoke to Falada, and how Falada answered; and then he went into the field and hid himself in a bush by the

meadow's side, and saw with his own eyes how they drove the flock of geese, and how, after a little time, she let down her hair that glittered in the sun; and he heard her say:

"Blow, breezes, blow!
Let Curdken's hat go!
Blow, breezes, blow!
Let him after it go!
O'er hills, dales, and rocks,
Away be it whirl'd,
Till the silvery locks
Are all comb'd and curl'd!"

Soon came a gale of wind, and carried away Curdken's hat, while the girl went on combing and curling her hair. All this the old King saw. So he went home without being seen; and when the goose girl came back in the evening, he called her aside, and asked her why she did so; but she burst into tears, and said: "That I must not tell you or any man, or I shall lose my life."

But the old King begged so hard, that she had no peace till she had told him all; and it was lucky for her that she did, for the King ordered royal clothes to be put upon her, and gazed on her with wonder, she was so beautiful. Then he called his son, and told him that he had only the false bride, for that she was merely a waiting-maid, while the true one stood by. And the young King rejoiced when he saw her beauty, and heard how meek and patient she had been; and, without saying anything, ordered a great feast to be got ready for all his Court. The bridegroom sat at the top, with the false Princess on one side, and the true one on the other; but nobody knew her, for she was quite dazzling to their eyes, and was not at all like the little goose girl, now that she had her brilliant dress.

When they had eaten and drank, and were very merry, the old King told all the story, as one that he had once heard of, and asked the true waiting-maid what she thought ought to be done to anyone who would behave thus. "Nothing better," said this false bride, "than that she should be thrown into a cask stuck round with sharp nails, and that two white horses should be put to it, and should drag it from street to street till she is dead." "Thou art she!" said the old King; "and since thou hast judged thyself, it shall be so done to thee." And the young King was married to his true wife, and they reigned over the kingdom in peace and happiness all their lives.

Goldmaria and Goldfeather

ONCE a nobleman had a beautiful daughter named Goldmaria. Her parents one day went on an excursion, and Goldmaria remained at home. On their return, they lost their way in a vast forest, when they were met by a large poodle. "I will lead you into the right path," said the poodle, "if you will give me that which first meets you from your house."

The parents instantly thought of their dear Goldmaria, and feared that she might be the first to meet them; but as the weather became worse, and they had lost their way, they at last consented, and promised the poodle what he required, thinking that the housedog might probably be the first to come to their carriage. They soon reached home; but the first that came to their carriage was Goldmaria. Said the poodle: "She now belongs to me and not to you." The parents besought him to take everything else, only to leave their dear Goldmaria; but the poodle would not hear them and would have Goldmaria, and no prayers were of any avail. A respite of three days would he grant them, and then fetch her away.

Goldmaria employed her time in taking leave of her friends. Amid their tears she was calm and content. On the last evening she said to her mother: "I will now bid farewell to our old neighbour." When she came, the old woman said: "Fear nothing, my child; if thou wilt sleep with me to-night, I will teach thee *to wish*, and that will be highly useful to thee." Goldmaria was quite rejoiced, and went back to her mother to tell her she would pass the night with her neighbour. When Goldmaria rose on the following morning she could conjure forth anything that she *wished*; and, having thanked the old woman, took leave, hoping that, by means of her art, she might be able to see her parents as often as she desired.

When she returned home, the poodle was already there to fetch her away. Goldmaria bade farewell to her disconsolate parents, but made no mention of her having learned *to wish*. On coming to the open country the poodle said to her: "Set thyself on my back, and I will soon bring thee to our journey's end." Goldmaria did so, and in a short time they came to a house, in which were two young maidens. When they entered, the poodle immediately transformed himself into an old woman, the mother of the two maidens.

"Now," said she, "I have three lasses in whom I can find pleasure. Thou, Goldmaria, will be very happy with me, if thou wilt be obedient."

Goldmaria promised to be so, and whenever the old woman said: "Goldmaria, do this, or do that," she would always do it quickly, as she had only to *wish* it.

One day when the old woman, in the likeness of a poodle, went into the forest, she met a comely young man, who had lost his way and was named Goldfeather. The poodle said: "I will conduct thee out of the forest, if thou wilt promise to return and abide with me." Goldfeather answered that he could make no promise, for that he was a king's son, and must speak with his father. At length, however, when he found himself quite unable to recover his path, he was obliged to say *yes*, and promise to belong to the poodle, who then conducted him out of the forest to his father's Court. But at the expiration of three days he returned to fetch away Goldfeather. The father at first would not deliver him up, but was at length forced to comply, when the poodle said: "Goldfeather has himself promised, and he must keep his word." So Goldfeather came to the place where Goldmaria was.

Goldmaria said to Goldfeather: "Be on thy guard against the old woman, for she is a bad one, and can do more than eat bread. To-morrow thou wilt certainly have to mow the grass."

"But," answered Goldfeather, "I cannot; I don't know how I am to do it."

And so it proved; for in the evening the old woman said to him: "Goldfeather, thou must get a scythe ready, for to-morrow thou shalt mow the grass."

Goldfeather then went to Goldmaria and said: "I am to get a scythe ready, and don't know how."

"Oh," said she, "just knock a little on the scythe, then it will soon be ready!" Goldfeather did so, and the scythe was instantly fit for use.

On the following morning the old woman said: "Goldfeather, go and mow the grass." He went first to Goldmaria, and asked her: "How am I to do it? I know nothing of the matter."

Goldmaria answered: "Only strike the scythe, so that it rings, about the time when the old woman brings thee food."

Goldfeather then went to the meadow and laid himself down to sleep; but at the time when his food was to be brought, he struck the scythe so that it rang, and in one

moment all the grass fell down at once. Now came the old woman, who, seeing that all was done, praised him, and promised that he should be rewarded.

On the day following, the old woman said to Goldfeather: "My son, go to-day and sharpen an axe, for thou shalt cut wood." He did not know how to sharpen an axe, and so went to Goldmaria for her instruction. She said: "Take a stone and rub it twice or thrice up and down the axe, and it will instantly be sharp." Goldfeather did so.

Shortly after, the old woman said to him: "Now go into

the forest and hew wood." He went, but could accomplish nothing.

At length came Goldmaria and brought him his breakfast. "Ah," said he, "thou must help me again, for I know nothing about woodcutting!"

"So," answered she, "it seems, then, that I am always to help thee and thou never helpest me."

"Oh, dearest Goldmaria," answered Goldfeather, "I will ever love thee and never forsake thee as long as there is a drop of warm blood within me! Help me but this time out of difficulty."

"Well then," said she, "only turn the axe round and strike the tree." He did so, and in a moment all the wood was hewed. The old mother was astonished at his diligence, and promised that it should be for his advantage. When Goldfeather returned home in the evening, he threw himself on his bed, thought much on his parents, but much more on Goldmaria.

The next day the old woman said: "Thou must get some rakes ready, for to-day, thou shalt all turn the hay and carry it in."

"Mother," said the daughters, "how can we carry in the hay? It is not possible."

"It shall be done, and you must do it," answered the mother. Goldfeather then went, and, with the aid of Goldmaria, prepared the rakes. When both the daughters, together with Goldfeather, were out in the field, where they were joined by Goldmaria, Goldfeather said to her: "How are we to carry in the hay?"

"Just do as I do," answered she; "only lay a stick on the nape of thy neck, and the hay will be soon got in." So when the two daughters were foremost with a small quantity of hay, Goldmaria and Goldfeather placed sticks on the nape of their necks, and all the hay came after them, and they soon had it all together in the place where it was to lie.

On the following day, he was ordered to bring wood home. But when he went for the purpose, he could bring only a very small quantity and was soon weary, so was obliged again to have recourse to Goldmaria, who said to him: "Do as thou didst with the hay;" and when Goldfeather had so done, all the wood was soon in the house Then said the old woman: "Now get some spades in readiness, for to-morrow thou shalt dig clay. Make also some moulds, for thou shalt also make bricks." Now must Goldmaria again give her aid, so that the spades and moulds were soon ready, and when Goldfeather set about digging clay, and could extract none, Goldmaria again came to his assistance, and told him he had only to thrust vigorously with the spade, and there would fly out clay enough. When Goldfeather had finished his task the eldest daughter came and praised him to the skies; whereupon Goldmaria said: "You praise him too much, for I have shared in the work." But the daughter still thought that Goldfeather deserved the greatest praise.

"It bodes no good to me," said Goldmaria to Goldfeather, when the daughter had left them, "that she praised thee so warmly."

But Goldfeather answered: "I will surely be true to thee, dear Goldmaria, as long as I live."

When the old woman came, she ordered the bricks to be made. Goldfeather made them, and, when they were dry,

would carry them to the house, but found them too heavy; recourse must again be had to Goldmaria. "Thou art truly a dolt," said she. "How often have I told thee that thou hadst only to take a stick and lay it on thy neck, and that then all would be easy."

Goldfeather then laid a stick across the nape of his neck, and all the bricks followed him. The old woman next asked him: "Dost thou know how to build an oven?"

"No," answered he, "but I will do my best."

So Goldfeather set to work, but could neither prepare the mortar nor lay the bricks, and must therefore again apply to Goldmaria to help him out of his trouble.

"Oh, thou canst do nothing!" said she. "Take a stick and beat the mortar with it, then it will be fit for use; and for the walls thou canst hammer a bit on a brick, and the oven will be ready." When he had finished, Goldmaria came to him and said: "We must now prepare for travelling; for I heard the old woman say we were too clever, and that when the oven was ready, we should be baked in it. Now I tell thee, Goldfeather, that, if thy life is dear to thee, thou must not leave me; for thou alone canst effect nothing against the old beldam. To-morrow she will allow thee to rest, and will bake thee the day after; be therefore on thy guard." Goldfeather was greatly alarmed, and it proved exactly as Goldmaria had said.

"To-morrow," said the old woman to him, "thou canst rest."

But quite early, just at the break of day, Goldmaria rose and waked Goldfeather. They soon made themselves ready, and when about to set out Goldmaria spat on each side of her chamber door and said: "When the old woman calls me the first time, do thou answer, *I am coming*; and if she calls a second time, answer, *I am coming directly*." In the morning the old woman screamed out for Goldmaria, and the door answered her: "I am coming." When she called a second time, the door answered: "I am coming directly." But no one came.

The old woman at length rose, looked into the chamber and into the kitchen, but no one was in either place. She then waked both her daughters, and said: "Rise up quickly;

Goldmaria and Goldfeather are away, and you must go after them. Go thou first," said she to the younger. "On the declivity of the Blue Mountain there stands a rosebush with a withered rose; that thou must on no account fail to pluck and bring to me." The daughter went in all haste after the fugitives, who had already proceeded a considerable distance, when Goldmaria said to Goldfeather: "Tread on my left foot, and look over my right shoulder whether anyone is coming."

Goldfeather did so and said: "The younger daughter is coming in all haste after us."

Goldmaria thereupon said: "I will then turn myself into a rosebush, and thee into a withered rose; but let not thyself be plucked, and prick her smartly; for if she plucks thee, we are both lost."

When the girl came to the rose, she was about to pluck it, but it pricked her so severely that she was forced to desist. She then returned home and was well scolded for her stupidity.

The old woman then said to the elder daughter: "Do thou now go, and when thou art over the Blue Mountain, thou wilt see a white church, in which there is a preacher in the pulpit: take him by the hand and bring him with thee."

Goldmaria and Goldfeather had in

the meanwhile proceeded farther; but Goldmaria soon said: "Tread on my left foot, and look over my right shoulder whether anyone is coming."

"Yes," answered Goldfeather, "the elder daughter is coming."

"Then," said Goldmaria, "I will turn myself into a church, and thee into a priest; but let her not lay hold of thee, else we are lost."

Now came the daughter and entered the church, but was unable to ascend the pulpit and obliged to return home. At seeing her the old woman's rage exceeded all bounds, and she ran forth herself. Then said Goldmaria to Goldfeather: "Tread on my left foot, and look over my right shoulder whether anyone is coming after us."

"Yes," answered Goldfeather, "the old woman herself is now coming."

"Then I will turn myself into a pond, and thee into a duck; but I beseech thee, Goldfeather, let not thyself be enticed to the edge, so that she may take hold of thee; but take the gold rings, which she will cast in for the purpose of catching thee, if thou canst get them without danger."

Now came the old woman to the pond, and would decoy the duck, which continued swimming about. She threw in her gold rings, one after another, but the duck was not to be so tempted; and when she had thrown in the last she was so angry that she resolved to drink up the pond, and, laying herself down for the purpose, drank so long that she burst. Goldmaria and Goldfeather now resumed their natural forms, and swore eternal fidelity to each other, and that they would never part. From the old woman there was now nothing more to fear.

They at length reached the city in which Goldfeather's father resided. When they came before the palace, and Goldfeather was about to enter, Goldmaria said to him: "Hear me, Goldfeather; I have only one request to make thee, that thou mayest not forget me when thou art in thy father's house, and leave me here without, standing on the broad stone. Beware that no one kisses thee; for then thou wilt instantly forget me." Goldfeather promised, and recollected the warning on entering the house; and when his father and mother hastened to welcome him, he did not kiss them. But when he entered an apartment, there sat his old betrothed, whose name was Menne, who, the instant she saw him, sprang up for joy and kissed him. In one moment all remembrance of Goldmaria was banished from his mind. She stood long without, expecting that he would send for her; but, finding that no one came, she wept for a long time, then took her departure, hired a neat little cottage opposite the palace, and gave herself out as a seamstress. Being admirably skilled in needlework, she soon got an abundance of work; no young person in the city being able to sew more curiously and beautifully.

The young sparks of the Court had in the meantime discovered what a handsome maiden Goldmaria was. But Goldmaria paid no heed to them, and never looked from her work, when they passed before her window. Among these young courtiers there were three brothers, all of whom were deeply in love with Goldmaria. They one day begged some fine linen of their mother, saying that Goldmaria worked so delicately, they wished her to make them some collars. The eldest was the first that went to Goldmaria, wished her a good day, and sat down to converse with her. "To-morrow evening you can fetch your collars," said Goldmaria. When the time came for fetching the collars, she invited him to stay awhile, and he remained till bedtime. When he was about to take leave, she said to him that he was welcome to stay there that night, which the young man was perfectly ready to do. When Goldmaria was retiring to rest, she requested him to go and lock the door of the house, and when he touched the lock, she cried out:

"Man to lock and lock to man,
Then go to rest I calmly can."

There he was obliged to remain the whole night. In the morning, when Goldmaria rose, she recollected that he was yet there, and said:

"Man from lock and lock from man,
Then give thanks for his sleep he can."

He then entered, returned thanks for his tranquil sleep, took his collars, with which he was much pleased, and went away. At home he made no mention of his

adventure. His younger brother then said: "This evening I must away to the seamstress."

He went accordingly, and said: "I wish to have some collars made like my brother's."

"Those you can easily have," said Goldmaria; "sit down and stay a little."

They then entered into conversation, while Goldmaria sewed. When it was time for him to depart, she told him that he was welcome to stay there that night; but before she withdrew, she said: "I have quite forgotten to fasten the garden door; would you have the kindness to fasten it for me?"

"Most willingly," answered he, and hastened away for the purpose; but the instant he touched the ring of the door, she cried out:

"Man to ring and ring to man,
Then go to rest I calmly can."

He was unable to get loose, and had to remain standing until morning, when Goldmaria rose and said:

"Man from ring and ring from man,
Then give thanks for his sleep he can."

Being released, he entered and thanked her for his comfortable sleep.

On his return home with the collars, his elder brother instantly asked him where he had been standing all night.

"What?" answered he. "Why, I have been sleeping."

"That's not true," said the other; "so tell me where thou

hast been standing, and I'll tell thee where I was standing."

He then said: "I have been standing by the garden door."

"And I by the house door," said the other. They then agreed not to say a word of what had befallen them to their youngest brother, that he might also be tricked.

In the evening the youngest brother went. "Good evening, Goldmaria," said he; "wilt thou make me two or three collars like those of my brothers?"

"Most willingly," answered Goldmaria; "just sit down a little while and stay."

When evening was over, she also requested him to remain there all night; but just as she was about to retire, she said to him: "Oh, my calf is not yet tethered, and is running about the yard! Do me the kindness——"

"With pleasure," answered he, running out; but on his touching the rope, she cried:

"Man to rope and rope to man,
Then go to rest I calmly can."

The calf then began running with him, over stock and stone, and through thick and thin, the whole night long. In the morning Goldmaria recollected that the young man was still running about with the calf, and said:

"Man from rope and rope from man,
Then give thanks for his sleep he can."

He then entered, thanked her for his comfortable sleep, and was exceedingly delighted with his collars, which were much handsomer than those she had made for his brothers. On his return home, and his brothers asking him how he had passed the night, he would not confess that he had been running about with the calf.

Matters had in the meantime proceeded so far with Goldfeather and Menne, that the day was fixed for their marriage. When the carriage with the bridal pair came down from the palace, and was passing by Goldmaria's window, she *wished* that it might sink in a deep swamp that was exactly before her door. The carriage stuck fast accordingly, so that neither horses nor men could draw it from the spot. At this the old King was sorely vexed, and ordered more horses to be put to, and that more men should assist, but all to no purpose. Among the retinue, which attended the bridegroom to church, were the three brothers before-mentioned, the eldest of whom said to the King: "Sir King, here in this small house there dwells a maiden that can *wish* whatever she desires; and she has surely wished the carriage to stick fast in this place."

"How dost thou know that she can do so?" asked the old King.

The young man answered:

"She lately wished me to the house door, and there I was obliged to stand all night."

"Yes," said the second brother, "but when she has wished anyone fast, she can also wish him loose."

"And how dost thou know that?" enquired the King.

"I was lately obliged to stand the whole night at her garden door; but in the morning she released me."

The old King would then instantly send to Goldmaria, but the youngest brother said:

"Sir King, the young woman has also a calf that has the strength of ten horses. Let the bridegroom go to her and beg her to lend us the calf; the carriage will then be soon set free."

"That I'll do most readily," said the bridegroom, at the same time alighting from the vehicle and going to Goldmaria, whom he besought to lend him her calf, which, as he had heard, possessed such wonderful power.

"The calf you can have and welcome," answered she, "but you must first promise that I shall be invited to the wedding, together with my doves."

This the bridegroom promised, and as soon as the calf was harnessed to the vehicle, it drew it forth with perfect ease.

After the ceremony, when the young couple had returned home, and many guests were assembled, Goldmaria also made her appearance with her two doves. She met with a friendly reception, and was conducted into the saloon, having a dove perched on each shoulder. At table the most costly dishes were served up, portions of which were set before Goldmaria; but she touched nothing, and sat sad and silent. At seeing so fair a damsel sitting so sad, and tasting nothing, the guests were astonished, and on asking her the cause, the doves answered:

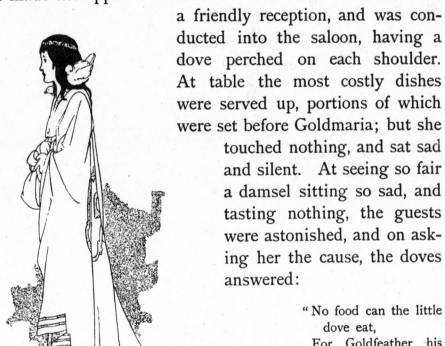

"No food can the little
 dove eat,
For Goldfeather his
 bride has forgotten,
And left on the stone
 in the street."

The bridegroom, hearing this, ordered the servants to place before her viands yet more costly; but Goldmaria touched nothing, and the doves repeated:

"No food can the little dove eat,
For Goldfeather his bride has forgotten,
And left on the stone in the street."

At this the bridegroom became lost in thought, looked steadfastly at Goldmaria, and recognized her. He then addressed his bride: "My dear bride, I pray thee answer me one question. I have a cabinet in which there are two keys, an old one, which I once lost, but have now found again, and a new one, which I procured in place of the old one, when that was lost. Tell me now which of the two I ought to use first, the old one or the new?"

She answered: "Thou shouldst first use the old one."

"Thou hast now," replied he, "pronounced thy own sentence; for this is my dear Goldmaria, with whom I have shared joy and sorrow at the old witch's in the forest, who at all times aided me, who saved me, and to whom I have sworn eternal fidelity."

Menne then, having no alternative, renounced Goldfeather, and all the people, and his and her parents, declared there was no one that so well deserved to be his wife as Goldmaria. They were then married and lived happily together for very many years

The Three Soldiers

THREE poor soldiers who, having fought hard in the wars, set out on their road home, were reduced to begging as they went. One evening they reached a gloomy wood, where they had to rest. To make all safe, they agreed that two should sleep while the third watched. When he was tired he was to wake one of the others, and sleep in his turn, and so on. The first one had not watched long before up came a little man in a red jacket. "Who's there?" said he.

"A friend," said the soldier.

"What sort of a friend?"

"An old broken soldier," said the other; "come, sit down and warm yourself."

"Well," said the little man, "I will do what I can for you; take this and show it to your comrades in the morning." So he took out an old cloak and gave it to the soldier, telling him that whenever he put it over his shoulders, anything that he wished for would be fulfilled; then the little man walked away.

When the second soldier's turn to watch came, the little man in the red jacket appeared again. The soldier treated him in a friendly way, and the little man gave him a purse, which was always full of gold.

Then the third soldier's turn came, and he also had the little man for his guest, who gave him a wonderful horn that made everyone dance to its beautiful music.

In the morning each told his story and showed his treasure; and they agreed to travel together to see the world, and for a while only to make use of the wonderful purse. Thus they spent their time joyously, till they tired of this roving life, and thought they should like to have a home of their own. So the first soldier put his cloak on, and wished for a fine castle. In a moment it stood before their eyes; gardens and green lawns spread round it, and flocks of sheep and goats, and herds of oxen were grazing about, and out of the gate came a fine coach with three dapple-grey horses to meet them and bring them home.

This was very well for a time; but it would not do to stay at home always, so they got together all their rich clothes and horses and servants, and ordered their coach with three horses, and set out to see a neighbouring king. This King had an only daughter, and as he took the three soldiers for king's sons, he gave them a kind welcome. One day the second soldier was walking with the Princess. Now this Princess was a witch, and knew all the wonderful things that the three soldiers brought. She set to work and made a purse so like the soldier's that no one would know one from the other, and then asked him to come and see her, and made him drink some wine that she had got ready for him, till he fell asleep. Then she felt in his pocket, and took away the wonderful purse, and left the one she had made instead.

Next morning the soldiers set out home, and soon after they reached their castle, happening to want some money, they went to their purse, and found to their great sorrow, when they had emptied it, none came in place of it. Then the cheat was found out; for the second soldier knew where he had been, and how he had told the story to the Princess, and he guessed that she had betrayed him. "Oh," said the first soldier, "I will soon get the purse back!"

So he threw his cloak across his shoulders and wished himself in the Princess's chamber. There he found her sitting alone, telling her gold that fell around her in a shower from the purse. The soldier stood looking at her too long, for the moment she saw him she started up and cried out: "Thieves! Thieves!" so that the whole Court came and tried to seize him. The poor soldier began to be dreadfully frightened; so without thinking of the ready way of travelling his cloak gave him, ran to the window, opened it, and jumped out. Unluckily, in his haste, his cloak caught and was left hanging, to the great joy of the Princess, who knew its worth.

The poor soldier made his way home to his comrades on foot in a very downcast mood; but the third soldier told him to keep up his heart, and took his horn and blew a merry tune. At the first blast a countless troop of foot and horse came rushing to their aid, and they set out to make war against their enemy. The King's palace was besieged, and he was told that he must give up the purse and cloak, or that not one stone would be left upon another. The King went into his daughter's chamber and talked with her; but she said: "Let me try first if I cannot beat them." So she thought of a cunning scheme, dressed herself as a poor girl, and set out by night with her maid, and went into the enemy's camp, as if she wanted to sell trinkets.

In the morning she began singing ballads so beautifully that the soldiers ran round in crowds and thought of nothing but hearing her sing. Amongst the rest came the soldier to whom the horn belonged. As soon as she saw him she winked to her maid, who slipped slily through the crowd and went into his tent where it hung, and stole it away. This done, they both got safely back to the palace; the besieging army went away, the three wonderful gifts were left in the hands of the Princess, and the soldiers were as penniless and forlorn as when the little man with the red jacket found them in the wood.

Poor fellows! they began to think what was now to be done. "Comrades," at last said the soldier who had had the purse, "we had better part; we cannot live together. Let each seek his bread as well as he can." So he turned to the right, and the other two to the left; for they

THE THREE SOLDIERS

"And set out by night with her maid"

said they would rather travel together. On he strayed till he came to a wood, and he walked on a long time, till evening began to fall, when he sat down tired beneath a tree, and soon fell asleep.

Morning dawned, and he was delighted, at opening his eyes, to see that the tree was laden with beautiful apples. He was hungry, so he plucked and ate first one, then a second, then a third apple. A strange feeling came over his nose: when he put the apple to his mouth something was in the way; he felt it; it was his nose, that grew and grew till it hung down to his breast. It did not stop there; still it grew and grew. "Heavens!" he thought; "when will it have done growing?" And well he might ask, for by this time it reached the ground as he sat on the grass, and thus it kept creeping on till he could not bear its weight, or raise himself up; and it seemed as if it would never end, for already it stretched its enormous length all through the wood.

Meantime his comrades were journeying on, till on a sudden one of them stumbled against something. "What can that be?" said the other. They looked, but could think of nothing that it was like but a nose. "We will follow and find its owner, however," said they; so they traced it till at last they found their poor comrade stretched under the apple tree. What was to be done? They tried to carry him, but in vain. They caught an ass that was passing by, and raised him upon its back; but it was soon tired of carrying such a load. So they sat down in despair, when up came the little man in the red jacket. "Why, how now, friend?" said he, laughing; "well, I must find a cure for you, I see." So he told them to gather a pear from a tree that grew close by, and the nose would come right again. No time was lost, and the nose was soon brought to its proper size, to the poor soldier's joy.

"I will do something more for you yet," said the little man; "take some of those pears and apples with you; whoever eats one of the apples will have his nose grow like yours just now; but if you give him a pear, all will come right again. Go to the Princess and get her to eat some of your apples; her nose will grow twenty times as long as yours did; then look sharp, and you will get what you want of her."

They thanked their old friend for his kindness, and it was agreed that the poor soldier who had already tried the power of the apple should undertake the task. He dressed himself up as a gardener's boy, and went to the King's palace, and said he had apples to sell, such as were never seen there before. Everyone that saw them was delighted, and wanted to taste, but he said they were only for the Princess; and she soon sent her maid to buy his stock. They were so ripe and rosy that she soon began eating, and had already eaten three when she began to wonder

what ailed her nose, for it grew and grew, down to the ground, out at the window, and over the garden.

Then the King made known to all his kingdom, that whoever would heal her of this dreadful disease should be richly rewarded. Many tried, but the Princess got no relief. And now the old soldier dressed himself up very sprucely as a doctor, who said he could cure her; so he chopped up some of the apple, and to punish her a little more gave her a dose, saying he would call to-morrow and see her again. The morrow came, and of course, instead of being better, the nose had been growing all night, and the Princess was in a dreadful fright. So the doctor chopped up a very little of the pear and gave her, and said he was sure that would do good, and he would call again the next day. Next day came, and the nose was, to be sure, a little smaller, but yet it was bigger than it was when the doctor first began to meddle with it.

Then he thought to himself: "I must frighten this cunning princess a little more before I shall get what I want of her;" so he gave her another dose of the apple, and said he would call on the morrow. The morrow came, and the nose was ten times as bad as before.

"My good lady," said the doctor, "something works

against my medicine, and is too strong for it; but I know by the force of my art what it is; you have stolen goods about you, I am sure, and if you do not give them back, I can do nothing for you."

The Princess denied very stoutly that she had anything of the kind.

"Very well," said the doctor, "you may do as you please, but I am sure I am right, and you will die if you do not own it."

Then he went to the King, and told him how the matter stood. "Daughter," said he, "send back the cloak, the purse, and the horn that you stole from the right owners."

Then she ordered her maid to fetch them, and begged the doctor to give them back to the soldiers; and the moment he had them safe he gave her a whole pear to eat, and the nose came right. And as for the doctor, he put on the cloak, wished the King and all his Court a good day, and was soon with his two brothers, who lived from that time happily at home in their palace, except when they took airings in their coach with the three dapple-grey horses.

The Frog Prince

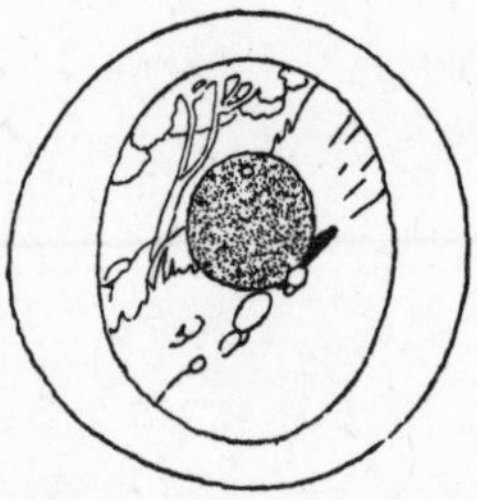

ONE fine evening a young princess went into a wood, and sat down by the side of a cool spring of water. She had a golden ball in her hand, which was her favourite plaything, and she amused herself with tossing it into the air and catching it again as it fell. After a time she threw it up so high, that when she stretched out her hand to catch it, the ball bounded away and rolled along upon the ground, till at last it fell into the spring. The princess looked into the spring after the ball; but it was very deep, so deep that she could not see to the bottom. Then she began to lament her loss, and said, "Alas! if I could only get my ball again, I would give all my fine clothes and jewels — everything that I have in the world." Whilst she was speaking a frog put its head out of the water and said, "Princess, why do you weep so bitterly?" "Alas!" said she, "what can you do for me, you nasty frog? My golden ball has fallen into the spring." The frog said, "I want not your pearls and jewels and fine clothes; but if you will love me and let me live with you, and eat from your little golden plate, and sleep upon your little bed, I will bring you your ball again." "What nonsense," thought the princess, "this silly frog is talking! He can never get out of the well: however, he may be able to get my ball for me; and therefore I will promise him what he asks." So she said to the frog, "Well, if you will bring me my ball, I promise to do all you require."

Then the frog put his head down, and dived deep under the water; and after a little while he came up again with the ball in his mouth, and threw it on the ground. As soon as the young princess saw her ball, she ran to pick it up, and was so overjoyed to have it in her hand again, that she never thought of the frog, but ran home with it as fast as she could. The frog called after her, "Stay, princess, and take me with you as you promised;" but she did not stop to hear a word.

The next day, just as the princess had sat down to dinner, she heard a strange noise, tap-tap, as if somebody was coming up the marble staircase; and soon afterwards something knocked gently at the door, and said:

"Open the door, my princess dear,
Open the door to thy true love here!
And mind the words that thou and I said
By the fountain cool in the greenwood shade."

Then the princess ran to the door, and opened it, and there she saw the frog, whom she had quite forgotten; she was terribly frightened, and shutting the door as fast as she could, came back to her seat. The king her father asked her what had frightened her. "There is a nasty frog," said she, "at the door, who lifted my ball out of the spring last evening: I promised him that he should live with me here, thinking that he could never get out of the spring; but there he is at the door and wants to come in!" While she was speaking the frog knocked again at the door, and said:

"Open the door, my princess dear,
Open the door to thy true love here!
And mind the words that thou and I said
By the fountain cool in the greenwood shade."

The king said to the young princess, "As you have made a promise, you must keep it, so go and let him in." She did so, and the frog hopped into the room, and came up close to the table. "Pray lift me upon a chair," said he to the princess, "and let me sit next to you." As soon as she had done this, the frog said, "Put your plate closer to me that I may eat out of it." This she did, and when he had eaten as much as he could, he said, "Now I am tired; carry me upstairs and put me into your little bed." And the princess took him up in her hand and put him upon the pillow of her own little bed, where he slept all night long. As soon as it was light he jumped up, hopped downstairs and went out of the house. "Now," thought the princess, "he is gone, and I shall be troubled with him no more."

But she was mistaken; for when night came again, she heard the same tapping at the door, and when she opened it, the frog came in and slept upon her pillow as before till the morning broke: and the third night he did the same; but when the princess awoke on the following morning, she was astonished to see, instead of the frog, a handsome prince gazing on her with the most beautiful eyes that ever were seen, and standing at the head of her bed.

He told her that he had been enchanted by a malicious fairy, who had changed him into the form of a frog, in which he was fated to remain till some princess should take him out of the spring and let him sleep upon her bed for three nights. "You," said the prince, "have broken this cruel charm, and now I have nothing to wish for but that you should go with me into my father's kingdom, where I will marry you, and love you as long as you live."

The young princess, you may be sure, was not long in giving her consent; and as they spoke a splendid carriage drove up with eight beautiful horses decked with plumes of feathers and golden

harness, and behind rode the prince's servant, who had bewailed the misfortune of his dear master so long and so bitterly that his heart had well-nigh burst. Then all set out full of joy for the prince's kingdom; where they arrived safely, and lived happily a great many years.